Lovin' a Virginia Bad Girl

Lovin' a Virginia Bad Girl

Racquel Williams

www.urbanbooks.net

Urban Books, LLC
300 Farmingdale Road, N.Y.-Route 109
Farmingdale, NY 11735

Lovin' a Virginia Bad Girl

ISBN 13: 978-1-64556-340-2
ISBN 10: 1-64556-340-5

First Trade Paperback Printing May 2022
Printed in the United States of America

10 9 8 7 6 5 4 3 2 1

*This is a work of fiction. Any references or similarities
to actual events, real people, living or dead, or to real
locales are intended to give the novel a sense of reality.
Any similarity in other names, characters, places, and
incidents is entirely coincidental.*

Distributed by Kensington Publishing Corp.
Submit Orders to:
Customer Service
400 Hahn Road
Westminster, MD 21157-4627
Phone: 1-800-733-3000
Fax: 1-800-659-2436

Lovin' a Virginia Bad Girl

by

Racquel Williams

DEDICATION

To my first born, Malik. Your strength and tenacity are unmatched. I am so proud of the man you've become. Continue reaching for the stars and know it's always us against them.

To Jehmel and Zahir, the ride hasn't always been easy, but no matter what, know I got y'all forever. I love y'all.

ACKNOWLEDGMENTS

First and foremost, I will continue to give all praises to Allah. This has definitely been a journey, and I'm forever grateful that He keeps on blessing me.

To my love, thank you for encouraging me and pushing me, even when I feel like giving up. It's only up from here. Love you, until I take my last breath.

To my readers, old and new. I appreciate all the support that you guys have given me. I'm forever grateful.

CHAPTER ONE

Nyesha

A bitch is tired of struggling by her damn self, I thought as I wiped the tears away from my eyes. I wasn't some trifling-ass female or anything like that. I just got knocked up by the wrong nigga. See, I met my baby daddy, Yohan, at Job Corps, where we were both studying a trade. I was studying to be a Certified Nursing Assistant, and Yohan took up painting as a trade. Well, I was studying, but he was there to hustle his dime bags of weed.

It wasn't love at first sight, or no shit like that. We met each other and then became good friends. We would hang out after classes and exchange stories about our lives. He was there because he had gotten in trouble with the law, and I was there because I had dropped out of high school. My mama was not having me laying around her house every day, so I signed up after I saw a Job Corps commercial about changing your life. I felt like the lady was talking to me. I grabbed my phone and dialed the toll-free number that flashed across the screen.

Our friendship developed into something more serious. He became my nigga, and I became his ride or die bitch. We eventually became inseparable, and soon I was going with him to his home in Boston. We were all over each other, fucking and sucking every chance that we got.

It didn't take me long to fall for that nigga, and I thought he was really digging me. I didn't have any reason to think he wasn't, because he treated me like his queen and all his time was spent with me. All that sweet shit changed months after I disclosed to the nigga that I was pregnant.

"What the fuck you mean, B?" he asked in his thick Southern accent.

"You heard me. I'm pregnant. We were fucking almost every day without using protection. Remember?" I asked in an annoyed tone.

"Man, don't you know I'm trying to go to college and shit? I just ain't ready for no baby. Shit, I still got my life to live," he yelled in a high-pitched tone.

"Are you fucking serious right now? I have college also. I mean, I'm the one carrying the baby, not your ass," I lashed out as tears welled up in my eyes.

"Man, I'on't mean to sound mean or anything. I love you, boo, but look where the fuck we at. Job Corps. We ain't got shit, so how we gon' take care of a baby?"

"You know what? Your ass should've thought about that before you busted all up in me. I didn't plan for a baby either, but I'm pregnant. To be honest, I begged you to use protection, but you insisted not to. The difference is, I'm gonna do what the fuck I need to do to take care of my child. I suggest you man the fuck up and stop whining like a little-ass bitch," I spat angrily with hurt in my heart.

I was shocked that my nigga, my rider, was talking to me like that. I mean, what the fuck did he think would happen if we were fucking around without protection? We were both careless, and this is what happened. We were having a fucking baby.

I looked at him, searching his face for an ounce of care, but I saw none. His big brown eyes that first drew me in to him showed nothing but coldness. I looked at him, shook my head, and walked off.

I walked in my dorm room, jumped in my bed, and started crying. It was like my heart was minced into tiny pieces.

"You all right, babe?" my roommate, Nerissa, asked me.

"No, I'm not. I just told Yohan that I'm pregnant, and his ass acted like he didn't give a fuck. He didn't want my damn baby," I cried.

"What? Are you serious? I thought you all were so in love."

"Hmmmm. I thought so too, but I guess not."

"Listen, girl. You're strong, and you can work to take care of your baby. My mama did it with ten of us, and we ain't have no daddy. Dry them tears and quit stressing yourself. Your baby needs you." She sat on my bed and hugged me.

I laid my head on her shoulder and cried. I'd never felt that broken before. I couldn't believe the way he'd reacted. It wasn't like I was just a bitch he was fucking. I was his woman, but that was how he treated me. I got myself together and eventually stopped crying.

"Girl, you're gonna be fine. Just pray to God and put your best foot forward. You're done with your program anyway. You know they give you a check when you leave. Just use that to get on your feet."

"Thanks, girl. You've been my rock."

"That's what friends are for. We gonna keep in touch when we leave here. Anyway, let me go hit the exercising room up." She grabbed her book bag and left the room.

I buried my head in the pillow and poured my soul out on the white pillowcase. I wanted to be strong for me and my baby, but I was feeling helpless. I was crying like we'd just broken up, but it was worse than that. I was carrying that nigga's child. A child that he didn't want.

***

I was all packed and ready to go. I had received my Certified Nursing Assistant license. I was awarded a scholarship to a two-year college, paid in full by Job Corps, but I was pregnant, and going to college was the last thing on my mind. I needed to get a job ASAP so I could take care of me and my unborn child. So, I gave up a two-year scholarship from Job Corps.

I grabbed my bags and hugged my roommate before walking out of the place that I'd called home for the last ten months. Tears filled my eyes, but I used every ounce of strength in me to hold them in. I was ready to go, even though I wasn't looking forward to where I was going.

I got in the bus that was transporting me to the closest Greyhound station. I kept looking out of the window to see if the love of my life would be walking in front of the bus. I mean, after all, he knew that I was leaving, because I had sent him a note the night before. All of my hopes quickly diminished when the bus pulled off the property and into the street. I hung my head down and allowed the tears to silently roll down my face.

I was so caught up in my thoughts that I didn't realize that we had reached the stop.

"Ma'am, we're here," I heard a voice yell out.

"Uh, oh, I'm sorry. Let me get my things." I jumped out of the seat and grabbed my purse along with my bags. I got off the bus and walked into the Greyhound bus station in Worcester.

"Can I get a one-way ticket to New York City, please?" I handed the clerk the money. She gave me my ticket and walked away from the counter.

I sat in the chair as I waited for my bus to pull up. My heart was heavy, and I felt like it was the end of the world for me. I wondered how things were going to turn out. For one, I did not call my mother to let her know I was coming back home. I also didn't tell her that I was pregnant. As much as I hated the fact that I had to face her, I didn't have much of a choice. I had nowhere to go, and no one else to turn to.

The ride to New York was a gruesome one. I was hungry, and my stomach was hurting. I was so caught up in my hurt that I forgot I hadn't had anything to eat since yesterday. However, my heart was hurting, and being hungry was the last thing on my mind. During the entire ride, I was playing different scenarios in my head about how I was going to break the news to Mama. I leaned my head on the windowsill and allowed my mind to wander.

Four hours later, the bus pulled up at Times Square, and I got off. I was happy that I was home, because I was a die-hard New Yorker. However, the occasion wasn't a happy one. I walked to the subway and jumped on the train to the Bronx.

The taxi that picked me up at 241st and Wakefield Avenue pulled up at my gate. I opened the door and took two steps inside. My legs were trembling as I walked up the stairs and then in the house.

I quickly walked past Mama's room and into mine. I closed my door and dropped my bags. I sat on the bed and nervously waited for Mama to come knocking on my door.

A few minutes went by, and there still was no knock. I was relieved that I would be left alone for a few more minutes, so I could get my thoughts under control. I took a shower and went to the kitchen to make myself a cup of hot chocolate. I realized that Mama wasn't home. That was when it hit me that it was after 7 p.m. and she worked the night shift at the hospital.

Good, I thought as I walked back in my room. It felt good to be home in my own bed, watching my TV. That didn't last long, though, because I was tired and didn't feel too good. Even though I was in the early stages of my pregnancy, it was already taking a toll on my body and mind. I had no idea what I had gotten myself into.

"Nyesha! Nyesha!" I heard a voice yelling my name.

Before I could wake up fully, I saw Mama busting in my room. I knew it was early because *Good Morning America* was on at the time.

"Yes, Mama. Why are you yelling? It's early as hell," I said in an annoyed tone.

"Why am I yelling? You are in my house without telling me you were coming, so that's why I'm yelling," she said at the top of her lungs.

"You don't have to yell—and I live here, so I didn't think I had to call you to let you know I was coming home."

"I'm not gonna sit here and argue with you. The last time I checked, you live at Job Corps."

"Well, I left Job Corps, and I'm not going back."

"What you mean you left? Didn't you just call me a few weeks ago and tell me that you got some kind of scholarship to go to some college out in Boston? What happened to that? I knew yo' ass was lying."

Tears welled up in my eyes as emotions gathered up in my heart. I'd been through enough, and I wished she wasn't coming at me with all those questions and accusations. All I really needed now was some kind of support, or a few kind words, you know?

"I wasn't lying, Mama. I . . . I'm pregnant," I stuttered while trembling with fear.

Her dark complexion turned dark purple, and her eyes widened. She took several steps toward me, looking at me like I was a two-headed animal standing in front of her.

"What the fuck did yo' ass just say? You pregnant? I know I didn't hear your dumb ass correctly."

"Yes, Mama, you heard me right. I'm pregnant, and I'm not going back to Job Corps. I'm going to work, and I'm going to take care of my baby." I instantly grew some balls. I was prepared for whatever action came after.

"Hmmmm. I always thought you was the one with some sense, but I see you're as dumb as yo' sister," she lashed out.

I was getting furious, and I wasn't going to sit there and listen to her degrade me. I remembered when my older sister got pregnant and Mama found out. She put her out in the rain one Friday evening. My sister had nowhere to go because her baby daddy was trifling and wasn't in the picture. I'd never forget the tears rolling down my sister's face as she pleaded with her. Mama didn't give a damn, though. Instead, she said that my sister was grown, and two grown bitches can't live under the same roof.

I stood up from the bed because it was getting hostile in there, and I didn't know where the argument was heading.

"So, where is this baby daddy at?"

"He's in Boston."

"So, not only did your dumb ass go and get knocked up, but you got pregnant for a man that's not even around. Who you think's gonna help you take care of this little bastard? I done raised mine, and I'll be damned if I'm going to be taking care of someone's children. Matter of fact, you're only here temporarily. Ain't no space for no baby up in here."

"I'm going to get a job so I can get my own place. I promise I'll be out before my baby is born."

"Uh huh, 'cause you know I ain't with that shit. You grown now, so put on your big girl panties and get out of my shit," she said before she stomped out of my room, slamming the door behind her.

I sat back down on the bed, giving myself a few minutes to register everything that had just happened. Tears rolled down my face. I never understood why Mama was always so cold toward us. Don't get me wrong, we never wanted for anything when we were growing up, and she always made sure we were taken care of. But she'd never hugged us or shown us any kind of love. To be honest, we needed to hear that more than all of the material things that she provided. I felt in my heart that was the main reason why I kept looking for love in all the wrong places.

I needed someone to talk to. I wanted to call Yohan, but I was angry at him also. He was supposed to be there for me, but instead, he was acting like an asshole and there I was, going through a pregnancy by myself.

I knew that crying wasn't going to help me, so I dried my tears and pulled up Google on my laptop. I was looking for any job that was hiring. I was desperate and didn't give a fuck if I had to clean toilets to make a dollar.

Three days later, I got a call to get interviewed for a job in Yonkers. It was a little distance, but I needed it and didn't mind taking the bus. I got dressed, ate a few crackers, and drank a cup of hot chocolate.

I'd been working non-stop since I got the job at a nursing home in Yonkers. I had gotten myself a one-bedroom apartment in the Bronx and moved out of Mama's house. It was sad as hell, because while I was still there, she barely spoke to me. I would work long hours, come in, and go straight to my room. Many days I was feeling sick, and I had no one to turn to or talk to about how I was feeling.

I was really looking forward to the birth of my first child. A few weeks earlier, I had learned that I was having a girl. I was overly excited, because now I had someone to love and care about. Someone that would love me unconditionally. I got a two-thousand-dollar check from Job Corps, and I started buying her pretty clothes. I couldn't wait for her to be born so I could spoil her behind.

I was lying in bed one night, catching an episode *of Law and Order,* when I heard my phone ringing. I hoped it wasn't my damn job because I was too tired and was not doing any overtime that day. I ignored the first couple of rings, but then the phone continued to ring. I rolled over, snatched it off the dresser, and answered without looking at the caller ID.

"Hello."

"Hey, babe," a voice that I knew so well echoed in my ear.

I removed the phone from my ear and looked at the number. It was an 804 area code. I didn't know anyone with that area code.

"Hello," I said, and it was obvious from my tone I didn't know who I was talking to.

"Aye, bae, it's me. Yohan."

It took me a few seconds to register what that nigga was saying to me. It had been seven months since I'd last seen him, and he had the audacity to call me. Was he fucking serious?

"Listen, I don't give a fuck about what you got to say. You didn't have shit to say to me before I left Job Corps, and it's seven damn months later. Do you think I want to hear some shit you got to say? For real, nigga, fuck you and the bitch that made you." I lashed out, not giving a fuck about anything.

"Babe, I know you mad at me and shit. I swear to you, I've been thinking about you, about us and our baby, and I want to be there for y'all. I admit I fucked up because I didn't know how to deal with you being pregnant. I was scared."

"So, your bitch ass ain't scared no more?"

"Come on with all that disrespectful shit, boo. I know I hurt you, but I'm trying to man up and right my wrongs with you."

"Nigga, you must think I'm a weak bitch. Where the fuck was you when I needed you? When I was alone, crying and shit?"

"Man, I'm sorry, babe. I had to leave Boston and shit. Now I'm out here in VA. I'm going to college and shit, but I'm grinding so I can take care of you and our baby."

"Fuck you, boy. You in college? While I had to fucking give up my dream to work and provide for my child? Fuck you, I swear." I hung the phone up in his ear and then turned it off.

I couldn't believe that I was busting my ass, working twelve-hour shifts when my stomach, back, and feet hurt, while my baby daddy was enrolled in college and living the free life. I threw the cup that I had in my hand into the wall.

"Damn you! How could you do me like this? You're getting a fucking education while I'm here carrying your child?" I cried out, louder and louder.

Pain ripped through my body as I lay down in the fetal position. Loneliness and hurt were only two of the emotions that I was going through. I swear, a year ago, my future was bright as hell, and I had everything going for me. That was until I fell for that nigga. Now, there I was, being a statistic, another baby mama knocked up, with a no-good-ass baby daddy. Now Mama was disappointed in me, and I couldn't say I blamed her. I was disappointed in myself.

CHAPTER TWO

Nyesha

My delivery date was steadily approaching, and I was too excited. I couldn't wait until I was able to see my baby girl's face. In another month, I would be able to do just that. A lot had been going on between her father and me. I tried my best to ignore him, but he was persistent and was not giving up. We started talking on the phone regularly, which ended up with us being on the phone late nights whenever I wasn't at work. At first, I thought he was still on his bullshit, but as time went by, I could hear the sincerity in his voice. I also believed him when he told me that he wanted to marry me. I knew we were young and still had a long way to go, but he was the love of my life, and if there was anyone that I wanted to say "I do" to, it would be him.

I dialed Yohan's phone, because I'd been missing him all day and wanted to talk to him.

"Hello," a female voice answered.

I was taken aback. Who was the bitch answering his phone?

"Who is this?"

"This is Kerry. Yohan's other baby mama. No worries. I know all about you."

The room started spinning, and it seemed like all of the oxygen had been sucked from my body. I swallowed hard.

"His other baby mother? Bitch, if you don't quit playing and put my nigga on the phone, I will come through this phone and rip your fucking head off," I said as I gasped for air.

"Ha, ha. You one funny ho. Where do you think he lives? He lives with me and my mama, and I'm eight weeks pregnant by him."

"Listen to me, you stupid little bitch. I don't give a damn about him fucking you. Like you said, you know about me. That means you already know that I'm the one that nigga loves, and trust me, if I have anything to do with it, he won't be in that unborn bastard's life. Now, go find you another bitch to play with, you country-ass ho." I hung up without waiting for a response.

I sat up in the bed and scrolled through my phone. My fingers trembled as I dialed Yohan's mother's number. While I was at Job Corps, she and I had become close, and she had always kept it one hundred with me.

"Hey, baby girl," she cheerfully said.

"Hey, Ma. Who is Kerry?"

"Why you ask that?"

"'Cause I just called your son's phone, and this bitch answered, talking 'bout they live together and she pregnant by him."

"That ho is lying. She ain't pregnant by my motherfucking son. Matter of fact, let me call you right back." Before I could respond, she hung up the phone.

I didn't know what to think at that moment. I was feeling hurt and was in my feelings. I knew his mother said the bitch was lying, but obviously she knew who that bitch was. Before I had a chance to put the phone down, it started ringing.

"Hello," I answered.

"Boo, what the hell just happened? What did that bitch say to you?"

"Fuck what she said to me. The real question is, who the fuck is she?"

"Boo, calm down. She ain't nobody but a fiend. Me and her got into it, and she just want to start some bullshit."

"Oh, and do you live with this bitch?"

"Nah, I'on't live wit' her ass. I trap out her mama house. That's all, boo."

"You know what? I don't need this fucking shit in my life. Me and you just started back dealing with one another, and now you got some bitch telling me she's pregnant and shit." I was feeling hurt, so I started crying.

"Please believe me, boo. That bitch is lying. I ain't never fucked her, so there's no way she can be pregnant by me. I swear, boo, don't let that bitch fuck us up."

I held the phone to my ear and just continued crying. Why did I have to go through that? I remembered when it was just us and I was the only person who mattered to him. What the fuck had happened to those days?

"Damn, man, you know I don't like it when you cry. Matter of fact, I'm going to handle a few things, then I'ma jump on the highway and come see you."

I wanted to tell him no, but part of me really wanted to see him face to face so I could address that bullshit. "Whatever. I don't want to hear your fucking lies anymore."

"Man, chill out. Text me your address and I'm getting on the road tonight. Man, and don't answer the phone if that bitch call back."

I didn't say anything. I just hung up, wondering what he was really hiding. Why didn't he want me to answer the phone if she called back? See, I wasn't a damn fool. I'd dealt with a few liars and cheaters before, and I knew that his ass was a liar. I also didn't believe bitches when they talked about my nigga fucking them. The truth was, some bitches would tell you that they're fucking your nigga so you would leave him, and then they could laugh about how dumb you were. I knew that there were three sides to this story. I heard hers and his, but I was curious to know what the fucking truth was.

I was up bright and early. Virginia was six hours away from New York, so Yohan hadn't arrived yet. I cleaned the apartment and took a shower. Feeling nervous because it had been months since I last saw him, I decided to listen to K. Michelle's latest CD. I was not sure why I did that, because her music only put ideas in my head and showed me how niggas were. The ringing of my cell phone took me out of the zone that I was in.

"Hello."

"I'm here."

"Okay, I'm going to buzz you in. I'm on the third floor, apartment C." I got up and walked over to the door and buzzed him in. I swallowed hard as I ran my fingers through my hair to straighten it up a little bit. I opened the door and anxiously waited.

I heard the elevator open, so I peeked around and saw him. I wanted to run to him and jump in his arms, but I didn't move. He walked up to me, dropped the small book bag that he was carrying, and grabbed me up in a bear hug.

"Damn, boo, I missed yo' ass," he said as he continued to hug me. I hugged him back because it did feel good to be in his arms again.

He finally let me go, and we walked inside my apartment.

"Damn, yo' stomach is big as fuck," he exclaimed.

"Really? What do you expect? I'm eight months pregnant with yo' child," I said sarcastically.

"I know, boo. I'm just shocked, that's all. So, how you been?"

"I'm living, even though you abandoned your child and me."

"Boo, I swear I'm sorry that I behaved like that. All that matters is I'm here now, and I ain't leaving you all no mo'."

"See, Yohan, I don't even know why I rock with you so hard and you treat me like shit." I couldn't believe I was considering giving him another chance after the shit he put me through, leaving me when I needed him the most.

"This is why you rock with me." He cuffed my nice, voluptuous ass with both hands and squeezed as his lips met mine.

No matter how bad I wanted to fight him off me, I couldn't because I missed him. I missed his smell and most importantly, his love.

His kiss took my breath away, and there I was, trapped in no man's land. My stomach was bulging out with his seed living inside me, and I was craving for more seeds to be planted inside my womb.

We moved over to my couch in the living room. I took my time to lay down on my back, careful not to hurt my stomach. I was missing his ass so much. Fuck foreplay. I assisted him with taking off my pajamas and my oversized T-shirt. I stuck my index finger inside my wet, warm pussy, and then pushed it inside of his mouth. Looking at him intensely, I teased him.

"Damn, you taste like peaches," he said, hopping on one leg, trying to take off his pants. One thing for sure was we were into that kinky sex, and when I said kinky, I meant kinky to the fullest.

I didn't waste any time getting into the spread-eagle position. My legs were parted like the Red Sea that Moses spoke about.

"Ohhh," I moaned out loud as soon as he entered my wet pussy. No matter how wet my shit was, this pregnant pussy was still virgin tight.

"Sssssshit, yes!" I screamed out, not giving a damn if my neighbors heard me. His dick was driving back and forth inside my pussy. I squeezed my muscles, locking them around his dick.

Oh my gosh. I wanted to scream as my juices flowed. He was hitting every single spot. I swear, his dick was tapping the baby's head, because I felt movement in my stomach.

"Damn, this pussy is on fire." He held my ass and pulled me up toward him as his dick plunged in and out my pussy. "Shit, baby, this pussy is so good," he groaned out between each thrust.

"This dick is sooo gooood!" I managed to shout out before exploding.

My sex drive was high as hell. I didn't know if it was because I was pregnant, but I wanted dick, dick, dick, dick, dick, dick. The words played out in my head in Rihanna's voice. Maybe it was the fact that I hadn't had any dick since I got pregnant.

"Let me get on top," I pleaded. I was hungry for the dick, and being pregnant wasn't stopping me.

Yohan was gasping for air, laying on his back with his dick standing tall while I sat on top of it backward. My stomach rested on his thighs, and my ass spread wide like wings as I slid down his pole.

I watched myself in the mirror on the wall in the living room as my pussy locked around his dick tight like a diamond ring. "Yesss!" I danced on his dick, grinding my hips with my hands locked on his kneecaps.

"Damn . . . sssss," he moaned in between breaths.

I was in full control of his dick, riding it to the tip of the head and then back to the base. I tightened my muscles as I came all over his dick continuously.

Now Yohan had his second wind, and my ass was long winded. I stood up and braced myself on the couch with my ass tooted up in the air. His hands slapped my ass, giving me a stinger.

"Shit, nigga. What you gonna do, fuck me, or beat me?" I swear I wanted both, because that shit turned me on.

"Shut the hell up and take this dick." He jammed his dick inside of my pussy. I loved it when he got rough with me. I saw that nothing had changed. Baby still knew how to handle the pussy. Each thrust he took ended with a slap on my ass. His dick was working magic as my pussy lips wrapped around him tightly, suffocating it.

"Yes, boo! Yes, that's my spot!" I sang out as his dick tickled my insides. "Oh, yes," I panted as his balls slapped my ass.

"Whose pussy is this?" he asked as he slapped my ass with his hand.

"Mine," I replied sarcastically.

Seconds later, I felt my hair being literally pulled from my scalp. His hands were tugging away, while his dick was digging deeper into my soul. I braced myself, because his pounding had me on a roller coaster ride. I felt my insides melting while the feel-good pain of ecstasy took over my body.

He pulled me closer to him. I felt his dick getting much harder, and I knew then he was about to cum. "This pussy is good, boo. Aaargggggh!" he yelled out as he exploded inside of me. "Damn, boo, pregnant pussy is the shit. I'ma have to keep yo' ass knocked up so I can get it on the regular."

He got up and walked toward his book bag with sweat dripping down his body. I was feeling weak, like someone had drained all of the energy out of me. I sat on the couch, hoping that I didn't mess it up with cum. He took out a washcloth and walked back over to me.

"You good? I ain't beat that pussy up too much, did I?" He laughed.

Nothing had changed. That nigga was as cocky as the day I met him. I wished I could burst his bubble, but the truth was, that nigga had that bomb-ass dick.

"Where's the bathroom at?"

"The first door on your right." I pointed.

I watched as that sexy-ass nigga walked off. I swear, that man had everything that a bitch dreamed of, but he couldn't be trusted. I was no fool. The dick was good and all, but I wasn't going to let that cloud my judgment.

After he came out of the bathroom, I decided to go take a shower. I got up to walk but noticed that my pussy was sore, so I limped to the bathroom. Shit, I knew the nigga was beating it up, but I didn't know he had done that much damage to my shit. I was happy to get in the water because I knew it would ease the pain a little.

The hot water wasn't making it better, so I turned on the cold water. After a few minutes, the water did magic and soothed my burning pussy. I quickly soaped up my body and was about to wash off when I felt a sharp pain, then the gush of fluid flowing down my legs. I knew it wasn't regular urine, so I bent down as much as my stomach allowed me to. I saw a thick type of fluid on my leg. I used my finger to touch between my legs, and when I looked, blood was on my fingers. Panic set in as I cut the water off and grabbed my towel.

"Yohan!" I yelled frantically.

"Boo, what's wrong?" He busted in the bathroom.

"I'm bleeding. I need to go to the hospital." I pushed past him and walked into my room. I grabbed a pair of underwear and a pad, then quickly got dressed.

He was already dressed and waiting on me. "You need me to carry you?" he asked.

"I'm good. Let's go." I grabbed the hospital bag that I had packed and my purse.

The contractions were hitting me back-to-back. I was in pain, and I couldn't wait to get there.

"We are going to Lady of Mercy Hospital. Just pull it up on your GPS." I was in so much pain as I tried my best to stay calm.

"I got it, boo. Hold on. We will be there real soon. I'm right here with you."

His words soothed my soul, especially at a time like that. He reached over and grabbed my hand, holding it. I pushed my seat back and closed my eyes. I was excited yet nervous.

An hour later, my baby girl, Emanyi Ellis, was born. She was a month early, so she weighed under four pounds. I cried tears of joy when the nurse handed her to me, and it didn't take a second for me to fall in love with her. I also saw the joy in her father's eyes as he stared at her. I saw that he had a soft side to him, but it was hard not to, because she was the most beautiful person I'd ever set eyes on.

The doctor informed us that our baby would be placed in an incubator until her lungs were fully developed. It was a bittersweet moment, because I was looking forward to taking my baby girl home with me.

After the nurse took her to the nursery and I cleaned up, I got back in bed. I was tired, mentally and physically. Yohan left to go outside for a few. I was happy to be by myself for a little while. Everything was happening quickly, and I needed to get my thoughts under control.

The day was a happy moment for us, but I couldn't help but wonder if it was gonna last. I heard all of the promises he was making; however, I couldn't believe him, because he'd left us before.

"You good?" he quizzed when he came back later.

"Yeah," I lied to him. My heart was heavy as hell. I was leaving the hospital, but I would have to leave my daughter behind. That was the hardest thing I would ever have to do. He reached over and squeezed my hand. It was a good feeling, but one that I was afraid wouldn't last too long.

The next couple of days were spent at the hospital, spending time with our baby girl and pretending like we were a happy new family. I still didn't trust him, and even though he tried his best to convince me that he was a changed man, something in the back of my mind kept reminding me that he was a cheating ass.

It was Friday, and he was getting ready to go back to Virginia. I didn't say much to him before he left. We hugged, and he kissed me. I felt like a part of me was leaving, but again, I tried to hide my true feelings.

After he pulled off, I ran back in the house with tears in my eyes. I took a glance at myself in the mirror and realized how old I looked. It was like the world was weighing heavy on my shoulders.

I was in physical pain from giving birth, and I was in mental pain because I wanted my baby with me. Her health was progressing, though, and the doctor told me that in a few more days, if she continued sucking on the bottle, she could go home. I was too excited when I heard that, and only hoped that she would.

The first day that Yohan was back in VA, I didn't hear from him. I didn't think anything of it. I knew that he'd driven over six hours and had to go to school the following morning. I was kind of missing him too. All of the old feelings that were buried were awakened all over again.

The doorbell rang, and I knew that it was my sister, Meisha. We'd spoken earlier, and she informed me that she was coming over. I swear, without her, I have no idea what I would've done. Mama called the day that I gave birth, but other than that, she wasn't supportive.

I opened the door, and she walked in. That chick never ceased to amaze me. Ever since we'd been grown, I'd never seen her without her hair and makeup done. Although she had kids, you couldn't really tell just by looking at her, because shawty was bad.

"Hey, chica," she said as she sashayed past me.

"Hey, sis." I locked the door behind me and went back to ironing my clothes.

"Damn, I know you just had the baby and all, but yo' ass look like one of those seventies housewives."

"Wow! I look that bad?" I rubbed my hand over my head, trying to lay my hair down.

"Girl, yes! You look like a train just ran over yo' ass. I know you wasn't looking like that while that boy was here?"

"Shit, he is the reason I look like this. You do know I just had his baby, right?"

"Nah, that nigga ain't right. His ass should've took you to the beauty salon and then to get you a mani and pedi. Girl, I was at the hospital asking for my MAC makeup. Ain't no way I was gon' look any ole way in the maternity ward."

I looked at her and shook my head. The crazy thing is, she wasn't joking. She was dead-ass serious. Meisha was a true glamour girl, especially since she had gotten a job as a stripper at one of Manhattan's elite gentlemen's clubs. She was determined to take care of her kids without her no-good-ass baby daddy. Mama didn't approve of her job, but oh well. My sissy was grown and on her own, so all that preaching that Mama did only fell on deaf ears.

"Anyways, how is my niecey-pooh doing?"

"She's finally sucking the bottle, so they said she can come home in a few days."

"Yayyyy! That's what I'm talking about. She a fighter just like her auntie. Oh, shit. I forgot to bring those cute Jordan booties that I bought her."

"Girl, aren't you tired of buying stuff?" I asked. "She can't wear none of the shit you bought."

"It's my money, so don't you start sounding like Mama."

We both busted out laughing. She was right. I did sound like Mama. God knows, I didn't want to sound anything like that miserable woman.

"So, missy, did you ask that nigga about that bitch that called the other day?" she asked me.

I rolled my eyes, having no idea why she had to remind me of that bitch. "Girl, I asked him and his mama. Both their asses kept denying that shit. They're acting like the bitch is lying."

"Hmm . . . take it from me. Not because I am the oldest, but because I have dealt with my share of sorry-ass niggas. I ain't saying the bitch is telling the whole truth, but there is some truth to her story. A bitch ain't gon' just hit you up unless she done got that dick and don't want to share no more," she said.

"That's the same thing I was thinking. I just ain't got no proof yet."

"Bitch, listen. You can fuck that nigga good, suck his dick, goggle on his balls, wash his dirty drawers, and cook his ass steak every fucking night and that nigga will cheat on yo' ass."

"You right," I said. "I just thought he was really trying to do right by me this time around."

"Girl, you need to put your foot down with his ass. Either he man up or get the fuck gone. Sis, you're too beautiful, you're smart, and I think you got some good pussy. So, you don't need no bum holding you back."

"Ha, ha. Damn, bitch, you not sure I got good pussy?"

"I'm just saying. I'm yo' sister, so I can only swear by what you tell me. For all I know, that shit could be garbage." She busted out laughing.

"Bitch, fuck you! Good pussy does not hold these niggas no more. They will leave you and go fuck a bitch who has no bottoms."

"That's so true, sis. That's why nowadays, a bitch like me is on straight pussy," she said.

I looked at that bitch like she was a strange animal. "What the fuck did you say? Mama gon' kill yo' ass." I was really shocked. I never thought my sis would ever fuck with bitches. Then it clicked in my head that most of the bitches who danced were bisexual.

"Girl, it ain't Mama's pussy, so why would she be worried? Matter of fact, Mama need to get that cat licked. You know it's been years, and that shit might have a ton of cobwebs all over it."

"Bitch, you a fool! Just shut the fuck up already." I busted out laughing. I swear I missed her ass. We used to sit up late, talking all kind of shit. I tell you, she didn't give a fuck about what she said out of that mouth of hers.

We ended up kicking it for a few hours. After she left, I got dressed and went to visit my baby. Even though I was drained, I still had to see my munchkin's face.

CHAPTER THREE

Nyesha

Two weeks later, my baby girl was out of the hospital and doing great. I was eager to get back to work also. I was running low on money, and I had no help. I called her daddy to help out, but he claimed shit was slow right now. That shit pissed me off. Just like I had to figure out a way to take care of her, he should've been held accountable also.

I started to get very irritated with him. He would call to check on his daughter and then try to tell me how much he missed me. While we were on the phone one night, that shit got to me so bad, I snapped.

"Aye, bae, are you keeping that pussy tight for me?" he said.

"Whatever, boy." I tried to brush him off.

"Damn, why you acting so cold towards me? You do know I love you, right?"

"Listen, I'm tired of hearing about love and keeping pussy tight. How about you get a damn job? How about you send money to buy Pampers, wipes, and soap to wash your daughter's behind? That's what the fuck I want to talk about," I snapped.

"Man, why the fuck you acting like a bitch? I told you things a little slow right now. Instead of supporting your man and uplifting him, all you do is bitch, bitch, bitch. I'm tired of hearing about your wants."

"My wants? Your daughter is almost a month old. Name one thing you did for her. Yet, when I saw your ass, you were dressed in designer clothes from head to toe. Boy, miss me with all that bullshit for real. You know what hurts the most? I always thought you was a real nigga. Well, guess what? A real nigga would make sure his seed is straight without giving a damn if he got it."

"Yo, bitch, you funny. So now I'm not a real nigga 'cause I don't have money to throw at your ass. Nah, bitch. You just a fucking gold digger for real. It ain't about my seed not having it. It's more about your greedy ass and you trying to control a nigga."

"Boy, fuck you." I hung up in his ear. I wasn't trying to sit on the phone and listen to him talk a bunch of gibberish.

I tried to find a babysitter for my child, but the hours that I was looking for didn't make it easy. I went to my boss and asked if I could switch to the a.m. shift, but I was told there was no opening. I wouldn't dare ask Mama 'cause she made it clear that we were not her problem.

I was feeling helpless. The little money I had was dwindling down. I decided to apply for public assistance just until I could figure out this job thing.

Fuck! I jumped up and threw the blanket off of me. The sound of my alarm clock constantly going off was starting to get on my last motherfucking nerve. I was not ready to get up out of my warm bed, but I had to be at the food stamp office early that morning. It was my first time ever applying for any kind of government help, and I was far from being happy about it. I didn't see any other option, though. I had my baby to take care of. It was bad enough that I had to scramble up my rent money every month. Sometimes it got so bad that I could barely pay that on time.

The welfare office was packed as hell. Although I got there early, it didn't make a difference. I looked around, realizing that there were females who were in a similar situation as myself. I felt nervous as I walked to the front to grab a number. As I filled out the information, tears gathered in the corners of my eyes. I knew it was going to be hard, but never in a million years would I have imagined that would be me.

It was almost dark when I finally stepped foot outside of that office. I dialed my sister's number.

"Hey, boo. I'm on my way. I had no idea that it would take this long," I said.

"Girl, you know this is New York and everybody and their mama is looking to get food stamps and free housing. The baby's 'sleep, so you can just go ahead and go home. I will drop her off in the morning."

"All right, chick. I so appreciate you right now, 'cause I'm dog tired," I said.

"Cool. Get some rest. Love you."

"Love you back."

After I hung up, I decided to jump in a cab. My damn feet were tired, and my stomach was touching my back. I realized that I had gone without food for the entire day, not even water.

As soon as I got in the house, I rushed to the shower. Shit, I was sweaty as hell and needed water to do my body some justice. As the water beat down on my tired soul, I couldn't help but think about my life. I mean, what had I done lately to change my situation? I was with a nigga who didn't have shit to offer me but some dick and sweet talk. The more I thought about our situation, the more the tears started to fall. I felt weak as my heart ached.

This can't be life, I thought as I continued pouring my soul out.

CHAPTER FOUR

TWO YEARS LATER

Nyesha

After not being able to work for almost a year, an opening finally came up for the 7 a.m. to 3 p.m. shift at the nursing home. I also found a great babysitter not too far from the crib. I was doing good in my eyes, and that might have caused me to let this nigga back into my life.

I was on my second baby with this nigga. Some might say that I was stupid, but I swear there was something about this nigga that just kept me going back to him.

It was the weekend, and Yohan had come up to visit us. We were kicking it as usual.

"Yo, babe, I think you need to move to Richmond with me. That way, me and you can be together, and I can be in the kids' lives," Yohan suggested.

I put my two-month-old son down on the carpet and turned to face him. He was sitting in the corner of my bedroom, rolling a blunt.

"Why would I do that? I got my job, my apartment, plus my family is here."

"Yo, I'm your man, and we a family. You keep saying how much you struggle by yo'self, so I'm givin' you a way out," he said.

I scooted over to the edge of the bed and looked that nigga dead in his eyes. I had no idea what had gotten into him or why he was saying this crazy shit.

"Come on, babe, for real. I love you, and I want to watch my kids grow up," he pleaded.

I searched his eyes to see if I could catch a little bit of deceit, but I saw nothing. My heart started screaming for joy, but a little voice in my head was screaming, *Bitch, you a damn fool!*

But I want this. I need this. I love this man. Shit, my babies need their daddy in their life.

I sat there in silence, trying to convince myself that it was the right decision.

"Yes, I will move to Virginia with you." The words rolled off my tongue without giving it much thought. Even though I told him yes, I was kind of nervous. I had no idea how I was going to break the news to Mama and my sissy. The only time I had been away from my family was when I went to Job Corps. I just prayed to God that I was making the right decision, because failing was not an option for me or my kids.

The next morning, he was up early to head back to VA to get things set up for us. The plan was for me to move in exactly a month. We hugged and kissed, and then he pulled off.

I was happy that he was gone. It gave me some free time to myself, so I could really think about the dramatic move that I was about to make. He was right, though. I needed help with the kids. When it was one child, it was kind of okay, but with two children, I was really struggling to keep my head above water. I was living paycheck to paycheck, and that wasn't cutting. Yes, I got food stamps, but they weren't really helping. That alone helped me to make up my mind about making that move.

I decided to visit my sister later that day. I'd been thinking of different ways to approach her. I was afraid of how she would react once I broke this news to her. We were sitting in her living room, kicking it, when I decided to tell her.

"Sis, I need to holla at you real quick."

"What, bitch? Don't tell me you pregnant again." She stood up and stared me down.

"Hell, nah! But for real, though, I need to holla at you." I paused, buying time and trying to put my words together. There was no easy way to say it.

"Sis, I'm moving to Virginia," I finally blurted out.

"You what? You moving to Virginia? Don't tell me you trailing behind that no-good-ass nigga." She lashed out and shot me a disgusted look.

"Meisha, chill out, sounding all judgmental and shit. You my sissy, and I need your blessings on this."

"You know what? You're right. I'm just shocked, though. You don't have no family out there. What if something happens to you or the babies out there?"

"Ain't nothing gon' happen. Stop acting like I'm leaving the country. We are only gonna be six hours away from each other. I know you gonna miss me and the kids, but I love him, and this is our chance to be a family. Who knows? You might come down to see us," I said.

"Hmmm, I know one thing. That fuck nigga better treat you and them kids good, or I'll be out there wreaking havoc on his ass."

"Sis, I love you," I said, trying to soften up her mood.

"Love you too, bitch. So, when y'all leaving?"

"In a few days."

She got up, walked over to me, and gave me a tight hug. "I love you. Please take good care of yourself and the babies. Please call me if you ever need me."

When she stepped away, I saw tears rolling down her face. My eyes started to gather water.

"Sis, don't do that. We gonna talk on the phone every day," I said.

"By the way, did you tell Mama?" she asked.

Lord, why did she have to mention that woman? I was still trying to figure out how I was going to break the news to her.

"Nah, I ain't told her yet."

"Uh huh. You know her ass gon' flip out."

"Well, you know what? It's been months since we have spoken. She ain't called or tried to see her grandchildren. I'm a grown woman, and I don't owe her ass no explanation," I said.

"Okay, grown woman. Take yo' ass on to Virginia then. Make sure you call me when you get settled in."

We hugged once again, and then I left. Tears rolled down my face, and I felt like I was leaving a piece of my soul behind. My sister and I had really gotten close over the past year, and she had become the rock that I could lean on when I was going through a rough time.

As promised, Yohan came back for us on the day we agreed would be best for me to move. We packed up all the kids' clothes and took my two flat screen TVs with us. I left the furniture and everything else behind. They were either broken or weren't worth selling We then placed the kids in the car, and he pulled off. I felt a sense of unhappiness come over me as I took one last glimpse at the place that I'd called home.

On the ride to Virginia, I noticed that Yohan was extremely quiet. The kids had fallen asleep, and the music was playing low. At first, I charged it to him being tired, but then it hit me that it was more than that. His phone kept ringing, and I watched as he looked at it and threw it down. That continued every five minutes. I looked over at him.

"Who is that blowing up yo' phone?"

"Come on, yo. That's a fiend tryna cop something."

I could tell by his tone that he was irritated. Doubts started filling my head, but I kept them to myself. I had a tendency to second guess myself. Some would call it self-destruction.

I tried to ease my mind by logging in on Facebook. There wasn't much going on, but the same old shit. It wasn't enough to grab my attention. My mind was still focused on the situation at hand. I could only trust God and hope that I'd made the right decision.

I must've dozed off, because I felt someone shaking me. I forced my eyes open and looked up. It was Yohan, standing on my side of the car.

"Where are we?" I asked.

"We are here."

I was wide awake then. I turned around to look at my babies. They were still asleep. I opened my door and stepped out. My heart started racing. The place looked like it had been abandoned years ago. I grabbed my chest, trying to calm my nerves down.

"You all right? Wake the kids up," he said as he walked toward the building with a few bags.

"Hmmmm . . ." I was seriously stuck, and it was like a big lump was in my throat, preventing me from speaking. I unbuckled the kids and led them inside.

"Mommy, where are we?" Emanyi asked.

"We're at our new apartment, baby," I answered quietly.

I was scared to enter, but I took a few steps inside. The first thing that grabbed my attention was that the room was empty. The floor looked like it hadn't been cleaned or polished in decades.

"Come on, bae. Let me show you the kids' room," he said happily.

I didn't say anything. I just led the kids into the room. He was standing in the doorway with a big, happy smile plastered across his face. Surprisingly, it looked much better than the front of the apartment. He had a bunk bed for the kids, and the beds were made up. I knew the kids were tired, and they had to be hungry by then. I proceeded to get them together.

"Babe, I'm about to make a run real quick. I'll be back later." He kissed me on the forehead before leaving.

I wanted to protest, but I was too busy tending to my children. I heard the door close, and his car pulled off. After I got them together and finally into bed, I sat down. I was tired as hell too, but I was too pissed off to sleep. Really, what was I expecting? I knew we didn't have a lot of money. Shit, all I had was $800 to my name. I knew I needed a job asap.

It was getting late as hell, and he still hadn't returned. It was our first night in that house, and my nerves were very unsettled. I decided to take a shower, get dressed, and get into bed.

Even though I was tired and hungry, I decided to log on to social media. I was being nosey for real. I wanted to see what lies those bitches and niggas were telling. I noticed my sister put up a status about how much she missed me and the kids. I started to call her but quickly changed my mind. I was too tired, and knowing my sister, her ass was going to have a million questions about everything.

Instead, I dialed Yohan's number. I was going to ask him to bring me something to eat. I tried to ignore the hungry feeling, but my stomach felt like it was touching my back. His phone went straight to voicemail. I dialed the number again, but the same thing happened.

Curiosity got the best of me. Why was that nigga's phone off? I sat up in the bed, trying to control my emotions. Tears started filling my eyes.

It was well after 7 a.m. when Yohan finally walked through the door. I was up and ready to confront his ass.

"Hey, babe," he said like he hadn't been out all night.

"Hey, babe? Where the fuck you been? You just drop me and your kids off and disappear?" I really didn't give two fucks about how I addressed him.

"Babe, I'm sorry, yo. I was grinding all night. I apologize. I should've called you."

"Nigga, you must think I'm a fool. I know one thing. I didn't bring my black ass all the way down here to be dealing with this bullshit. You hear me?" I snapped.

"Mommy, why you yelling?" Emanyi asked as she walked into the kitchen.

"Come to Daddy, baby girl." He picked her up and walked away.

I was so heated, I started pacing the floor. I took a quick glance around, and the tears started flowing. All we had was a fucking bed. I mean, I wasn't the richest person in the world, but I worked and made sure my kids and I were comfortable. I was happy that I'd put two of my flat screen TVs in the car, or else my kids would not have had anything but a fucking bed. I hated to sound ungrateful, but that nigga claimed that he was out in the streets hustling and that was all he could come up with? Shit, he needed to give that shit up, 'cause he was definitely hustling backwards.

"Bitch, don't you ever talk to me like that in front of my kids."

I felt the slap as his hand connected with my face. I grabbed my cheek with my left hand and then used my right hand to punch his ass. He grabbed me and pinned me against the wall. I tried to claw at his face, but he grabbed my hands. My strength wasn't enough to fight him off.

"Baby, I'm sorry I hit you. Oh my God! What have I done?" He started crying and then tried to kiss me, but I moved away.

"Baby, please forgive me. I don't know what has gotten into me. I think it's school, grinding out in these streets, and dealing with these fuck niggas. Life is just weighing down on me," he cried.

I swear, I was angry as fuck that he put his hands on me. Still, another side of me felt compassion for him. I'd never seen him like that before.

"Please, baby, please! I love you. I promise it won't ever happen again," he pleaded as tears and snot rolled down his face.

I raised my hand to touch his face, caressed his cheek, and wiped a tear away. I hated to see him hurting like that and wished I could take some of his pain away.

We moved away from the wall and got in the bed. He continued to express how bad he felt for putting his hands on me. I wasn't sure if he was being sincere, but I also didn't have any proof that he wasn't either.

That night, we ended up making love. He ate my pussy from the back to the front. Then he dicked me down properly. After the sex ended, he was knocked out.

I laid on my back, thinking. It really bothered me that he had the nerve to raise his hand at me. I looked over at him. He looked so calm, as if nothing had happened earlier. I shook my head in disbelief and rolled over. I was tired mentally and physically.

CHAPTER FIVE

Nyesha

Things didn't remain good between me and Yohan. He would wake up, go to school, come home, chill with the kids for a little, then claim he was going out to hustle.

"Hustle? How the fuck you keep claiming you hustling, but you don't bring no money in? What kind of fucking hustler are you?" I confronted him one day while he was getting dressed to leave.

"Damn, man. All you do is fucking complain. Shit, when you gon' get off yo' ass and go find a fucking job? Shit, you got all that mouth, so you can start paying some of these goddamn bills 'round here."

"You really funny. Who the fuck's supposed to watch yo' fucking kids while I work? You ain't never here. Shit, you barely change a fucking diaper, never give them a bath or nothing. I do every fucking thing. So, before you sit up here trying to check me about paying bills, check your motherfucking self!" I spat.

"Yo, B, I'm gone," he said as he walked out the door. I ran behind him, but I was too late. He jumped in his car and drove off with the music blasting.

I ran back in the house crying. My daughter walked up to me and wiped my tears.

"Mommy, don't cry," she said in the most innocent voice.

I looked at her, smiled, and gave her a big hug. I hated that my baby had to see me like that.

That night I waited on him to come home, but as usual, I waited in vain. I tried calling his phone, but it rang until the voicemail came on.

I dialed my sister's number. I needed someone to talk to, and my sister was the only one that I could confide in.

"Hey, bitch. What you doing up?" she asked.

"Just need to talk to my favorite girl, you know?Wait, what time is it? Why you not at work?"

"I go in late tonight. Babysitter had an emergency. Fuck all that, sis. You good? You sound like you've been crying." She sounded concerned.

I couldn't hold it in. I busted out crying, letting all my emotions out.

"Nyesha, you okay? That nigga didn't hurt you, did he?" she inquired.

"Sis, I think it was a mistake for me to move out here," I confessed.

"Why? What happened?"

I went on to tell her everything that had happened to me since I made the move. Well, almost everything. I deliberately left out the part about him hitting me. I knew my sister, and she would hit the roof if I told her that shit.

"Sis, dry those got-damn tears. I know you grown and you gonna live your life, but like I always tell you, you better than that dude. You need to start thinking about your babies. They don't need to be around that nigga if he's treating you like that."

I sat on the phone, weeping quietly. My sister was reading my ass, and there was nothing I could do about it. The fact was, I needed to hear it.

Things only got worse between me and Yohan. The fights got louder, and his absence was felt. I was feeling lonely because I didn't know anybody in Virginia. My kids were my only company and the only reason that I kept my sanity.

I wasn't feeling too hot one day. Each time I stood up, I felt dizzy. Also, when I was taking a shower, I noticed discharge. I wasn't alarmed at first, but three days later, as I was getting out of bed, I started feeling a bad pain in my abdomen. I didn't say anything about it, but I took two Tylenol and lay back down in the bed.

I had the kids in the room with me because I was in no state to watch them. I tried to stay alert, but I was getting weaker by the second. I grabbed my phone and dialed Yohan's number.

"Hey, boo," he answered.

"You need to come home. I need to go to the hospital."

"Why? Something happen to one of the kids?"

"No, it's me. I'm in pain, and I got a fever," I barely got out.

"Damn. I'm on the way."

Twenty minutes later, he was at the house. He had to help me to the car. He then got the kids in the car and pulled off.

"Yes, ma'am, may I help you?" the receptionist asked when we got to the hospital.

"I need to see a doctor. I am having abdominal pain, and I think I have a fever."

"Okay, fill this out and then bring it back to me."

Didn't that bitch hear me say that I was in a lot of pain? Filling out a fucking paper was the last thing that was on my mind. I took the clipboard from her and walked over to where Yohan and the kids were. I filled the paper out and took it back to her.

Minutes later, the nurse called me and checked my vital signs. "We need to take her back there. She has a fever of 105 degrees," she hollered to another nurse.

"Let's go, honey." She helped me to my feet and took me to a nearby room.

I noticed two doctors rushing in. I explained what was going on to them.

"Let's get her on an IV with antibiotics. Get a urine sample also," he said to the nurse.

After getting examined and giving a urine sample, I was hooked up to an IV. I texted Yohan to let him know what was going on with me and to check on the kids. I knew they were his kids also, but he'd never had to care for them on his own before.

I was no longer in pain, and the IV seemed to be working. Suddenly, I wasn't burning up like I had been when I came in. I was still feeling weak as I nervously waited for my lab results to come back.

After about three hours, I heard the door open. It was the doctor, along with a nurse. My heart skipped a few beats as I braced myself for what he was about to tell me.

The doctor greeted me and then said, "Your lab results are back, and it appears that you contracted an STD. Chlamydia."

The room started spinning around me as I tried my hardest to digest what the fuck that nigga had just said to me.

"Chlamydia? Are you sure? I mean, how is that possible? I only have one sex partner. . . ." My words trailed off.

"Yes, I'm sure. We already started you on antibiotics, and now you should start feeling better. Your partner should also get tested and treated, because if he doesn't and you have intercourse with him, you will only re-infect yourself."

I was listening to the doctor, but I wasn't hearing him. All I could think about was this dirty-dick nigga that was sitting out front.

"I'm gonna put you on antibiotics for seven days, and please refrain from any sexual activities," the doctor said.

The IV was finished, and I was ready to go. I sat there impatiently, waiting on the nurse to discharge me. I swear, I was running all kinds of different ideas through my head.

"Do you have insurance?" the nurse asked as she filled out papers.

"Nah, just send me a damn bill," I said in annoyance.

I was given my discharge papers. After that, I quickly got up and got dressed. I noticed that I was feeling a little better than I had been when I first came in.

"What they say, bae?" Yohan asked when I got to the waiting room.

I didn't tell him anything because I didn't want to cause a scene up in that hospital.

"Come on. Are y'all ready?" I snatched the kids' hands.

"Babe, what's wrong?" He followed me outside.

I remained quiet. I was trying to get the kids in the car without them listening to any of the shit that was going to take place. He got into the car while I strapped the kids in. I got in and turned to look out of the window.

"Babe, talk to me," he said as he reached over and grabbed my hand.

I snatched my hand away from him. I was careful not to let my kids see that shit. I looked over at him and could see that he was angry. At this moment, I didn't give a damn about his feelings. That nigga sure didn't give a fuck about slinging that dick up in those nasty-ass bitches. Now my ass was sitting there paying for that shit.

Oh my God, and I sucked his dick. I instantly wanted to vomit.

As soon as he parked the car, I jumped out, opened the back door, and got the kids out. I hurriedly took them inside and put them in their room.

I ran to the kitchen and grabbed the biggest knife that was available. He walked in the house, and I approached him.

"Yo, who the fuck you been fucking?" I yelled.

"You tripping. What you talking about?"

I shoved the papers from the hospital in his face. "I fucking hate youuuuuuuuuu!" I screamed as I lunged toward him with the knife.

"Damn, bitch, what you doing? You stupid bitch. You just cut me!" he grabbed my hand.

I tried to hang on for dear life, but my strength was nothing compared to his. "I fucking hate you. You hear me? You out here fucking these stanking-ass bitches and don't even have the fucking decency to wear a fucking condom. You know what? You nasty just like them hoes."

"Man, I ain't got shit. How I know yo' ass ain't the one that's been fucking? Matter of fact, the other day when I was fucking you, your pussy felt a little loose."

"Ha-ha, you a funny-ass nigga, you know that? Fuck you with yo' old burning-ass dick. Maybe I should've fucked and sucked a few niggas."

"Bitch, I don't give a fuck what you do," he snapped. "Shit, I'm only around 'cause of my seeds."

I was ready to rip that nigga's head off, but he still had my hands held together. "Let me go. Get yo' nasty ass off me!" I screamed out while kicking to get away.

He finally let me go, and I ran to the bedroom. I swear, I hated his ass for real. What kind of man would do that to a woman, especially the mother of his kids? That's when reality hit me. He wasn't a man at all. He was just a dirty-ass nigga who was selfish and didn't give a fuck about me.

Tears flooded my face as I buried my head in my pillow. My heart was broken because I had trusted him to a certain extent. I never expected him to fuck around and bring that shit home.

A little while later, that burning-dick nigga was in the shower. I was on my phone, browsing Facebook, but his phone kept on ringing. First, I ignored it, but whoever was calling wasn't easing up. I jumped off the bed and grabbed the phone. I was about to press the ignore button, but the screen caught my eyes.

BABY GIRL.

I held the phone away from my face, blinked, and looked at the ringing phone that was still in my hand.

"Hello," I answered.

"Hello, good afternoon. Can I speak to Yohan?"

"Who is calling?"

"This is Zaria."

"Okay, Zaria, and why are you calling my man's phone?"

"Oh, you Nyesha, his baby mama, right? Well, I'm his woman, so now that the introduction is over, can you put my man on the phone?" that bold bitch said.

"Your man, bitch? I live here with him and his kids. Trust me, I'm the only woman he got. Just because he fucking you don't mean he wants you, you silly bitch."

She laughed. "Ha-ha, you big mad or little mad? He told me all about you and how you were homeless out in New York with his kids, dirty and hungry. Of course, I support my man, so I agreed for yo' broke ass to move out here. The only reason why you're there is because he needs to keep an eye on his kids."

"Bitch, you a silly ho if you believe that shit. I see you one of those gullible-ass bitches out here that keep allowing these cheating-ass niggas to run back and forth. Bitch, I'm done addressing you for real. Oh, by the way. Make sure you go check out that burning-ass pussy of yours."

Hanging the phone up on that ho, I hurriedly took the number and put it in my phone. Then I heard the water turn off, and I knew that he would be coming out of the bathroom soon.

"Yo, who the fuck is Zaria?" I asked as soon as he came in the room.

"Why? She called?"

"Answer my fucking question. Who is this bitch?"

"Man, she ain't no bitch. She's my friend."

"Friend? You told that bitch that I was homeless and shit. Talking 'bout my kids were hungry and dirty? I don't give a fuck about you trying to get pussy, but how low can you get, lying on my kids?"

"What the fuck you doing answering my phone?" he snapped.

"All you worried about is me answering your phone. Be a fucking man and let me know if you don't want me anymore. I deserve fucking better than this shit that you dishing out."

"You know what, Nyesha? You're right. I want out of this relationship. I'm not happy anymore. All you do is bitch every day. Let's just be friends and co-parent," he said.

"Nigga, fuck you! You brought me all the way to Virginia to tell me you ain't happy? So, this bitch is who you wanna be with?"

"Man, I'm tired of lying. I love her, and I want to be with her."

I leapt off the fucking bed and sprayed that nigga with the bottle of Mace that I had hidden under the cover.

"Awe, you bitch! What was that? I'm going to kill you!" he screamed as he held his face and dashed out of the room.

"Mommy, what is wrong?" My daughter ran into the room.

"Baby, go back in your room," I said, not wanting to burn her eyes. I didn't want my baby to experience any of the drama. I quickly put on a pair of sweatpants and stood up. I knew that nigga was angry, and he might come back up in there.

A few minutes later, he stormed up in the room. I was ready for whatever. I knew I couldn't beat him, but I would die trying.

"Bitch, you Maced me. I should beat yo' motherfucking ass, but that's too easy, I'm done with you. Pack yo' shit and go back to New York, yo. I'm done trying," he yelled.

I wanted to jump on that nigga again, but his words caught my attention. That nigga just told me to pack my shit and go, just like that. I watched as he started throwing clothes into a duffle bag.

"Where the fuck you going?" I ran over to him, grabbing onto his shirt.

"Bitch, get the fuck off me. I'm leaving yo' ass for good."

"Please, Yohan, don't do this. I swear we can work it out. I will be with you even if you with her, pleeease." I fell to my knees and held on to his leg.

He kicked his leg to get me off. "Get off me, you pathetic bitch. I never want to see your fucking face ever again."

His words echoed in my head.

"Please, baby, please. I need you. The kids need you. You can't leave us!" I cried. My chest was tightening up on me, and I felt like I couldn't breathe. I wanted to fight for my man, for us and our family.

I stood up with tears rolling down my face. I looked him in the eye and begged him to give me another chance. He looked at me with disgust in his eyes.

"Fuck you! I hate you, bitch. Ever since you came in my life it has been nothing but hell." He hawked and spit in my face.

I fell to my feet, and he walked off.

"Noooo, God, no!" I cried out while trying to wipe my face. I felt disgusted and wished God would just take me. My heart was hurting and felt like it had been broken into a million pieces.

"Mommy, don't cry. Please don't cry," I heard my daughter say as she knelt down beside me and wiped my tears away. I tried my best to stop the tears, but to be honest, I was too hurt and couldn't hold it back. My daughter then hugged me close to her while patting me on the back.

"Mommy, it's goin' to be okay," her little voice whispered in my ear.

I didn't respond. Instead, I hugged her tightly while using my might to fight back the tears.

"Come on, baby. Let's get up off this floor," I finally said.

I walked into the bathroom and washed my face with soap. I still couldn't believe that nigga spit in my face like I was a regular bitch in the streets.

After I cooked dinner for the kids, bathed them, and tucked them in their beds, that's when everything hit me. A year ago, I was doing okay without that nigga, and he popped his ass out of nowhere. Now look at me. I had nothing, and I meant nothing. The money that I had saved up was gone. If I needed anything, I had to ask him, and half the time, he caught an attitude before giving it to me.

I held my head as the stress of life came pounding down on me. Everything flashed in my mind. I could hear my sister's voice in my head, warning me. I could hear mama's voice telling me how stupid I was. Lord, I wasn't ready to face any of it.

I got up and went to the kitchen where he had a bottle of Hennessy. I didn't even drink anymore, but I needed a few drinks to help me deal with the bullshit that I was dealing with.

CHAPTER SIX

Nyesha

I had K. Michelle's "These Men" blasting on repeat. Each word was sinking into my veins, but the alcohol sure was helping. I went from feeling pitiful to feeling empowered. All of the tears were gone, and anger took its place. Funny thing was, I wasn't angry at that nigga. I was more disappointed that I had allowed myself to get played by him a second time. How many times did that nigga have to hurt me in order for me to leave his ass alone? I looked up to God, searching for answers.

I was a single mother for a while before I left New York. Now, there I was in a new state with a few dollars and nothing else. I couldn't call my mother because I didn't want to hear her mouth, and I didn't want to put a burden on my sister. Most days, all we had to eat was noodles and milk for my baby.

I was sitting in the living room, trying to come up with a plan, when I heard a knock at the door. That was strange because I didn't know anybody in VA. I grabbed my phone just in case I might need it. I walked to the door and looked out.

"Yes, may I help you?"

"Hello, ma'am. My name is Charles. I'm the landlord, and I'm looking for the gentleman that rented this property," the man on the other side said.

I opened the door to speak to him. "He's not here right now, but you can leave a message."

"He's two months behind on the rent. I've been calling his phone, but there's no answer. Are you his wife?"

"Wife? Umm, no. I'm his kids' mother. I will call him and let him know that we're behind on the rent," I said.

"Thank you, ma'am, because the next step is to take him to court. Here is my card with my number. I'll be waiting on him to call." He handed me a business card before walking off.

I walked away, closing the door behind me. I flopped down on the couch. As if the fucking day couldn't get any worse. That nigga just left us high and dry. I dialed his number, but the phone just rang.

I texted him. You need to call me now.

I sat there with the phone in my hand, waiting, but the phone never rang. I tried calling a few more times, and nothing happened. I remembered I had his cousin's number, so I pulled it up and called him.

"Yooo," he answered.

"Aye, this Yohan's baby mama. I was wondering if you seen him?"

"Oh, hey, how you doing? Ummm, nah. I ain't seen that nigga in a minute. How the kids doing?" he asked.

"Don't worry about how my kids doing. Tell that no-good-ass cousin of yours that I'm looking for him." I didn't wait for a response. I just hung up.

I knew that nigga was lying because he and Yohan were too tight. When you saw one, most times, you saw the other one. I really didn't have time for games when me and my kids' future was up in the air.

Days went by, and I still hadn't heard from Yohan. Day after day, I watched as the little food we had disappeared. The night before was the hardest. I had to split a pack of noodles between my daughter and me. My baby was down to his last few scoops of Enfamil. I couldn't go to sleep, because as their mother, I wanted to do better. It felt like I was failing them.

I really didn't know anyone in VA, but I noticed that there was a chick about my age who lived next door. While the kids were sleeping, I walked over to her apartment. I nervously knocked on the door.

The door flew open. "May I help you?"

"My name is Nyesha, and I'm new around here."

"I know who you are. You Yohan's baby mama."

I was shocked that she was aware of who I was. We'd never exchanged any words before, and I'd never seen him talking to her.

"You know Yohan?" I was curious now.

"Yeah, well, he and my boyfriend grew up together over by Blackwell. I'm from Churchill," she said.

"Oh, okay. I see."

"So, where is Yohan, by the way? I haven't seen him in a while. Shit, he must be back with Zaria."

"Huh?"

"Oh my God. You didn't know about her?" She looked at me strange before she continued. "Girl, I probably shouldn't be talking to you, but you know we women need to support each other more."

"I agree. So, tell me why is this so important to Yohan?" I asked.

"Girl, he been fooling around with that bitch for a while now. She's a little young schoolgirl, and I heard he took her virginity."

"Really?" I was disgusted.

"Girl, I was wondering how he was going to work it out. I mean, with you and the kids coming and all."

I stood there listening to her run her mouth. Shit, it seemed like she knew all that nigga's business.

"Do you know where the girl lives?" I asked.

"She live somewhere over on Sand Susie, but I'm not sure. I do know where she works, though. One day when Ryan and I went grocery shopping, we saw her," she said.

"Can you give me the address?"

"Nah, girl, 'cause I think you about to cause some drama. Just Google that shit. It's the only Winn Dixie on the south side."

"Thanks. Anyway, I was wondering if you can watch the kids for me while I go to the social service building tomorrow?" I asked.

"Girl, of course. All you got to buy me is a Pepsi and a pack of Newport Lights."

"Bet. It's a deal."

"By the way, I love your New York accent." She giggled.

"Bitch, what the fuck you doing outside? You left the got-damn noodles on the stove. Now them shits is burnt!" A dude that I assumed was her man yelled as he walked outside.

"Girl, excuse him. His mouth off the chain," she said, looking like she wasn't bothered.

I just smiled. I wasn't sure what to say. After all, I had my own problems.

"Anyway, it was nice meeting you. What's your name again?" I asked.

"It's Karen."

"Okay, Karen. You can come over around nine a.m. to watch the kids. I'll try my best not to be there all day."

"All right, honey. See you in the morning."

As I walked off, I couldn't help but think she was one hell of a character. She seemed like she knew everybody's business. I made a mental note not to let her into mine.

Karen came through for me and watched the kids. I got dressed and headed to the bus stop. I sure missed the subway and the dollar buses in New York. As I stood there waiting for the bus, I couldn't help but think about Yohan. I wondered what the motive was behind him moving us out to Virginia. If he knew he was in a relationship, why couldn't he just leave us alone? He could've visited his kids without putting us through that. I felt my eyes starting to gather water. I let out a long sigh, trying not to cry again.

I looked at my phone. The bus would be arriving in less than five minutes. I put the phone back in my purse and waited. I saw a car coming toward me with the music pumping loudly. As the car got closer to me, it looked familiar. It was a BMW X6.

Man, I swear I know that car, I thought as the car flew past me. I focused my attention back on the bus that I saw coming down the street.

Honk! Honk! Honk!

The sound of a horn startled me, bringing me out of my thoughts. I looked up and saw that the same money-green BMW that flew past me had reversed back. I stood there wondering what the fuck that person wanted. The windows were tinted, so I couldn't see who was inside, but I didn't have to wait long to find out who it was.

"Yoooo!" I heard a familiar voice with a northern accent holler. Only then, I bent down to see if it was who I thought it was. I was surprised as hell to see my homeboy, Sean.

"What the hell you doing down here, B?" he asked.

"Shit, I should ask you that same question, Mr. Harlem."

"Yo, get in real quick."

Without hesitation, I jumped in his car, happy to see a familiar face. He was not just anybody that I knew from back home. Sean was a big-time dope boy from Harlem. I remembered walking down White Plains Road before, and this dude pulled up and tried to holla at me. We exchanged numbers and kept in touch. I knew he wanted to fuck, but I was so caught up with my baby daddy, so I never gave him no play.

"Yo, B, what's good? How long you been out here?" he asked.

I couldn't respond to his questions. Instead, I busted out crying.

"Yo, B, what's good with you?" He reached over and grabbed my hand.

I was a hot mess and was at my breaking point. I needed a listening ear and a broad shoulder to lean on.

"Yo, you scaring me. Talk to me, B."

I guess that was all I needed to hear, because I started pouring my heart out to him. I told him about everything from the time my baby daddy came to New York to when I moved to Virginia with him.

"Yo, that nigga wicked as fuck. How can that nigga treat you and his seeds like that? Man, you need to leave that nigga alone, yo," he said in his thick Harlem accent. New York niggas were hype as hell, but those Harlem niggas were cocky as fuck. I swear, when a Harlem nigga entered a room, he was going to make sure you knew he was there.

"Yo, let's go get something to eat and chill for a minute," he offered.

I quickly forgot where I was going. "Yes, sure."

He took me to Red Lobster for lunch. We ate, and he mostly listened to me talk about all my problems. It felt good to have a familiar person listen to my issues and not judge me.

Sitting across from him made me more aware of his manly presence. My pussy started jumping as his voice echoed in my ear. I tried to ignore it at first, but the feeling wouldn't go away.

The nigga ended up getting a room. I knew I shouldn't have been there, but fuck it. My pussy was throbbing, and I needed to be fucked. I closed my eyes and tried not to think about where my baby daddy had been and whose pussy he'd been digging in all night.

Sean didn't waste any time. As soon as we got inside the room, he rolled two blunts, and we smoked. Suddenly, he started rubbing on my legs. My mind was telling me no, but my pussy was in total control. His hand traveled from my thighs to the wetness between my legs.

"Oh, oh, oh my goodness." My entire body felt like hot lava was about to erupt. I realized how backed up I really was. I hadn't fucked since I found out that my baby daddy had burned me.

Sean got up and started undressing me, first with his eyes, and then with his hands. He lifted my legs and put them on his shoulders while his tongue brought life back into my soul. I didn't try to figure out why and how Sean ended up between my legs. Maybe because he had the sexiest lips I'd seen on a brother.

"Yesss, daddy," I cooed with my hand on the back of his head, guiding it back and forth while rubbing my hard nipples with my other hand. "Eat this pussy, daddy." My body felt like I was floating on clouds. I was higher than a motherfucker, and my eyes rolled back in my head as Sean continuously sucked on my clit.

Shit, what the fuck was he doing to me? My body tensed up, and I was trying to hold back my nut, but Sean's tongue plunged in and out of my pussy.

"My Lord!" I called on his name because he made me repent and sent me a savior. My juices flowed from my body like a running river.

I opened my eyes, realizing that I'd zoned out. It felt like I was about to pee on myself, and sweat was pouring down my face. My body was numb, and I couldn't move. I was paralyzed from the waist down.

"Shit, I gotta pee," I mumbled under my breath, but I couldn't move my body. I couldn't believe I was about to pee on myself. I could not hold it any longer.

"Oh, shit," I groaned. The sensation of liquid leaving my body felt so different. It was soothing and relaxing.

"You like that, baby?" Sean asked while he did what was he doing between my legs. "Skeet, baby, skeet."

The everlasting stream that flowed from me caused my body to shiver and shake uncontrollably. My body was experiencing the best orgasm ever. I went from crying to his tongue digging in my insides. He had me squirting like a busted pipe.

"What the fuck did you just do to me? Damn, Sean, do it again." I begged for more. I wanted to have that pleasurable feeling forever.

I laid there, restless, wanting Sean to have his way with me. He rubbed my clit, which sent chills through my body. My pussy was still on fire. He started nibbling on my clit, and my body shivered again in ecstasy.

Each kiss felt like my body was yearning for him to be inside of my pussy, soul searching. Sean's lips and tongue traveled up my stomach as he kissed my skin. My mind was lost in love. My perky nipples wanted some attention as his tongue made circular motions around them.

"Shit, babe." I didn't want him to ever stop. The pleasurable sensation had my toes tingling.

Sean kissed the other nipple, giving it some unconditional love. He kissed my hotspots, which made me melt over and over again. His rock-hard dick rubbed against my thigh, making my hips automatically start to grind in a circular motion.

My pussy was starving for dick like a Kindle starving for readers. "Fuck me, daddy," I whined like a baby.

He lifted up one of my legs, placing it over his shoulder. His dick entered into my soul, sending magic to my world. I held my breath, taking him all in, inch by inch.

"Damn, this pussy feels so good," Sean said as he penetrated me deeply.

With each thrust, I squeezed my pussy muscles, hugging his dick. My lips looked like the lips on my mouth while sucking on a pickle, as they wrapped around his dick.

"You love it, don't you?" I purred.

"Hell yeah," he responded, kissing my lips. His tongue toyed with my tongue. I was experiencing out-of-body type shit.

As my juices flowed, my pussy was making splashing sounds. My breathing became heavy, and my body felt like it was shutting off and on. Sean's dick penetrated in and out of my pussy. I really didn't know this nigga that well, but I was loving him right now. Or maybe I should say that my pussy was loving him. His dick game was on point. My body shook and trembled uncontrollably as I reached multiple orgasms.

I was tired after I busted numerous times, but he was still going. That nigga balled my little ass up and had me all over the room. Even on the bathroom sink, that nigga was dicking me down. I tried to keep up with him by matching each stroke that he was throwing.

"Aaarghhhh! Damn, babe, I'm about to cum. Open up and take this dick." He squeezed my ass together and pulled me closer to him, straight applying pressure to the pussy.

"Ahhh, ahh, fuck this pussy, daddy," I whispered in his ear. I knew that would speed up the process. Shit, the dick was good as fuck, but the pain was becoming unbearable.

"Aaaarrgghh! Open up yo' legs." He moved my legs farther apart while he was all up in me.

It was in that quick second that I realized he wasn't wearing a condom, and my dumb ass was not on the pill.

"Yo, B, you got that Aquafina flow pussy. You had my whole dick wet." He broke my train of thought.

I smiled at him, hoping that meant he was going to help me financially.

I got up and went in the bathroom to take a quick shower. I tried my best to wash all of his cum out of me. I knew that was bullshit, but I was hoping and wishing that I wouldn't get pregnant by him.

When I came out of the bathroom, he was on the phone, handling some business. I sat on the side of the bed and browsed Facebook.

"Aye, yo, I figured out a way that you can make some money," he said.

"You did? Do you know somebody that's hiring?" I turned around to face him.

"Nah, B. You know what kind of business I do."

"Yeah, and?"

"I'ma throw you three pounds of Loud. You can flip that and keep the money so you can get on yo' feet."

I was confused, although I tried to conceal it. I had never sold anything before, so why the fuck was that nigga talking about giving me some pounds to sell? Shit, I wasn't trying to go to anybody's jail for real.

"I ain't never sold no drugs before. Shit, I wouldn't know the first thing to do," I said.

"Listen up, B. You ain't got too many choices right now. I can teach you this shit and you can make yo' money, or you can continue being broke," he said in a harsh voice.

"Damn, you ain't got to say it like that," I said in an annoyed tone.

"My bad, yo. I ain't mean it like that. I'm just trying to help you out."

"I guess so," I responded reluctantly.

Hustling class was in full effect. He spent the next hour teaching me to sell drugs. He showed me what a nick, dime, and dub bag should look like. He also showed me what an ounce looked like. Before he left, I had full knowledge of how to sell weed.

"Yo, I'm about to bounce" he told me. "Here goes some money to get you and the kids some food. Take my number and hit me when you're ready to re-up."

I called a cab and went home. I hoped that chick Karen wasn't mad because I was gone longer that I'd intended to be. I got out of the cab and entered the house.

"Mommy, Mommy!" both of my kids yelled in unison as they ran to me. Even though I needed the little break, I was happy to see my babies.

"How did it go? I hope they didn't give you a hard time," she said to me.

"How did what go?"

"Social services, girl." She busted out laughing.

"Oh, yeah. My bad. I'm tired as hell. It went fine," I lied.

"Oh, okay. Those motherfuckers be stingy with the food stamps and shit, like it's coming out of they pocket."

"I know, right?" I smiled.

"All right, girl. Let me get on over there before this man start tripping. You know how these niggas do," she said.

I reached in my purse and grabbed a $50 bill. "Here you go, chick. Thank you again."

"Damn, you balling, bitch. If you paying like this, you can hit me up anytime for babysitting duties."

I didn't respond. I just walked her to the door and locked it. I was happy to be home with my kids. I let them bathe, then ordered pizza for their dinner. I spent the remainder of the evening watching television with them.

After they were tucked in safely in their bed, I sat at the kitchen table, thinking about how I was going to pull off selling the weed. Sean made it seem so easy, but I was terrified.

God, but what choice do I have? My back is against the wall, and this is the only way I see out for me and my kids.

CHAPTER SEVEN

Kymani

"Ky, where the fuck you think you going? It's seven o'clock in the damn morning!" Simone yelled.

"Man, don't worry about where I'm going, as long as I'm getting far away from yo' ass. All you fucking do is bitch, bitch, bitch. Damn, a nigga just came in the house!" I yelled while putting on my jogging pants.

"Nigga, you must think I'm stupid. I know you out there fucking and sucking everything with a pussy. Nigga, keep fucking playing with me, and I'ma roll up on yo' ass."

I wasn't trying to hear that shit that Simone, my psychotic-ass baby mama, was spitting. Simone and I had been messing around for about a year before she got pregnant with my seed. Shawty wasn't the kind of chick that a nigga was proud to call his baby moms, but shit happened. One night, I was drunk as fuck and busted all up in her. I was praying that she wasn't pregnant, but a month later, she hit me up, telling me she was carrying my seed. Being the nigga that I was, I stepped up and started fucking with her on the regular.

At the time, she was living in Jackson Ward with her mama. It wasn't a great living situation to bring a baby into, so when she was five months pregnant, I moved her into an apartment over on 32nd Street. I knew the old dude that was the manager, so I dropped a few bills on him, and he got her up in there.

It wasn't my intention to move in with her, since I had my own crib on 33rd Street. I started spending a few nights here and there because I was trying to do the right thing, but that soon proved to be a fucking mistake. That bitch stayed checking my pockets when I was asleep. I would wake up to yelling and screaming about other bitches. Damn, what the fuck did she think? We were not together. We were only fucking.

A few months later, she gave birth to my seed. I couldn't lie. When I visited the hospital and saw my daughter, a nigga like me was emotional. Shit, she was the most beautiful human being I'd ever seen. On that day, I made a promise to God that I was going to do right by her for the rest of her life.

Simone was still yelling some shit as I jumped in my ride. I put the windows up and turned up the music. Lil' Boosie's CD was blasting as I pulled off. It was too fucking early for that bitch to be doing all that fucking yelling.

I decided to grab something to eat at Waffle House. The plan was to get a few hours of sleep before I hit the block again. The next day was the first of the month, and Richmond's streets were going to be jumping with fiends trying to get that hit. Shit, I was good because I had hit my connect up in Petersburg the day before, and he made sure I was straight.

My phone kept ringing. Looking at the caller ID, I saw that it was Simone blowing me up. I pressed ignore, but her ass kept calling.

"Yo, what the fuck you want?" I yelled into the phone.

"Boy, what the fuck I want? You just gon' up and fucking leave like you ain't got a fucking baby up in here?"

"Yo, cut it out, Simone. Little mama's sleep."

"So fucking what? She'on't never get to fucking see you. The only fucking time you come over here is late night when you trying to fuck."

"Man, fuck all that. Do you want me to come get my daughter? Is that what you fucking want?" I said.

"Fuck you, boy. My daughter won't go nowhere with you."

"A'ight then, bitch. What the fuck you want from me?"

"You know what, Ky? You ain't gon' stop until I bring a nigga up in here and fuck him while yo' daughter is on the bed. See, you think you know me, but trust me, you got the wrong bitch!" She spoke with venom in her voice.

I didn't respond, even though that bitch had just woken up the beast in me. See, I murked niggas on a regular, and that bitch had no idea what the fuck she'd just said to me. Man, I needed to stay away from that old dumb-ass bitch before I had to kill her ass too.

I put out the black I was smoking, turned my phone off, and walked into Waffle house.

God, I can't keep dealing with this ole dumb-ass girl, I thought.

CHAPTER EIGHT

Nyesha

Selling drugs was not as hard as I first thought. After I made a few sales, word spread like wildfire that I was the chick with that exotic. Before you knew it, the whole apartment complex was copping smoke from me. I had to thank Karen because she helped spread the word. I went from selling dimes of weed to twenties to ounces. In no time, I upgraded to selling pounds.

The money was coming in so fast that I started to feel paranoid. Richmond niggas were known for robbery. The fact was, I wasn't one of them, and I wasn't sure if I was going to become one of their victims.

"So, what you gonna do with all that money?" Karen asked.

"I don't know, but my plan is to find a house to rent for me and kids. You know, get from around here," I said to Karen as we sat outside. The kids were playing, and she and I were just sitting there kicking it.

"Great idea. I wish I could make some of that damn money you making. Shit, we struggling our asses off."

"You, selling drugs? Girl, stop it." I busted out laughing.

"Bitch, you just don't know. Shit, I done sold pussy before, so selling drugs can't possibly be that damn hard."

"You sold pussy before?" I was kind of shocked by how open she was about selling pussy.

"Hell yeah. When my kids were hungry and my baby daddy was off doing one of his many bids, I ain't had no choice but to fuck this nigga that I went to school with. Shit, he had money, and I had product. Ain't no shame in my motherfucking game. I'ma do whatever to make sure my kids eat."

"I hear you. Well, I can front you a pound, but I need my money back," I said.

"Are you serious? Bitch, I love you, and of course. I got you." She hugged me tightly.

"A'ight, chick, chill out. You almost choked me to death."

After spending a few more minutes talking, I decided to take the kids in the house.

"Mommy, why we got to go inside?" they asked.

"Because it is hot as hell out here. Plus, Mommy got some work to do."

"You always got work to do, Mommy," my daughter whined.

I looked at my ungrateful-ass little girl. Did she know how hard it was? Just months ago, all we had were ramen noodles, peanut butter, and Kool-Aid. Lately, they didn't want for anything. The fridge was full, they got their favorite snacks all the time, and all of their clothes were designer. I knew that she might not understand it then, but one day, she would thank me.

After I bathed the kids, fed them, and got them settled, I decided to do some work. The next day was the first of the month, and I needed to bag up some work. I got my scale, my scissors, and my baggies, and flopped down on the couch in the living room.

I picked up the remote to turn the TV on, but before I could do so, I heard a loud bang on the door. My heart almost jumped out of my chest. I wondered who was knocking like that. I grabbed the large garbage bag of weed along with the baggies and ran toward the back room. I threw everything under the bed and then rushed to the front, where the knocking was getting louder.

I looked through the peephole and realized that it was the landlord. Fuck, what did he want? I had just paid the rent for three months in advance. I opened the door.

"Yes. How may I help you?"

"Miss, I need to talk to you about some complaints I've been getting," he said.

"Complaints about what?" I was surprised.

"A few tenants have been complaining that you are dealing drugs over here in the complex. At first, I ignored it, because you don't seem like a drug dealer, but the complaints are becoming more frequent. I even have a tenant that's been with me for a long time who's threatening to leave if I don't do something about it."

"That is a lie. I don't sell no drugs. Honestly, I think they just jealous of me because I don't sit around and gossip with them all day," I said.

"That might be true, but I can't have that kind of rumor spreading around here. Most of my tenants are Section 8 tenants, and the last thing I need is to have the government or the police snooping around. If this continues, I'ma have to give you notice to vacate the premises."

"All right, I hear you. Is that all?" I asked.

"Yes, ma'am. Have a good day." He titled his hat and walked off.

I locked the door and leaned against it. Who the fuck was running their mouth? I mean, most of those motherfuckers smoked or hustled weed, so why was my name being mentioned? I caught an instant headache, because what if he wasn't the only one they were running their mouth to?

Fuck, I got to move ASAP, I thought as I walked into my room and grabbed a Black and Mild off my dresser. I quickly lit it and grabbed the garbage bag from under the bed. I had heard what that fool had said, but tomorrow was a money-making day, and I wasn't going to miss out.

A few days later, the kids were at the park with Karen and her kids. I decided to kick it with Sean for a little while. As usual, we went out for lunch and then back to the room. I was kind of getting tired of fucking him, but my loyalty to him was at an all-time high. If it wasn't for him, I wouldn't be able to make all that money.

"Yo, B, you seem a little distant. You good?" he asked.

"Yeah, I'm good. It's just that the other day, the landlord stopped by to warn me that some of the tenants are complaining that I'm hustling over there."

"Yo, B, I told you before that it's time to move around."

"I know, but I am used to those people over there. Plus, I was trying to stack some more dough, you know?"

"Stop being stupid," he said. "You been killing it. I know 'cause you been hitting me up back-to-back. You definitely moving that work. You need to find you a house or a new apartment and get the fuck outta there."

"Yeah, you right." I sat there thinking about what he was saying.

"Listen, yo. This game can be grimy and cutthroat. The same bitch-ass niggas that laugh in yo' face be the same ones working with twelve. In this game, trust no one, and I mean no one. You hear me?"

"I got you."

"Sean, I need to talk to you on a personal level," I said.

"Speak."

"I know you helped me and everything, but I don't think that every time I re-up I should have to suck your dick or fuck you."

He looked at me like I was crazy. "Damn, B, it's like that? I thought you loved fucking me."

"It's not that. It's just that you have a woman, and all we're doing is fucking. I mean, I want more."

"What? You want money?" he asked.

"No, I got money. I want a man to call my own, you know. Someone to make me feel special on the regular."

"Oh, a'ight, I feel you. So, your baby daddy must be back in the picture."

"No, he's not. I haven't heard shit from him since he left me and the kids. This has nothing to do with him. I'm grateful that you helped me, and I want us to remain cool on a business level."

"You got it. No worries, B." He didn't sound as cool about it as he wanted me to think he was.

"Sean, please don't be upset. I just been thinking about this for a while."

"Nah, B, you good. You got my number. Hit me up when you need that work." He picked up his cell phone and walked out of the hotel room without saying another word.

I leaned back on the bed, looking up at the ceiling. *Damn, what did I just do?* He was the only nigga who showed me that he cared and made sure I got back on my feet. My mind was telling me one thing, but my heart was telling me I made the right decision. I knew that I deserved better than just meeting up with a nigga and fucking.

First thing first, I needed to find somewhere to live. I knew that my days at the apartment were numbered. I was also on pins and needles. I kept replaying Sean's words, warning me not to trust anyone.

I had a few errands to run, so I asked Karen to watch the kids. I hated going down to Richmond, but I had a dude from over Jackson Ward who would cop a pound of weed every other day. I sure wasn't going to let that money fly past me, especially because he was a regular customer.

I spotted him as soon as I got out of the cab. I looked around to scope out my environment. The street was crowded, which was kind of good. I clutched my purse closely as I walked toward him.

"Hey, boo," I greeted him.

"Whaddup, shawty? Damn, you look sexy as fuck," he said as he gave me a quick hug.

"Come on. Let's walk up here real quick."

"Bet."

We proceeded to walk up Broad Street, which was away from the crowd.

"So, how is business doing?" I asked.

"E'erything good, shawty. Shit, the weed's moving so damn fast that I can't keep up for real."

"That's a great thing." I smiled.

"Boss lady, I was gon' ask you if you could front me about two pounds and I'll bring you back the money in four days."

I stared at him. "You know I don't be on no fronting shit. I need my money up front."

"Yeah, but we been dealing with each other for a minute now. Man, I swear you can trust me. I've always been one hundred with you. It's just that my girl pregnant, and I need to make some more money to buy the baby things."

"Dre, you putting me in a tight spot and shit. Man, come see me tomorrow and I got you. But for real, son, don't be playing with my money, yo," I said.

"Boss lady, I'm a real nigga. My word is e'erything, and I give you my word."

"Here you go." I took out the pound that I had in my purse and threw it in his book bag. He then hurriedly stuffed the money in my pocketbook.

"That's all my money, right?" I asked.

"Yup, all twenty-four hundred of it."

"Ok, cool. I'm about to bounce. Come see me tomorrow."

"Ok, cool, boss lady. Be easy," he said.

I walked off in the opposite direction, pulled up my Uber app, and requested a cab. It was the first of the month, and my phone had been blowing up. I had a few more stops to make before I headed home.

It was a little after dusk when I got home. I was beat from running around all day, but I had to say that it had been lucrative. I was so grateful that Karen had been helping me out with the kids. Her boyfriend violated probation a few days before, and her mama had her kids. Therefore, she had free time to babysit the kids for me whenever I had errands to run.

"Hey, chica," I said as I entered the apartment.

"Hey, boo." She jumped up off the couch.

"Where the kids? It's quiet as hell."

"They 'sleep."

"This early?" That was strange being that it was only a little after seven.

"Yeah, I had them outside running around. We came inside, I made them something to eat, and then bathed them."

"Well, I guess that explains it. Well, here you go, and thank you, man. I don't know what I would do without you." I handed her $150 dollars.

"You're more than welcome. You have been nothing but good to me," she said.

"All right, girl. I'm about to jump in the shower. Long-ass day."

"Shit, at least you making money, right?" She laughed.

"True. Close the door behind you."

I turned my back to walk to my kids' room to check on them. I was missing my babies.

"Don't move, bitch!" I felt a gun poking me in my back, and I stopped dead in my tracks.

"Bitch, I need all the weed and the money too!" a male voice yelled.

I swallowed hard as I tried to make sense out of what was going on.

"Please lower your voice. My kids are sleeping," I said.

"Bitch, shut up before I blow your motherfucking brains out." He poked me harder in my back.

I didn't know who it was, but he sounded really serious. I couldn't take any chances with my kids in the next room.

"It's in my room, under my bed, and the money is right here in my purse," I said as my voice trembled.

"Bitch, go."

I walked to my room, knelt down, and grabbed the large bag of weed that I had left. I handed it to him.

"Give me all the fucking money that's in your bag, too, and this better be e'erything, bitch, or I'll be back to kill you and them little bastards."

My body trembled as I heard his cold threat toward my children.

"That is all the money and drugs that I have," I told him.

"All right, bitch, now get in that closet." He pointed the gun at me.

I got up from the carpet, but not before trying to get a quick glance at his face in the mirror. He had a mask on, so I couldn't see anything. I could tell by the complexion of his hand that he was a light-skinned nigga.

I got in the closet and kept my head down the entire time, trying not make the nigga angrier.

"Bitch, you better not mention this to nobody. You hear? I swear you'll regret it." His words echoed as he waved the gun around.

I put my head down while praying silently to the man above. It was just too much. He closed the closet door, and then I heard my back door open. I waited anxiously for a few seconds. He seemed to have left.

I ran out to check on my babies. They were still asleep. I ran over to them and checked their pulses, making sure that they were really asleep. They were okay.

I made my way to the back door and locked it. I peeped through the window, but no one was there, which was strange.

Where the fuck did that nigga disappear to that fast?

I walked to the front door and made sure that it was locked also. I fell to my knees and started crying. I felt violated in the worst way. Who was that nigga who'd just walked up in my shit and took my weed and money? All kinds of thoughts were running through my mind.

How the fuck did he get inside? My back door was locked and my front door . . . my front door . . .

I tried to remember as I retraced my steps. I locked the door behind me when I came in, but Karen had just left seconds before the dude held me up. Literally seconds. I jumped up from the carpet, ran to the bathroom to wash my face, then checked on the babies. They were still asleep. I closed the door and ran over to her apartment. I rang the doorbell, but there was no answer. I started banging on her door and still got no response.

"Karen, open up the door!"

"Aye, stop all that got-damn noise!" a bitch a few doors down hollered.

"Bitch, shut up and mind your business!" I yelled back.

I waited a few minutes and then rushed back to my apartment. I grabbed my cell phone and pulled up her number. The phone just rang and then went to voicemail. That was crazy. She was always at home, and when she left my house, that was where she said she was going.

"Could she be behind that shit? Oh God, no!" I yelled out as I grabbed my head. I hoped I was wrong for her fucking sake, because if I found out she had anything to do with it, I was going to rip that country bitch into pieces. I was terrified of the way I was feeling, because it wasn't good at all.

I wasn't going to spend another night in that apartment. I didn't know if dude was planning on coming back to finish what he started. I grabbed two suitcases and started throwing our clothes in them. I didn't have no other place to go, so a hotel was my only option.

I grabbed the phone to call Yohan but quickly changed my mind. Fuck that nigga, too. His ass had straight abandoned us, and calling him would only make him think a bitch needed him.

I got us a room at a hotel on Midlothian Turnpike. The kids wanted to know why we were there. I couldn't really tell them, so I just made up a story.

After I got them settled, I dialed Sean's number. I knew that we didn't part on good terms the other day, but I was hoping our relationship was in good standing.

"Aye yo, what's good?" he answered.

"Hey, I got robbed earlier."

"You for real? By who?"

"I was gone all day, handling some business, and when I got back, some nigga was in the crib waiting on me, yo."

"You see the nigga's face? And what did he get?"

"He got e'erything and all the work," I lied.

Truth was, the nigga did get all the work that I had left and the money I made earlier, but his ass was too dumb to check anywhere else. All the money that I had saved up was still in the shoeboxes in my kids' closet.

"Damn, B, that's fucked up."

"Yeah, I have a feeling that it was a setup. The bitch who babysits my kids was just in my apartment. I think her ass let him in. I swear I'ma find that ho and I'ma beat that motherfucking ass."

"Yo! Yo! You not thinking straight, B. You beat that bitch ass and then what? She tells the police e'erything she know about you. Then what you gonna do, B? You got to use your brain when you in this line of business. Fuck that shit. I'ma drop you off some more work in the morning. Start from scratch and build your shit back up. That shit is minor compared to you getting indicted on some shit because the bitch started running her mouth," he explained.

"All right, man. I get what you saying. I'm just pissed the fuck off right now. I left the apartment, and I'm on Midlothian right now at one of the hotels. Hit me in the morning when you on the way."

"A'ight, one."

I guess what he said made sense, but I was fuming with anger. I had fed that hungry bitch, gave her money, and even put her on. I could see that bitches nowadays didn't give a fuck if they bit the hand that fed them. That bitch had better pray that I didn't bump into her again. Fuck what Sean was talking about. She was going to feel these hands all over that ass.

I decided to take a shower. It had been a long-ass day, and my damn feet were hurting. After my shower, I ordered some food from Dominos and decided to chill. Tomorrow was another day, and I needed to find us somewhere to live asap.

CHAPTER NINE

Kymani

"Yo, my nigga, twelve just did a bust on the boulevard early this morning. They got Jay B and Mo," Beenie yelled into my phone.

"Say what?" I jumped up out of the bed. "You serious, dawg?"

"Hell yeah. I been calling yo' phone all morning, trying to let you know."

My head started hurting. The house on Chimborazo Boulevard was where I and a couple niggas grinded and kept our work. My nerves were fucking bad after hearing that news.

"Man, where you at now?" I asked.

"I'm at the store on Thirty-third."

"On my way," I said as I threw my phone on the bed.

"Fuck!" I yelled out. How the fuck did the trap get busted like that? Shit, we kept a low profile. The people that we dealt with were people we'd been dealing with on the regular.

The next thought that came to my mind was that somebody was running their motherfucking mouth. Man, I was lucky as fuck, because if the bust had been conducted the day before, all of us would be gone.

I jumped in the shower and washed off quickly. In about ten minutes, I was dressed and out the door. I jumped in my car and pulled off. I had a leftover blunt from last night, so I lit that shit. I took a few pulls, trying to calm my nerves.

I peeped my nigga Beenie's Lexus truck and pulled over. He saw me and walked across the street.

"What's happening, babe?" he greeted me, and we exchanged dap.

"Man, how the fuck did that shit happen?"

"Yo, dawg, I was in the crib when shawty from next door hit my phone. I immediately got dressed and headed down there. They had Chimbo blocked off. I stood from a distance, but I saw when they put them niggas in the police cars along with large garbage bags. Man, I was fucked up when I saw that shit. That means all the money that was made last night is gone along with the work."

"Fuck!" I slammed my hand on my steering wheel.

"I know, dawg."

"Yo, check if them niggas got a bond. Send Nia down to the courthouse. I'm sure they'll go in front of the judge this morning. If they got bonds, just hit me and let me know. Let's lay low for a few days until this shit die down. Trust me, dawg, I think this is an inside job, or somebody's running their motherfucking mouth."

"That's the same thing I was thinking," he said. "But I'm about to hit Nia."

"A'ight, yo, I'm out."

"A'ight, babe. Be easy."

"Fa sure." I busted a U-Turn and went in the opposite direction. My mind was racing a million miles per minute. That was a big-ass loss to take at the time when shit was booming. I estimated between the work and money loss, that shit had to be over fifty grand.

I was so caught up in my thoughts that I didn't see that Richmond PD jumped behind me until I heard the sirens. My heart skipped a few beats as my mind jumped on the loaded burner that I had hidden under my seat. I thought about running but decided against that with the way those pigs were killing niggas nowadays.

I pulled over on the side of the road while reaching for my insurance information. I saw the officer approaching my vehicle. I put the window down and kept my hands on my steering wheel.

"Good morning, sir. License and registration."

Without hesitation, I handed it to him.

"I'll be right back."

I knew my shit was legit, because my mama made sure I kept up to date on everything. The truck was in her name also. After about five minutes, I saw him approaching my vehicle again.

"Here you go, sir. I pulled you over for going seventy-five in a fifty-five mile-per-hour zone. I'm going to give you a ticket for going twenty miles over. Your court date is three weeks from today. The information is on the back. You can pay it in advance and avoid going to court. Sign right here," he handed it to me.

I hurried up and signed that shit.

"Please watch your speed and have a nice day."

Fuck! As soon as he walked off, I caught a breath. I was sweating fucking bullets. I watched as he pulled off, then I pulled off. Damn, that was a close call.

After that, I tried my best to maintain the speed limit. I thought about going back to the crib because I was kind of paranoid after just getting pulled over. I knew it was early, but knowing my mama, she was probably up cleaning or washing.

See, Mama was my favorite girl. The first lump sum of money that I made from trapping went into buying her a nice three-bedroom house. My whole life, I'd watched her struggle to make ends meet for me and my older sister. I used to sit back and watch her make something out of nothing, and that was one of the reasons why I went so motherfucking hard in the streets. One of these days, she wouldn't have to work anymore because her son made sure she was good.

I pulled into the driveway and banged on the door.

"Boy, you done lost yo' mind. What the hell you doing banging on the door this early in the morning?"

"My bad, Ma. I just wanted to see my favorite girl." I walked over to hug her, and she cringed. I pulled back and looked at her. There was a bruise on the side of her face.

"Ma, where did that come from?"

"The other day I bumped into the wall." She couldn't look me in the eye.

"Bullshit. Did that nigga hit you again?" I was referring to my mama's on again, off again, worthless-ass boyfriend, Deano.

"Baby, just let it go, please. I'm begging you."

"Nah, fuck that. I told that nigga if he even breathes on you hard again, I was gon' murk that ass."

"Ky, please stop."

I wasn't trying to hear that shit. I knew the nigga was in the house because his work truck was outside. I slightly pushed my mama to the side and headed for her room.

I walked in on that nigga getting dressed. I didn't give a fuck. At that point, my rage was uncontrollable.

"Yo, pussy nigga, didn't I warn you not to put your dick beaters on my mama no more?" I said.

"Look who is here. Little nigga, you better watch yo' mouth before I beat yo' ass the way I beat that—"

I pounded on that nigga, knocking him back into the wall.

"Ha-ha, nigga, you dead. You and that bitch is dead! You hear me?" he threatened.

I pulled my gun and aimed it at that nigga's head.

"Ky, no! Oh my God, don't do it!" My mama jumped between me and that nigga, but not before I squeezed the fucking trigger. I tried to stop the bullets from hitting her, but it was too late. In front of me, the woman that gave me life, my black queen, my everything, fell to the floor.

"Noooooooooooooooooooooooooooo!" I growled with every fiber in my body.

I fell on the floor beside her. Holding her, I checked her pulse, but she didn't have one. I laid my head on her lifeless bosom. "Mama, please. You can't leave me, please."

"Nigga, don't cry now. You done killed the bitch."

I stood up, looked at that fool with tears in my eyes, and emptied the clip in him. I stood over him as he took his last breath. I then walked back to where my mama was, knelt down, and kissed her face. I then stood up and walked out. I was careful not to speed away because I didn't want to bring any attention to me being there.

Tears flooded my eyes as images of my mother's dead body kept playing over and over. How the fuck did I mess up like that? Man, my mama's blood was on my hands.

"Oh God, please take me now!" I cried out. I thought about calling the police but got a reality check real fast. Mama was dead, so what sense would that make? I would be charged with murdering her and that fuck nigga.

I stopped at the liquor store and grabbed a big bottle of Paul Mason. I needed something strong to drown my emotional pain. After I got back in my ride, I popped the bottle open and took it straight to the head. The strong hit of the alcohol burned through my chest, but that didn't deter me from drinking. That pain was nothing compared to what I was actually feeling.

I managed to get myself to the crib. I fought with my keys for a good minute before I stumbled inside and onto the hardwood floor. I didn't even move. I just sat there, continuing to drink and bawl.

"Mama, please, I need you, man. I swear, Mama, I didn't mean to . . ." My words trailed off as I banged my head against the wall. I just wanted to fucking die.

I kept hearing my phone ring, and I thought I was tripping, but the rings got louder in my head. I tried to lift my head, but I was too fucked up to maintain my balance. I glanced around and saw my phone on the floor close by.

"Yo . . . yo," I stuttered into the phone.

"Yo, where the hell you been? I just found Mama and Deano shot to death." It was my sister Claudia.

"What? Dead? You sure?"

"Boy, did you hear what the fuck I said?" she screamed into the phone, triggering my headache more.

"I heard you, dammit."

"Well, bring yo' ass. Our mama is gonnnnne," she cried into the phone.

"A'ight man, I'll be there." I knew I was lying. I was too fucked up to drive and mentally I wasn't prepared to face my sister, knowing damn well I was the cause of her pain.

It had been days since my mama passed, and the pain wasn't getting any easier. I couldn't sleep at night, because every time I closed my eyes, I would see Mama's eyes staring at me. The only time my mind was a little at ease was when I was fucked up and high.

I finally found the courage to visit my sister. All we did was cry and hug each other. There were several times when I came close to confessing to her, but I quickly caught myself. Even though my sister and I were close, she was hurting, and there was no way that I was confident she wouldn't run to the police.

"You have to promise me that you will find whoever did this to Mama. You have to find them and kill them. You hear me?" she hollered as she hugged me.

I stood there, fighting my own damn tears. I was the one who was responsible for bringing such heartache to my sister. It was me who took our mother's life. I felt so low that I wanted to pull out my burner and blow my brains out.

After we left the funeral home, my sister decided to go home, and I drove to my baby mama's house. She'd been calling me since my mama died, but truthfully, I wasn't in the right frame of mind to deal with her. She had sent me a text earlier to let me know that my daughter needed Pull-ups and money for food. I parked and knocked on the door.

"Yo, what's good?" I said.

"Baby, look. Yo' daddy finally decided to show his face."

I didn't pay her ass any mind. Instead, I walked over to the couch where my daughter was sitting down, watching television.

"Hey, Daddy's baby." I picked her up and hugged her tight.

"Love you, Daddy," she said as she planted kisses all over my face.

"Boy, don't be popping up in here, acting like you the fucking proud daddy of the year. You ain't seen your daughter in days. Fuck that. Not even a fucking phone call," she snapped.

"Yo, chill out. Now is not the time for this." I was trying my best not to go there with her for real.

"Nah, nigga, you chill the fuck out. I understand yo' mama dead and all. Shit, she gone, but your daughter's still here and needs her daddy. I see you can be e'ery motherfucking where else, but you can't come see yo' daughter."

"Bitch, I just said chill out. I just lost my mama, and you up in here running yo' mouth about some irrelevant shit."

"Boy, I don't give a fuck about you losing yo' mama. Shit, it ain't like she liked me or my motherfucking daughter anyways. So, now that she dead, you think e'erything should stop for her ass. Boy, bye."

I looked at that bitch, and the first thought that entered my mind was to blow her motherfucking head off.

"Daddy, can you buy me this?" My daughter pointed to a Dora toy on the television.

"Yeah, baby, I sure can."

I looked at that dumb bitch and regretted ever sticking my dick up inside of her. She was right. My mama couldn't stand that ho.

"Hey, baby girl, daddy got to bounce. I'll be back tomorrow to see you, a'ight?"

"Yeah, right," that bitch said. "Don't hold yo' breath, boo, but no worries. Mama got you."

I took a stack, peeled off $500, and threw it on the couch. I was ready to get away from that old, dumb bitch.

"You think you can just throw money around here and think shit is good. You know what? You can keep yo' money. We good over here, boo boo."

I started walking out when she jumped in front of me, blocking my path. "Who is you fucking?" she yelled. "Why are you acting so stank with me lately?" She grabbed my shirt.

"Man, get the fuck off me. All you want to do is bitch. I ain't got time for little girl shit. Grow the fuck up." I snatched my shirt out of her grip.

"Grow up? I'm more woman than you could imagine. I don't run these streets, and I'm always home with my baby. Unlike her so-called daddy."

"Well, maybe if you get off yo' ass and get a job, Daddy can leave these streets alone." I made my way to the door, not listening to a damn word she was saying.

I pulled off immediately. I swear, tomorrow was the day to put my mama in the ground, and I wasn't ready. I didn't feel like being around the niggas, not right now anyways, so I decided to hit the crib. Lately, that was the only place that I found any kind of peace.

CHAPTER TEN

Nyesha

"Come on, children!" I hollered as I carried the bags into our new apartment. I was happy that we had found something because truth was, living out of a hotel was for the birds. I knew that my children were tired of eating KFC and McDonald's every damn night. Shit, I knew I was.

I was trying to stay on the south side, because that was all I knew, but I couldn't find anything decent. Our new place was in Churchill. Yes, you heard me right, Churchill. I was kind of leery at first, but when I saw the apartment, I realized that it was just right for me and the kids.

"Damn, shawty, you need some help taking them bags in?" a sexy-ass, down-south accent asked.

I closed the trunk of the Uber car and turned around to address that nigga about that shawty shit. He was so close to me that I bumped into him.

"Well, excuse me, but aren't you a little too close?" I said.

"Nah, I was tryna help you take those bags in the house and introduce myself, you know."

I stared up at the stranger's face and wondered what the fuck he really wanted. He had to be around 6 foot 9, light skinned, with a head full of hair. I sized that nigga up quick. I also peeped that he had a grill in his mouth. I could tell he was a hood nigga from the way he talked and his demeanor.

"Well, I'm good, and I don't need your help." I sashayed off into the apartment building. I walked inside and locked the door. I had no idea who that nigga was, nor did I care to know. Shit, my mama always warned me not to talk to strangers, and in my book, he was a stranger.

I sat waiting for the furniture to be delivered. God only knew that I was ready to take a shower and dive in my queen-sized mahogany bed that I ordered from Ashley Furniture. I had also ordered brand new beds for the kids, along with living room and dining room furniture. I really felt good that I was able to do everything on my own.

I was up bright and early the next morning. I had made doctor's appointments for the kids, so I could get their immunization records updated. It was time to get them in daycare, so I could have more free time to rip and run whenever I wanted to. After what happened with that bitch on the south side, there was no way that I was going to allow another bitch to come up in my shit. I swear, I was still hoping that I bumped into that ho one day.

The kids and I were standing outside waiting on Uber when I spotted a bunch of dudes standing a few yards away. It was different from when I moved in the day before, because the block was quiet then.

Hmmm, I hope this block isn't hot, I thought.

The Uber pulled up, and we got inside. I was impressed by how quick we got out of the doctor's office.

Within two hours, we were back at the crib. As soon as we stepped out of the cab, I noticed the same nigga from the day before approaching me. I tried to push the kids to walk faster while I clutched my purse.

"Aye, shawty, hold on. I know I approached you wrong the other day, but listen, yo, my name is Ky." He stretched his hand out.

I didn't want to come off ignorant, so I extended my arm. "Nyesha."

"Nice to meet you, Nyesha." He stared in my eyes and rubbed my hand.

"Oh, okay, can I go now, Ky?" I asked sarcastically.

"Shawty, just give me five minutes of yo' time. I just need to holla at you real quick," he said.

I looked at the kids, who were clearly ready to get out of the heat. "Listen, Ky, let me get my kids in the house, and if you are still out here, I'll come back out and talk to you for five minutes." I shot him a suspicious look.

"A'ight, bet, shawty. I'll be here waiting." He flashed a devilish grin at me.

I walked off on that nigga, but something inside was screaming at me. I wanted to know what the fuck he had to talk to me about. It had been a minute since a nigga took interest in me, and I had to admit that it had my stomach doing flips.

"So, what do you want to talk to me about?" I asked a while later when I walked up behind him.

"Damn, I almost shot yo' ass." He smiled.

"A'ight, calm down, killa."

"Yo, you not from around here."

"What makes you think that?"

"For one, your accent screams that you from up north, and two, I know e'erybody from my hood."

"Ohh, so this your hood?" I asked.

"Born and raised 'round here. So, was I correct?"

"Yes, I'm not from here. New York born and raised," I said proudly.

"Now I see where that attitude comes from. You know you New York chicks be fly out the mouth."

"Is that so? So, you had a New York chick before?" I wasn't going to lie, standing there talking to him was definitely doing something to me. It was something about that down south accent that was pulling me in.

"So, Ky, let's cut all the small talk. Do you have a woman, and if so, what in God's name do you want from me?" I cut straight to the point. Yeah, he was cute and everything, but I had a million and one things that I could be doing with my time.

"I'ma keep it one hunnit with you, shawty. I got a baby mama. My daughter is two years old, but shawty and I don't be fucking with each other on no personal level," he said.

Lord, here we go. Where were the single niggas without children or baby mamas at? I guess I was not being fair, since I had two damn kids, but shit, I didn't have any baby daddy drama.

"Hmm, so where yo' nigga at?" he asked. "I know a beautiful woman like you got somebody who already cuffed yo' fine ass up."

"Well, thanks for the compliment, but I don't have nobody cuffing my fine ass. However, I do have a baby daddy somewhere out there, but he is not in my kids' lives, and he's definitely not in my life."

He started smiling.

"What's so funny about what I just said?"

"Damn, and you aggressive. That shit is sexy as hell. But nah, I love that you ain't got no nigga. That mean I can go ahead and slide my bid in," he said.

"Ky, you cute and all, but I ain't looking for no nigga and definitely not no hood nigga."

"Damn, that was harsh. I mean, why are you so against a hood nigga?"

I stepped closer to him. "'Cause the last hood nigga I dated wasn't shit. All he wanted to do was fuck, smoke, and run the streets," I said bluntly.

His phone started ringing. He pressed ignore, but it kept ringing.

"Somebody looking for you? Go ahead and get it before you get in trouble," I said with a grin.

"Nah, that's just my baby mama being annoying and shit."

"Oh, okay." I decided not to speak on the subject.

"Listen, Nyesha. Let me cut to the chase. A nigga is feeling you, shawty, and I would love to get to know you a little more, if you don't mind."

"Do you mean you're looking for a new piece of pussy?"

"Man, cool out wit' all that. Pussy? Look at me. I'm a fine-ass nigga with major rep in these streets, so I can get bitches on the regular. I need a woman in my life. It's a difference between getting pussy from different bitches e'ery day and having that one special woman that you can come home to every night," he said.

I smiled at him. His conversation was different from most of the niggas I'd dated. His eyes were piercing my soul while screaming at my heart. I needed to get away from him.

"Well, it was nice talking to you. Here's my number, so you can call me sometime."

He took the number and put it in his phone. "Aye, shawty, I want you to think about what I just said, though. I mean, at least let me take you out on a date."

"A'ight, I'll think about it. Also, if you know anybody that need some smoke, tell them to holla at me via phone. Don't want nobody knocking on my door."

"Oh, word. Shit, I'ma need some in a few. What you got?"

I hesitated, because for all I knew, he could be a stick-up nigga or the damn police.

"Man, come on, shawty. What you think I'ma do? Rob you?" He must've read my mind.

"Hmmm. Can't be too sure these days. Anyways, I'll have whatever you need," I told him.

"A'ight, fair enough. I'll holla at you, shawty," he said and walked his cocky ass off to the corner of the street.

I walked back in the house. The kids were still in their room, playing with their toys. I stood at the door, smiling. It made me feel good inside to see that I was able to keep a smile on my babies' faces, even though we'd been through hell since we came to this damn state.

I was in the kitchen preparing dinner when I heard the phone ringing. I washed my hands off quickly and ran to get it. I thought it was Ky but quickly realized it was my sissy. I picked it up because it had been weeks since we'd talked, and I sure was missing my boo.

"Hey, bitch. What you doing?" she asked.

"Nigga, I'm cooking. What's going on with you?"

"Nothing. Missing my right hand and thinking about coming to visit you."

"Bitch, don't be playing with my emotions like that. You know I got heart problems. You know how much I miss you and the babies," I told her.

"I'm dead-ass serious, and the babies are with their grandma for about two weeks."

"With who? Ma?"

"Nah, wit' their daddy mama. You know that bitch lives in Florida, so she up here visiting. She wanted to see her grandbabies. I was goin' say hell no, but I needed the break. Shit, it ain't like they do anything for them anyways. Anyway, I'm dead serious. I'm going to book a flight tomorrow for next Friday," she said.

"Bitch, you just made my day. Just let me know."

"All righty. I'll call you tomorrow."

Lord, my sissy coming to visit was definitely a great thing. The thing was, I had never told her I was selling drugs. I was just going to be very discreet when she got there.

I finished cooking, fed the kids, cleaned up afterward, and took a shower. That nigga Ky was invading my thoughts. I tried not to think about him, but I kept hearing his accent loud and clear in my head. That nigga was definitely easy on the eyes, and I couldn't help but wonder how big his dick was. He was tall and had big feet, and you know what old people said about niggas with big feet.

CHAPTER ELEVEN

Kymani

Y'all know I pulled bitches on the regular and could fuck a different bitch every night if I wanted to. Lately, I'd been chilling on bitches. After we buried Mama, I just dug myself deeper into my grind and focused on bitches less. That was until I peeped this one shawty moving into one of the apartments on the block.

"Who the fuck is that?" my nigga asked.

"I'on't know, but I'm about to find out, though."

I walked off as my niggas continued talking shit. I wasn't stuttin' them niggas. Shit, my only goal was getting at shawty.

When we first started rapping, all I was thinking about was smashing and bouncing, but the more we conversed, the more I fell for shawty. She wasn't your average chick. Her physical appearance pulled me in first, but her mind kept me interested. I went against every code that I lived by. We would talk on the phone for hours at night while I was in the trap. Anyone that knew me knew that you couldn't catch me on the phone for more than five minutes unless it was my mama.

We would talk about our past relationships and what we were looking for. To be honest, it was the first time in my life that I'd ever considered settling down with a chick. Even though she already had two kids, I was willing to step up to the plate. Shawty made her own money, which was a plus for real. All I needed to find out was if she had some good pussy.

For days, I'd been ripping and running the streets. We had to find a new trap after the police busted the other one. Mo was out on bond, but Jay B had a probation violation, so he had to sit it out.

"Yo, we need to be extra careful about who we bring up in here. Trust me, somebody is talking for real," I said to my niggas.

"Yo, I was thinking the same thing. I think it's one of those bitch-ass niggas that done got pissed off 'cause we running up checks over here," Malik answered,

"More than likely, but you know those old police-ass niggas ain't gon' really show their hands. I know one thing. If I ever find out who the fuck singing to the people, I'ma murk their ass for real."

"You ain't saying nothing but a word. I got them niggas," Malik said while pointing his 9 mm at the wall.

"Nigga, put that shit up before you shoot yo'self," I joked with him. That nigga was about that life and wouldn't think twice about pulling that trigger.

"A'ight, my nigga." He laughed.

"Yo, y'all be easy. I'm about to take shawty to lunch," I said.

"Who, Simone?" Malik asked.

"Hell nah, the new chick from up the street."

"Nigga, you lying. Did you smash? I know you ain't spending on no bitch unless you fucked."

I laughed, shook my head, and walked out. My nigga thought he knew me. Matter of fact, he knew the old me. Like I said, shawty was different, so I had to treat her different. I wasn't a wait-forever-to-smash type of nigga, but for the time being, I was in no rush.

CHAPTER TWELVE

Nyesha

I thought the south side was booming. Bullshit! Churchill was where the money resides. I was selling pounds of weed daily, plus making extra from dimes and twenties. I was back on and was able to give Sean his money from the pounds he had fronted to me. You couldn't tell me shit, because it took me no time to have Churchill on lock. Even my niggas from Jackson Ward were glad that I was back on.

I was at the Richmond Airport, waiting for my sister to land. I was happy to see her, but I was also nervous. I saw her walking toward me, and I quickly made my way over to her.

"Sisssyyy!" I jumped up and down and started hugging her.

"Damn, bitch, you almost knocked me over."

"Come on, let me request an Uber car real quick."

"A'ight. You look good, boo. I thought I was gon' come out here and see you barefoot and pregnant," she joked.

"Yeah, right. You know damn well my ass ain't having no more children. Shit, I can barely manage the ones I got."

"Man, I am ready to see my babies. I bet you my niece's ass is all grown up," she said.

"Girl, yes. She is grown and thinks she's somebody's mama."

We continued talking about what had been going on in New York, and she updated me on how Mama was doing.

After we ate dinner, she and I sat in the living room, talking. I decided it was time for me to let her know what had been going on with me.

"Girl, what time that baby daddy of yours is coming home? Don't tell me he's still running these streets," she said.

"Sis, I'm so happy you're here, but I need to talk to you."

"Oh, shit. Here we go. Don't tell me you killed that motherfucker, 'cause, bitch, I ain't going down with yo' ass."

"Girl, shut up and listen."

I started off by telling her about how Yohan left me and the kids for dead, how I bumped into Sean, and how I started hustling. I expected for her to start screaming any minute now.

"Bitch, you telling me yo' little scary, raised-in-the-suburbs ass is a drug dealer?" She looked at me with excitement in her eyes.

"Sis, I didn't want to sell drugs, but it was either that or sell pussy. God knows I couldn't lay down for that."

"Bitch, aren't you scared? What if the police catch on?"

"At first, I was scared as hell. But the more I did it, the better I got at it. I love the money for real."

"Listen to you," she said. "Do you know you will get a lot of time if you get caught?"

"Key words, sis, *if I get caught.* I am not out in the streets being careless or nothing like that. Plus, I saved over fifteen grand already. Shit, I would've had more if I didn't have to buy all this furniture."

"Sis, you grown, and I can't tell you what to do, but please be careful out here. It's not just the police you got to worry about. You got to worry about them jack boys also. Don't think 'cause you a female them niggas won't jack you. Trust me, little sis. These streets don't love nobody at all."

I sat there listening and remembering how I got robbed a month ago. I was glad that I didn't mention it to her because of how she was talking.

"A'ight, enough of the preaching, bitch. What's been going on with you lately? Still twerking on them poles?" I asked.

"Bitch, you know me. I'm gonna be old and gray, still twerking this old-ass pussy. Don't no retirement fund come with dancing."

"Ha, ha, I hear that."

We continued laughing, drinking, and smoking. I was happy that she was there with me. I really did miss her crazy ass.

Over the first few days that she was there, I didn't handle any business. We went out to eat a few times, and I took her shopping. It was funny to me that a few days ago, that bitch was screaming that I needed to quit, yet she had no problem picking up those $350 Gucci slides. I wasn't tripping. I was just happy to be able to buy my sister something expensive.

By Thursday, I was itching to get back to the grind. My phone was jumping nonstop. I knew that if I didn't get back to business, my customers would go to someone else.

My phone started ringing, and I looked at the caller ID. It was Ky.

"Hey, boo," I quickly answered.

"Whaddup, shawty? I ain't heard from you in a few days."

"Oh, my bad. My big sis is here visiting from New York, so I've been ripping and running."

"Oh, okay, that's what's up. Well, I ain't gon' interrupt yo' family time. Hit my line when you free," he said.

"Okay, boo."

I really missed talking to him every day. I swear, I was really digging that boy, even though I tried hard not to let it show.

"Hmm, who was that on the phone? I see you all smiles," my sister commented.

"Girl, nobody."

"Mm-hmm."

I wasn't trying to entertain her ass, so I walked out of the living room. Even though he gave me chills, I wasn't ready to get into another serious relationship.

I peeked in on the kids. They were being quiet, watching television in their rooms. I then walked in my room to bag up some work. The next day was Friday, and I needed to make some money. I cut up a pound into dime and twenty bags. I was tired, so I decided to leave the rest for the next day.

I heard my phone ringing. It was this dude named Troy from up the street. He'd been getting an ounce a day. I thought he would not fuck with me anymore because he tried to holla at me the other day, but I turned him down.

"Yo," I answered.

"What's good, shawty? You straight?"

"Yeah, I'm good."

"A'ight. I'm coming through in five."

"Okay." I hung the phone up and grabbed an ounce of weed. I then walked out to meet him in the hallway.

"What's good, shawty?"

"Nothing." I handed him the ounce of weed and he handed the money.

"This a new batch?" he asked.

"A new batch?"

"Just asking if this is different from the batch that you sold me the other day."

This was kind of strange that he was asking about a different batch of weed. "Was something wrong?"

"No, boss lady. I was just curious. Anyway, I got to bounce."

"All right. I stood there counting my money while he ran down the stairs and out the door. My money was straight, so I stuffed it in my bra, opened my door, and walked inside.

My sister was still on her phone, whispering and shit. I looked over at her, smiled, and walked back to my room. I sat on the bed and grabbed my phone. I was about to text Ky when I heard a commotion.

First, I heard a couple thumps, then I heard footsteps. Lots of footsteps. Then I heard my door breaking down. I realized that it was a bust. I jumped up, grabbed the bag of weed that I had under the bed, opened my back door, and threw the bag over the fence. I then tried to run away from the door.

"Richmond Police! Richmond Police! Get down!" they yelled.

"Mommy, Mommy!" I heard my son running towards my room. I grabbed him up in my arms.

"Richmond Police! Get down!" It was a big, burly officer with a rifle pointed at me and my son.

"Please, don't shoot my mommy. Pleeeease." My baby started crying.

By then, the rest of the pigs were all in my room, tearing it up.

"Nyesha Smith, you're under arrest for the distribution of marijuana. You have a right to remain silent." The cop proceeded to read me my rights.

It was like an out-of-body experience. I heard him talking, but I was not understanding what he was saying. Tears started rolling down my face as an officer grabbed my son and took him out of the room.

"Look what we found outside," a female officer said as she walked inside with the bag that I had thrown out.

"Do we take the other lady also?"

"No, she ain't got nothing to do with this. She's just here visiting," I said in a hurry. I swear, I wouldn't be able to live with myself if she was to get locked up behind my bullshit.

"Since she's claiming the drugs, we don't need to charge the other lady."

I was relieved when I heard the officer say that.

My sister carried my kids out of the apartment, and I was led out in handcuffs. The minute I walked outside, I noticed that the entire hood was out witnessing my sad demise. I hung my head down in shame as they led me to one of the police cars that was waiting.

At the station, I was charged and processed. "You need to take off your clothes and cough," the guard said with an attitude.

"What the fuck you mean? Like strip all my clothes off? Cough?" I shot that bitch a dirty look because I was shocked to hear what she'd just said.

"You heard me. Take your clothes off, spread your butt cheeks, and cough," she said with a slight grin plastered on her face.

I could see that the bitch was enjoying that shit a little too much. I stepped out of my clothes, grabbed my ass, stooped, and coughed. I knew that my body shocked that old burly-looking bitch. I shot her old hating ass a dirty look.

"Here. Put this on. You on G Block," she said.

I didn't respond, but I took the orange jumpsuit and put it on. I grabbed my mat and walked to G Block.

It wasn't until I stepped into the actual pod that fear and anxiety hit me. The strong smell of human sweat and urine hit my nose. I saw bitches laid out on the bunk beds, just staring at me.

"Over here!" the guard yelled.

I pulled the mat and stood there, looking around.

"Welcome, newbie," a dyke-looking bitch said to me.

"Hello," I barely whispered.

"This must be your first time in jail. Give me your stuff and let me make your bed up." Before I could respond, she grabbed the little, flimsy sheet and started making the bed up. When she was finished, she jumped off the bunk.

"By the way, my name's Niecey. What's your name, shawty?"

"Nyesha."

"A'ight, Nyesha. What you in here for? Boosting?"

"Why the fuck would you think that? Do I look like a thief?" I asked.

"Damn, nah. I just thought it was something simple."

"Nah."

I wasn't into chatting or making any new friends, for real, for real. I didn't want to be there.

CHAPTER THIRTEEN

Kymani

Man, I couldn't believe what the fuck had happened. I was standing on the corner of 32nd Street. All I heard was tires screeching, and when I looked up, police cars were coming from both directions. I thought they were coming for me, but they didn't stop where I was at. Instead, they pulled up at the apartment complex. I was relieved to know that they were not coming at me. Whoever they were going after was in some deep shit.

I didn't stick around. Instead, I jumped in my car and pulled off. I hit my boy's phone.

"Aye, yo. Where you at?"

"Over here at the spot. What's good, babe?" he said.

"Yo, them people just ran up in the apartments on Thirty-second. Yo, maybe you need to cool out for a little while. It's hot out here."

"Oh, word. Ain't that where shawty live?" he asked.

"Fuck yeah. Man, I'm going in the house. Be easy, yo," I told him.

I hung up the phone and dialed Nyesha's number. There was no answer, which was strange.

Maybe she's out with her sister, I thought.

I pulled into my driveway and jumped out of the car. Churchill was on fire lately. I felt like those fuck niggas were running their mouths too much. I swear, I needed to get the fuck away from around there asap.

I must've dozed off because the ringing of my phone woke me up. I answered it.

"Yo."

"You know it was shawty house they busted up in and they got her?" my boy said.

I jumped off the couch and walked over to the window. "Man, are you fucking serious, bro?" I was hoping he wasn't.

"Yeah, I just came from 'round there. They got shawty."

I swear, that had fucked me up. Shawty didn't fuck with nobody, so who the fuck would rat her out?

"Yo, this snitching shit is getting outta hand. You can't tell me that the police just ran up in there on their own. Ain't no motherfucking way. Shawty don't even be out there like that," I said.

"Bro, that's the same shit I was saying earlier. I don't think it's no crackhead either. I think it's one of these fuck niggas."

"Man, this shit got me looking at niggas sideways and shit. It could be any nigga. Even the ones we breaking bread wit'."

"That's real, my nigga. That's why you the only nigga I trust one hundred," he said.

"Shit, bro, you already know. Ain't no bitch in my blood."

"Bro, I'm about to hit Golden Corral with this li'l bitch from Creighton that I been smashing."

"A'ight, yo. Be easy," I said and hung up.

I walked back to the couch and sat down. That was fucked up. I knew shawty was hurting. Shit, I needed to call to see if she had a bond. I grabbed my phone but then remembered that I didn't know her last name. There was only one way to find out.

I took a quick shower, got dressed, and headed out. I walked up the stairs and immediately saw that the door was halfway off the hinges. I heard someone inside, so I banged on the door.

"Who is it?"

"Ky."

"Who are you? My sister not here."

"I know, but I need to talk to you," I told her.

"I don't know who you are, and I don't want to talk."

"Come on, shawty. I want to help yo' sister."

A few seconds later, a chick opened the door. I could see the resemblance immediately.

"Who are you, and what do you want?" she asked.

"I know yo' sister is locked up, but I need to know if she got a bond."

"I don't know. I'm not from here. Her kids are crying for her, and I don't know what to say to them." She was crying.

"Give me her last name. I know this dude that can bond her out."

"Thank you."

"No worries, and I'ma get somebody to fix this door asap."

After she gave me the last name, I dialed the county jail to check on shawty and to find out if she had a bond. It was my first time doing that, but it was needed. I knew how it felt to get locked up and have no one on the other side.

"Hello, Richmond City Jail."

"Aye, I need to know if Nyesha Smith has a bond, and if so, how much it is?" I said.

"Okay, sir, hold on." After a minute, the person came back on the line and said, "Yes, she has a bond of thirty-five thousand dollars."

"A'ight. Good looking out." I hung up.

I hit Big Jazzy up. He was a bail bondsman I'd been dealing with for a minute, and I knew that he was definitely the man for the job. He wanted $3,500, so I headed to the crib. He already knew my ass didn't have a job and couldn't sign for shit. So, as usual, he worked his wonders. I knew it was going to cost me some work, too, because when that nigga wasn't bonding out dope boys, his nose was buried in powder cocaine.

I wasn't going to the jail, so I hit up Nia. See, she was the chick in our clique who was also a college graduate. She mostly handled shit that had to do with the police and anything legal.

"Hello, boss," she said.

"Yo, where you at?"

"Umm, just leaving the nail shop. You know it's club night, so a bitch got to get right."

"Yo, meet me 'round the way."

"All right. I'm on the way," she said.

I pulled up on 30th, waiting for her. I couldn't help but wonder what the fuck was really going on with me. I had just met shawty not so long ago, and all we had been doing was talking. I had never gone that long and not smashed a female that I was interested in.

I saw Nia pull up behind me, and then she walked up to my side of the car. "Hey, boss."

"What's good, shawty? I need you to run down by the city jail and give Big Jazzy this money," I told her.

"Who got knocked?"

"This chick. Here is her name. I want you to wait until she comes out and take her home."

She looked at the name on the paper. "Hmmm, who the fuck is this? A new bitch you fucking?"

"Nah, I ain't fucked her yet." I laughed.

"Mmm-hmmm. A'ight, I'm on it. Oh, and you owe me, 'cause I was on my way to get a massage, but instead my ass got to play captain save-a-ho." She walked off before I could respond.

I swear, I fucked with her the long way. She was a bad bitch who was street smart and book smart. Those were the reasons why I put her on the team. She was always ready to ride when it was time. She pulled off, and I pulled off right behind her.

CHAPTER FOURTEEN

Nyesha

I was laying on the top bunk, trying to figure out how I was going to get out of the shit that I'd managed to get myself into. It had only been hours, but it seemed like forever for real. I was quite sure they'd found all the money that I had in the shoe box and under my mattress. So many days, I'd thought of banking the money, but my ass never got around to doing it.

I couldn't imagine how my sister and my kids were doing. I really felt bad that the one time she visited me, this shit happened. I felt my eyes gathering water, and a tear fell down my face. I quickly turned my head and wiped it away.

Oh, man, I needed to get out of there. Those bitches were loud and obnoxious. They stayed up all night and slept all day. It was even more ridiculous to see those bitches making out with each other. I mean, that was their lives, but shit, to do it out in the open like that was just nasty.

"Nyesha Smith," I heard a guard say.

I was sure that it wasn't me, since I'd just been there a few hours.

"Nyesha Smith. Grab your things."

"Girl, you got bond," my bunkie yelled up at me.

"Huh, me? You sure?"

"That's your name, right?"

She was correct. That was my name, unless someone else was in there with the exact same name. I jumped down from the bunk and quickly put my slippers on. I grabbed the mat and speed-walked up to the front.

"Let's go. You got bond."

I hoped that wasn't some sort of mistake and I was really being bonded out. It felt good being back in my own clothes. It was something about that orange jumpsuit that made my skin crawl.

I knew it was my sister who'd posted my bond. God, I knew that I was going to hear her mouth. That was the only time that I wasn't going to fuss back, because I was happy that she came to get me.

"Hi, Miss Smith, I'm your bondsman. Please read this and sign your name," a man said.

"Hello." I read the requirements of the bond and then instantly signed my name. I handed him the paper. He thanked me and left.

I walked out of the door, looking for my sister and kids.

"You must be Nyesha." A light-skinned, bougie-looking chick walked up to me.

"Yeah, and who the fuck are you?" I balled my fist up. I didn't know the bitch and was wondering how the fuck she knew my name.

"I'm Nia, the bitch that bonded your ass out. Come on."

I looked at that bitch like she was crazy. "I ain't going nowhere with you 'til you tell me who the fuck you are."

She examined me from head to foot, "Ha, ha. I see why Ky fucks with you hard. You have a smart-ass mouth. Kind of reminds me of myself."

Now it made sense. My sister did not bond me out. I guess that bitch was one of Ky's flunkies.

"Come on. I hate to be down here. The police make my big red ass itch," she said.

I followed her as she walked to a candy-colored BMW. She got in, and I got in on the passenger's side.

"What the hell you doing selling drugs? You damn sure don't look like no drug dealer," she said.

"Drug dealers have a special look?"

"You know what I mean. You don't look like no hood bitch. You look like you should be working up in somebody's office, answering phones and shit."

"Hmm, looks can be deceiving. Don't be fooled by my looks. I can be just as ruthless as a nigga in this game." I shot her an evil grin.

"Damn, you remind me of myself. Shit, I might need you on my team."

"Thanks, but I'm my own team," I told her.

She didn't respond. She just dialed a number on her phone.

"Yo, boss, I got your chick."

I knew it was Ky on the phone. I thought of thanking him but decided to wait until I got home. I swear, I appreciated him so much.

"A'ight, Miss Thang. Here you go." She pulled up at my apartment complex.

"Thank you." I exited her car, and she pulled off.

I looked around and then looked up. "Thank you, God," I said before I proceeded up the stairs and then rang the doorbell.

"Who is it?" my sister asked.

"It's me."

"Mommy, mommy!" Both of my babies jumped on me, almost knocking me to the ground.

"Hey, babies." I stooped down and hugged them close to me. I wished I didn't have to let them go.

"Damn y'all. Can I get a hug too?" my sister asked.

"Ha ha! Of course you can, boo." I let the kids go and hugged her too.

"Welcome home, boo."

"Thank you."

"Well, I cooked dinner. I know yo' ass is starving."

"Girl, yes, but lemme take a quick shower. I need to wash that dirty-ass jail funk off me," I said.

As the water beat down on my body, the tears rolled down my face. I was so happy to be home that I was crying tears of joy. That was my first time in jail, and I swear, that shit was horrible. I had no idea how bitches and niggas kept running in and out of jail.

I heard the bathroom door open.

"Mommy, I missed you so much," my daughter said.

I cut the water off and grabbed my towel. "And you know that Mommy missed her baby too, right?"

"Yes. We cried for you all night, but Auntie let us get in the bed with her."

"Baby, I am so sorry. Mommy ain't never leaving y'all again."

I could see tears forming in her eyes, which made my eyes watery. "Listen, you got to be strong right now, baby. Mommy is here with you and your brother."

I hugged her for a few minutes. "A'ight, get out so Mommy can get dressed. You know your auntie's gonna start fussing in a few minutes."

After she left the bathroom, I wiped my eyes and washed my face. Then I got dressed and joined them in the living room.

"Damn, bitch. Either the food is good, or you just hungry," my sister said.

"I think I'm just hungry." I busted out laughing.

"So, bitch, who is this dude? What's his name? Ky?"

I smiled at the mere mentioned of his name. Soon as I finished eating, I was sure going to hit him up.

"Girl, he's just my friend. I see you met him."

"Friend my ass. He came up here acting like he lost his woman and shit. Whoever dude is, he really cares about you for real. He even got somebody to fix the door. I was scared and didn't know what the kids and I were going to do."

"I'm happy he came through and helped out. Dude likes me and everything, but I am not ready for a relationship yet," I said.

"Really? I hope you ain't sitting around waiting on that no-good-ass baby daddy to come back into your life. You deserve a real nigga that can stand up and handle business like a real man. I don't know this nigga, but he made sure you came home and we were okay. Girl, don't miss your blessing by waiting on that fool," she told me.

"Oh, damn, my sister done graduated and became a relationship specialist. How come your shit don't be working out?"

"Girl, I done gave up on love. But little sister, you have been through too much and deserve to experience love."

Before I could respond, I heard banging at the door. I got up and walked out to the living room. I looked through the peephole and opened the door with my heart racing.

"What's good, ma?" his sexy ass asked me.

"Hey, you. I was going to call you and thank you for bonding me out."

"Man, that's nothing, shawty. I just had to make sure you got on up out of there."

"Aww, well, I do appreciate you."

"I wanted to see if you wanna go grab a bite with me. A nigga's famished for real," he said.

"Well, I just ate."

"Shawty, come on. Even if it is just to sit with me. I just want some company for real."

"Okay, let me put on some clothes real quick and I'll be right down."

"Bet."

I closed the door behind me. My sister was in the kitchen with the kids.

"I need a favor," I said.

"What's up?"

"Ky wants me to go to dinner with him. I told him I just ate, but he insists."

"B, you better take yo' ass on. You might get some loving!" She yelled after me as I walked out of the room.

I looked in the mirror. My hair wasn't done, but I brushed it and put a little grease on it, so it was good to go for the moment. In about ten minutes, I was dressed in a skin-tight body con dress and some Michael Kors slippers. I grabbed the matching purse. I was feeling like shit on the inside, but I wasn't going to let my physical appearance reflect that.

I stepped outside and saw him leaning against a black Charger with black rims.

"Ready?" I asked.

"Yup." He went around to the passenger side and opened the door for me. That made me feel so good. I swear, I'd never had a nigga who opened doors and didn't mind being a gentleman. Damn, a bitch could really get used to that.

"So, where we going?" I asked.

"I was thinking Buffalo Wild Wings. I mean, you don't want to eat, so I can just grab something simple."

"Okay." I closed my eyes. There was still a lot of things on my mind, but I was trying my best to enjoy the little company.

At the restaurant, we took a seat, and then he excused himself to answer a phone call. I decided to log on Facebook to see what was going on.

"You a'ight?" He startled me when he came back.

"Yes, I'm good. Was just seeing what's going on on social media."

"You mean Fakebook?" He laughed.

"Yup, that's it."

"Shawty, how you feeling?"

"I'm good. Thanks to you, I'm home."

"I'm just happy you had a bond. So what the fuck happened?" he asked.

"Man, I really don't know. My paperwork said I served an undercover informant."

"Word. Who the fuck was that?"

"I don't know, but I know the only person I served that day was yo' boy Troy. I also remember that he was acting fidgety and asking me some dumb-ass questions," I told him.

"You serious? You know I heard some rumors before that he was working with the peoples. I never had any proof, though, and the nigga grinds, too."

"I'm pretty sure it was him. I sold him a pound, and that was the exact amount on my paperwork."

"Yo, you just fucked me up wit' that one right now. Not Troy? I grew up wit' that nigga. Damn, yo." His face tightened as he bit on his lower lip.

"I'm mad as fuck because I never did anything to that nigga, so why set me up? I'm just a bitch trying to take care of her kids," I said.

"Yo! Don't ever let me hear you describe yourself as no bitch. You're a queen, and a bitch is a female dog."

"I know that. That's how I talk. If you want a proper-talking female, you need to go find a church bitch."

"A'ight, shawty, I see where this is headed." He laughed.

Man, he just didn't know, but that in-control attitude just turned me on. His cocky ass was pulling me in.

I wondered what it would be like to fuck a real nigga. I felt my clit pulsating as the thought entered my mind. My pussy was screaming at me to just get fucked already. I tried to ignore it, but the more I sat there, the more I wanted him.

After he ate, we left. As he drove down the road, I reached over and started massaging his dick in his shorts. It was a good size. Not too big and not small.

"You good, shawty?" he asked.

"Yup. I just want to massage your dick real quick." I smiled up at him.

"Shit, lemme help you out." He unzipped his shorts, releasing his rock-hard dick. It was a caramel color with a hook to the left.

I started massaging it slowly, wasting no time. Leaning over in his lap, I started licking the tip of his dick.

"Fuck," I heard him say as he used one hand to cuff my butt cheek, which was halfway out of my dress.

I swear, I licked that dick up and down, eventually taking the whole thing into my mouth. I felt the tip touch my throat. I didn't ease up at all. Hungry for his dick, I sucked on it like a starving bitch.

"Damn, babe, you got a nigga weak right now. Yo, I'ma get a room so you can do your thing," he told me.

I didn't respond. I just kept on making sweet love to that pretty-ass dick.

"Aarghhh! Damn, I'm about to bust."

His encouragement caused me to suck harder and apply a little pressure with my teeth. Within seconds, his sperm spurted out. I opened my mouth wide, catching every drop of his creamy cum. I swallowed it and then used my tongue to wipe his dick clean. After that, I sat up and wiped my mouth.

He didn't say anything. He just pushed his dick back inside of his shorts and zipped them back up. The car stopped. I looked up and realized we were at the Holiday Inn over on the west end.

"You ready? Make sure you wipe that cum off yo' mouth." He busted out laughing.

"Oh my God. Really?" I looked in the mirror.

"I was joking, shawty." He continued laughing.

"Boy, you play too much." I shoved his arm.

We got out of the car and walked into the hotel lobby. I was ready to see what that nigga was hitting for. Most of those gangsta niggas weren't good in bed like they pretended to be.

As soon as we entered the room, Ky's hands were going up and down my leg. Good thing I had shaved, because my legs were looking rough hours before.

"Stop," I muttered, trying to act like I wasn't loving it. No lie, his hands were not rough, but not soft. They were strong, and I loved the way he touched my body.

"Damn, baby, you're so freaking sexy, and those thighs, oh my God, are *phat*. My hands are addicted to them." He started rubbing his hand up my thighs again.

I inhaled, my heart tingled, and butterflies fluttered in my stomach as he planted small kisses all over my neck. He didn't waste any time as he threw me on the bed.

I spread my legs and tried my best to relax my body. He slid my panties to the side and slid his index finger inside of my throbbing, wet pussy. He pushed his finger deep into my pussy and then pulled it out before tasting my goods.

"Damn, baby, this pussy taste so damn good." He licked his finger clean before inserting it back inside of my pussy.

"Yes, daddy. Mmm." I moaned as his finger tapped against my clit.

The sensation of pleasure caused my eyes to roll in the back of my head continuously, and my breathing became heavier. He added his middle finger.

"Oh, yes," I panted, feeling good pain. I was loving his fingers moving in and out of my pussy as it made gushy sounds.

"Damn, this pussy is so wet and good," he said as he planted kisses on my neck, sending more chills through my body. I caught myself grinding on his finger as if it were his dick.

"Damn, it feels so good." My voice grew louder. My moans and breathing became heavier. My pussy was soaked with juice, and his fingers started moving faster.

"Oh, shit!" I shouted out. I couldn't hold back as my juices flowed onto his fingers.

I was anxious to fuck him. He licked his fingers while he rubbed my pussy. His dick was out already as he pulled my body farther up on the bed. I arched my pussy in the perfect position for Ky to enter me. My legs were folded, and my knees pushed backed, touching my chest. His hands were braced on my knees for balance.

"Sssss, mmmmm, shit, yes." He slowly made his way inside of my goodies.

"Fuck this pussy." I wanted him to have his way with me. I wanted to feel his dick in my stomach, touching my guts.

He slow-fucked me gently, grinding in and out of my wetness expertly.

"Ky!" I screamed because he was deeper than I thought. It felt like I was suffocating. With each stroke, he took my breath away. I tried to run from the dick, but there was nowhere for me to go.

"Don't you run now," Ky said, applying more pressure to my body. He had me pinned against the headboard. His dick was searching for my hidden treasure because he was hitting my walls.

With each thrust he took, that feel-good sensation traveled through my body. It felt like I was having multiple orgasms even when he touched my face.

"Awww, baby, fuck this pussy!" I screamed out.

"I got you, babe," he replied before going deeper.

God, that nigga was touching my soul. I put my hands on the headboard, trying to brace myself.

CHAPTER FIFTEEN

Nyesha

Damn, that was some good-ass fucking, I thought as I tried to wash between my legs. I didn't realize how bad that shit was burning until the soap encountered my pussy. I couldn't lie, though. I needed that in my life.

I walked out of the bathroom with the towel wrapped around me. He was sitting back on the bed, smoking a blunt.

"You want to hit this?"

"Yeah, let me hit that shit. You know a b—" I was about to say bitch, but I caught myself quickly. "You know I'm stressed the fuck out." I took the blunt from him and took a few drags.

"Sit down, shawty." He motioned for me to sit beside him.

"What's up?" I was nervous. I hoped that nigga wasn't about to tell me that he had a bitch. I swear, I was prepared to swing on his ass.

"Yo, shawty. I told you before I'm digging you. This ain't about getting no pussy. I want you. Fuck that, I need you in my life."

I sat there looking stupid. I really didn't know how to respond to what that nigga was spitting to me. I looked at him and let out a long breath.

"Ky, I don't know what to say. I mean, I've been down that road before, and I trusted the wrong nigga. I can't put myself through that again. I'm just now getting myself together."

He reached over and grabbed my hand in a not-so-romantic way. "Listen, baby, I'm tryin' not to sound corny. I'm not that nigga that hurt you. Whoever the fuck that nigga is, fuck him. Look at me. I'm a real nigga, and I need a woman of your caliber to be by my side. I know you've probably heard all this shit before, but yo, shawty, just give me a chance to show you that I'm not yo' average nigga." He squeezed my hand.

Tears spilled from my eyes as I tried to get an understanding of what that nigga was saying to me. I swear, I wanted to believe him, but thoughts of Yohan were in my mind. All of the lies he told me and especially how he abandoned us was still fresh. How could I know if that nigga was telling me the truth? He sounded so convincing, but so had my baby daddy.

He let my hand go and got up from the bed with his dick still hanging. I quickly turned my head. I was feeling emotional and didn't want to be tempted to get some more of that dick.

He walked around to me, picked me up, and sat me down at the edge of the bed. He threw my legs apart, and before I was aware of what he was doing, his head was buried deep inside my love cave. I had no idea how he was breathing because my pussy was suffocating his ass. He started licking me aggressively, then he stuck his tongue inside, tasting my strawberry.

"Mmmm, ohhh," I moaned.

He latched on to my clit and started sucking on it like he was famished. My toes started curling as I tried to get away, not because it wasn't good, but because I was under pressure. That shit was so good.

"Damn, boo. Yes, oh my God. I'm about to cum."

He sucked my pussy harder as my body trembled and juices flowed from my body into his mouth. He started lapping up my juices. My pussy was throbbing as I screamed out.

"Awww, yes, I want to be your woman!" My legs shook uncontrollably.

After he was finished, he got up, grabbed his phone, and walked off into the bathroom.

Fuck, this nigga's tripping, I thought. That nigga was a beast at sucking pussy. That was the kind of shit that would have you chasing a nigga down. I shook my head in disgust. I swear, that nigga had no idea that he had just sucked the life out of me.

I heard the shower running, so I got up and got dressed.

"You ready to go, aren't you?" he asked as he walked his old, sexy ass out of the bathroom.

"Yeah. You know I just got home, and my sister got the kids."

"A'ight, cool. Just let me get dressed real quick."

We left the hotel and were about to get in the car when I saw a car pull up fast, blocking us in. I was confused about what was going on, but not for long.

"This is how you do, nigga?" A skinny, dark-skinned chick ran up on Ky, catching him by surprise.

"Yo, what the fuck you call yourself doing? And where the fuck is my daughter?" he yelled.

"Fuck you, Ky. Your fucking daughter? Nah, nigga, who the fuck is this bitch that you coming out of a hotel with?" She poked him in the face a few times.

I was ready for whatever with that ho. See, I didn't say shit when she was addressing her baby daddy, but the minute that ho turned her attention to me, it became my business.

"Look, bitch, I'm Nyesha. And you are?" I asked sarcastically. That bitch had no idea that I was a beast and didn't give a fuck if that was her baby daddy or not.

She ran around him and got all up in my face. I quickly punched that little ho so hard that she staggered into the car. However, she didn't stay down. She got up and tried going for my face. I balled my fists up and started pounding that ho in the face.

"Chill out, shawty. Chill out. She ain't worth it." He grabbed me up and pulled me away from her.

"Fuck you, bitch. I'ma get your ass. I promise on my daughter, bitch," she yelled.

"Next time you run up, your baby daddy ain't gon' be able to keep me off your little ass. Bitch, get your weight up before you come gunning for me," I shot back.

"Fuck you, bitch. You think he wants you? All that nigga want is pussy. He'll be right back at home with me and his daughter. Tell her. Let this ho know she ain't nothing but a piece of ass. Tell her, Ky!" she yelled.

"Yo, stop making a fool out of yourself. Get in your car and go home," he told her.

Her facial expression changed from angry to hurt. I swear, I kind of felt bad for her, but then again, fuck that ho. She should've stayed in her lane.

"You know what? Fuck you and your dead, stupid-ass mother. You won't ever see my daughter again!" She tried swinging on him.

He grabbed her arm and dragged her toward her car. She was still cussing and carrying on. He ran back to his car, jumped in, and pulled off. He wasted no time speeding out of the parking lot.

As soon as we got out of there, he turned the radio down. "Yo, I'm so fucking sorry about that. I'on't know how the fuck she knew where I was at. Man, I think she followed us or something."

I was pissed the fuck off and really wanted to go off on his ass, but I thought carefully about what I was about to say to him. "Listen, I ain't got no fucking time for you and yo' bitches. I got my own fucking baby daddy if I want to be in some drama. Man, I knew I shouldn't have got into this shit."

He stopped the car suddenly and looked at me. "Yo, chill out. I ain't bring you into no drama. I'm not fucking around wit' shawty. I told her ass that I just want to be in my daughter's life, but she wanna be childish and shit. Shawty, I'm keeping it one hunnit wit' you."

I didn't say anything because I was still feeling angry. That bitch had no idea how much anger I had built up. I could really kick a hole in her head.

The rest of the ride was spent in complete silence. Not even the music was playing. I closed my eyes, just thinking about how I was going to bounce back from everything that was going on.

As soon as he pulled up, I tried to jump out of the car. He got out quickly, blocked my path, and then grabbed my hand.

"Shawty, hold up. I'm sorry that this happened, but I'm not going to leave you alone. I told you I'm gonna make you mine, and I meant that shit, yo."

I snatched my hand away. "Listen up. I'm not one of your little country-ass bitches. Certain shit I'm just not going to tolerate. I suggest you get your shit together before you come trying to be in a relationship wit' me. 'Cause guess what? I'm done being in relationships wit' little-ass boys that don't know what the fuck they want," I lashed out.

I didn't wait to hear anything else he had to say. Instead, I walked off to my building. I hated that I had to handle him like that, but God knows that I was tired of dealing with sorry niggas and their shenanigans.

I walked in the house and threw my purse down on the couch. I wasn't sure if I was tired from fucking or from fighting that bitch. Either way, a bitch was beat.

"Damn, bitch. You look like you been through hell. Let me find out that nigga put that dick on you like that," my sis said.

"Girl, you have no idea. That dick was so gooood, but his stupid-ass baby mama showed up when we were leaving the hotel, and me and her ass got into it."

"What you mean, y'all got into it? Do I need to put my boots on?" She had a serious look on her face.

"Girl, no. You should see that old, skinny-ass bitch. She called herself running up on me. I promise you, I dealt with that ho the proper way. You know I don't like to pick fights, but if a bitch comes for me, I'ma shut that shit down quick."

"Yo, so what did that nigga say? And I just knew that nigga was the real deal."

"He was tight as fuck. He checked that bitch and then drove off," I told her.

"Well, fuck her then. As long as he knows you ain't wit' that shit."

"Yeah, I told his ass that I ain't the one. I done had my share of no-good niggas. I swear, I prefer to be myself. Shit, I fuck myself and make my own money. What the fuck do I really need a nigga with drama for?"

"Girl, these niggas don't hear you, though. Dildos done took over, and bitches are self-sufficient now. Sooner or later, we won't need them for anything."

"I see you got them in the bed early," I said.

"Girl, I have them on a schedule." She busted out laughing.

"I'm tired, so I'ma go lay down."

"Uh-huh. That nigga tore that pussy up."

I didn't respond. I just got up and walked toward my bedroom. My damn sister was as crazy as they come, but I really appreciated her being here. I mean, for the last couple of days, she had become my rock.

I was beat, and sleeping was the only thing on my mind. In no time, I was in bed, pulling the covers over my head.

CHAPTER SIXTEEN

Kymani

That bitch Simone was really getting on my mother-fucking nerves. How the fuck did she know where the fuck I was? I swear, the more I thought about it, the more I hated that bitch.

"Yo, dawg, I heard Simone ran up on yo' ass the other day," Mo joked as we sat on the steps of his crib, smoking a blunt and drinking beers.

"Damn, how you hear that?"

"Man, you know Simone and Monique are tight, and I be fucking Monique when her baby daddy is at work."

"Yo, you a dirty nigga. You be up in that man's shit when he at work, pounding his old lady? Damn, dawg."

"Yo, shit, he knew that bitch was a ho when he decided to wife her, so I mean, what do he expect?"

"You right. Just be careful. If I was you, I wouldn't trust that bitch," I said.

"Nigga, I trust no bitch. Not even my mama, 'cause her ass done did some suspect shit before."

"I hear you, dawg." I took a few more pulls and then handed the blunt to him.

"Yo, dawg. What's good with you and shawty?" he asked.

"Man, ain't shit. I'm trying to cuff her ass for real, but after what Simone did, I'm not sure she still want to fuck wit' a nigga."

"Man, that bitch ain't going nowhere. E'ery bitch wanna fuck wit' a real nigga, so they can brag to their friends."

"Nigga you a fo—"

Before I could finish my sentence, I saw a dark-colored Charger creeping toward us. I pulled my gun out of the waist of my jeans.

"Yo, dawg, get down." I pushed Mo down.

Gunshots were flying in our direction. I ran to the side of the house for cover, then lifted my head up and peeped around the corner. I fired back at the car that was now speeding off.

I ran down the street, firing while making a mental note of the car. They sped off, and I stopped in the middle of the street with my gun in my hand. That's when it hit me that I didn't see my nigga.

"Noooooo!" I yelled as I ran back to the steps. I fell to my feet. My nigga was slumped over with gunshot wounds all over his body.

"My nigga, hold on. I got you." I took my shirt off and tried to stop the blood. I was only doing some shit that I saw them do on TV. I grabbed my phone to call for help.

"Nine one one. What's your emergency?"

"Can you send an ambulance?" I rattled off the address and held on to my homey.

"Hang on, dawg. I swear, the people coming. Hang on," I cried.

I rested his head on the steps, and then I got up. I jumped in my car and took off. I had his gun and my gun, and there was no way that I was going to stick around for the police.

I tried wiping my tears as I made my way down 33rd Street. I saw an ambulance zoom past me, followed by a fire truck and police cars.

"God, please let my nigga make it," I whispered as I grabbed my phone to call Nia.

"Hey, boss man," she answered.

"Yo, get up there on Thirty-third Street. Mo just got shot."

"Oh my God, are you fucking serious? I'm on the way."

I hung up and pressed the gas. I got home in no time. I got the guns out of the car and jumped right back in.

I dialed Nia's number again. "Yo, which hospital they took him to?"

Nia didn't say anything.

"Did you hear me, shawty?"

"Boss man, he's gone. . . ." Her words trailed off.

I hit my fucking steering wheel, hung up, and pulled over on the side of the road. Everything around me seemed black. I put my head on the steering wheel as my emotions took over.

A while later, I felt something warm hit me in the arm. Then I felt the same thing a couple more times. I lifted my head up and realized that I had been shot. I reached for my gun but remembered that I had left my guns at the house.

I used all of my strength to open my door, and I fell out of the car. I started feeling dizzy. That's when I saw the same dark-colored Charger pulling away in a rush. I guess it was time to go to my mama. That was my last thought before I collapsed on the sidewalk.

CHAPTER SEVENTEEN

Nyesha

Days went by, and I couldn't get Ky off my mind, no matter how hard I tried. I was still irritated with him, but I was missing him, nonetheless. I tried fighting the feeling, but it would not leave. I picked up the phone and dialed his number. I was nervous as hell because I'd been avoiding him.

The voicemail came on. I felt disappointed because I was hoping to hear his voice. I lay in bed, staring up at the ceiling. I hoped I hadn't lost my chance with him.

My phone started ringing. I jumped up and grabbed it from underneath my pillow.

"Hello," I said without looking at the caller ID.

"Yo, somebody just call this phone?" an unfamiliar male voice asked.

"Who is this? I just called for Ky." I was sure I had dialed the right number.

"This is Ky's phone."

"This is Nyesha. Can I talk to him?"

"Shawty, he got shot. He's in the hospital."

The phone fell out of my hand. I tried to grab it, but my hands were shaking uncontrollably. I managed to pick it up.

"Which hospital is he in?"

"He up here at MCV."

"A'ight."

I ran into the living room, where my sister was sitting, talking on the phone.

"Ky got shot!" I yelled out.

"What? Lemme call you right back." She hung up the phone.

"What are you talking about?"

"Ky got shot and is at the hospital right now."

"Oh my God. What happened?"

"Sis, I don't know, but I need to get up there."

"Go ahead then and let me know what's going on."

I ran back into my room and threw on a pair of shorts, a white T, and a pair of slippers. I googled the address of the hospital, and then I requested an Uber.

I stood outside, praying and hoping that he wasn't in critical condition. The Uber pulled up, and I jumped in. I swear, everything around me seemed so strange. It was like I was losing my mind.

"God, please, don't let him die. Please, God, just give him one more chance," I whispered as the tears started rolling down my face.

Once we made it to the hospital, I hopped out of the car and ran straight into the hospital entrance. I looked around and saw a bunch of niggas standing around. I walked to the front and asked the receptionist if someone named Ky was there.

"Do you have a last name?" she asked.

Embarrassment suddenly kicked in when I realized that I had fucked that boy, but I couldn't tell that lady if that was his correct name or just his street name.

"Lady, I don't know his fucking name. I just know him by Ky," I said angrily.

I felt a tap on my shoulder. "Aye, his name is Kymani Lee," a tall dude said.

"Oh, you're, the one I talked to earlier? How is he doing?" I turned my focus to him.

"Man, my nigga got hit three times. They say he's in surgery right now. I'm waiting on his sister to get here 'cause she's family, and they will give more info to her."

As soon as he said that, a chick walked in and made her way over to us. "What happened to my brother? First Mama and now my only brother. Oh my God." She walked off to go talk to the clerk at the front desk.

I could tell that his niggas were genuinely hurt. "Do you know what happened?" I asked them.

"Nah, I was over on the west end," one answered. "He called me and told me that some niggas killed Mo and he was on his way to the hospital. I was on my way to meet him when I got the word that he was brought up here with gunshot wounds. I swear, whoever the fuck did this to my nigga gonna be fucking dead by morning."

"I just want to see him. Does his mother know?" I asked.

"His mother got killed a few months ago."

"What? This is crazy. I see why his sister was going off like that."

"Yo, they better pray my nigga make it through." His lips trembled as the words left his mouth.

I sat in the waiting room, hoping and praying that baby boy pulled through. I hadn't known how much I cared for him until that moment. My heart was hurting, and I couldn't stop the tears from flowing.

"He is in surgery, and I got to wait to see my mother-fucking brother," his sister said as she took a seat.

I wanted to hug her and console her because I could see the pain written all over her face.

It was a little after 2 a.m. when the doctor came over to us and told us that he was out of surgery. He stated that he was in critical but stable condition.

"So, when can we see him?" his sister asked.

"He's being moved to a room in the ICU, so give them a few minutes, and then you will be able to go up," the doctor answered.

I waited for the doctor to leave. I got up and walked over to where his sister was sitting. "Hey, my name is Nyesha. I am a friend of your brother's. I was wondering if I could go up with you to see him. I know that they are only allowing family to visit, but I really do need to see him." I looked at her with tears rolling down my face.

She looked me up and down. "I guess if you're a friend of his, it's okay."

I sat there, waiting and praying. I swear, I needed strength because I wasn't sure what I was about to see when I went up there.

The nurse came to get his sister, and I tagged along as if I were a close family member. We entered the room. He was hooked up to a machine with tubes running all through his body.

"Damn, bro, what did they do to you?" His sister leaned over him and started crying.

It was hard to stand there and watch her break down like that. My own heart was hurting also. I took a few steps closer to the bed, and the sight of him made my body cringe. The once bright yellow dude was now dark, and his face was swollen to the point where he was unrecognizable.

The door opened, and two doctors entered the room. "Miss, I'm Doctor Obohoa, and this is Doctor Wilson."

"Doctor, please tell me my brother's going to be all right. Please," she cried.

"Your brother was shot three times. One of the bullets missed his heart by a few inches. I was surprised that he wasn't in worse shape than this. We removed two of the bullets, but we couldn't get the one that was close to his heart. He is in critical condition, but we've managed to stabilize him for now."

His sister started bawling louder as she walked back over to her brother. "Hey, Doctor, is he going to make it?"

"Well, the bullet close to his heart could've been critical. If he pulls through, with the proper care and rehabilitation, I think he will be able to go on to live a normal life. Let's just see how the next few days go."

"Thanks," his sister said gratefully.

Standing there listening to him, I really didn't like how he sounded. He was the doctor. Why couldn't he just let us know straight up, instead of beating around the fucking bush?"

That morning, I left the hospital with a broken heart. I wished I could do more, but sitting there wasn't helping.

I dragged myself up the stairs and walked into my building. The kids and my sister were asleep, so I tiptoed into my room, buried my face in my pillow, and cried myself to sleep.

That morning was bittersweet because my sister was getting ready to go back home to NY.

"Sis, I'm going to miss you so damn much," I said.

"I know, babe, but you do know I'm just a phone call away. You can hit me up anytime."

"I know," I said as I choked back the tears.

"Bitch, quit all that damn crying. You better save them tears for when I fucking die. Nah, I'm coming back soon. You take care of yourself. You hear me? Just know that I'm praying for him, and I hope he pulls through."

"Thank you, Sissy."

The taxi arrived. She got in, and they pulled off. I wiped my tears as I walked back into the building. I decided to clean up the house and make my kids some breakfast to keep my mind occupied. So much shit had happened in such a short period of time that I often slacked on my mommy duties. I decided to change that shit. No matter what was going on, my babies were my life.

After the kids got up, I fed them and bathed them. Their daycare van arrived, and they got on. I was kind of happy to be alone, so I could gather my thoughts.

First thing first, I needed to call a lawyer. My court date was coming up in a month, and I needed to see what my case was looking like. The next call I made was to Sean. I hadn't heard from him in a while, but I needed to get back on, and I had no one else to turn to. When I was locked up, I had made a vow not to hustle again, but there I was, broke as hell because the police took all my money and drugs. There was no way that I was going back to being a broke bitch who could not support her children.

His phone started ringing. I really hoped he didn't start talking about getting some pussy. I mean, I needed help, but I was not going to fuck anymore to get it. The older I got, the less bullshit I wanted to deal with.

"Yo, stranger, what's going on?" he said.

"Hey, boo, you ain't heard from me 'cause my ass got torn off," I told him.

"Damn, you good now?"

"Yeah, but I lost e'erything, so I'm trying to see if you can front me something."

"You know I got you. You in the same spot?" he asked.

"Nah, I moved over here by Churchill."

"Churchill? Around them hot-ass niggas?"

"I know, but I ain't have no choice. I had to find something for me and the kids."

"I feel you. Well, shoot me your address and I will stop by in 'bout two hours," he said

"A'ight cool."

That was easier than I thought. I was ready to get back into the groove of things. My adrenaline was rushing as I mopped the floor.

This time, I was going to be more careful. I hadn't seen that fuck nigga Troy since the day that I served him. I damn sure wasn't going to fuck with him anymore. This time around, a bitch was going to be on point.

I stood outside as Sean pulled up. "Hey, you," I said as I sat down in the passenger seat.

"Yo, what's good, ma? I got four pounds that I can front you."

"A'ight, that's cool. I will hit you up soon as I get rid of this," I said.

"Aye, yo, be careful out here wit' these niggas. 'Member, you from up top and they'on't fuck wit' up-top niggas like that. Plus, you a female, and them niggas will definitely try you," he said.

"Trust me, I know. I ain't gon' be around here for long. I just need to bounce back real quick and then find somewhere else to go. Thinking about going back up top for real."

A police car drove by us. "That's my cue to bounce. It's hot as fuck over here," Sean said.

I waited until the police car turned the corner and was out of sight, then I grabbed the large garbage bag and got out of the car in a hurry. "I'll call you," I said as I closed the car door.

He wasted no time pulling off. I hurriedly walked into the building, unlocked my apartment door, and went straight to work, cutting up dimes and twenty bags. I wished I could sell just weight. However, I needed to make enough money so I could give him his cut and have money to get my own shit.

It didn't take me long to bounce back. It was like I didn't even take a break. I had Churchill back on lock. In about a week, I sold what Sean had given me, gave him his money back, and re-upped.

My plan was to stop selling weed. See, I had it on lock with the weed, but that shit was hard to get rid of if the police busted up in there. The only thing was, I knew nothing about hustling crack. I knew that was what Ky dealt with, but he was still in the hospital, so he couldn't show me how to do it.

I sat there pondering who I could go to, and that was when it hit me. Ky's boy shouldn't have a problem showing me how to cut up crack and bag it.

I was tired as hell, but I had to make it to the hospital to see my boo. He was doing so much better, and I was hoping he could go home soon. Most days, I would sit up there with him, just talking and joking.

My feelings for him were extraordinarily strong, and I was just waiting on him to get released, so we could start our lives together. Ky getting shot made me realize how easily I could've lost a nigga that really showed me nothing but love.

"Bitch, I see you everywhere but the fucking casket," his old, stupid-ass baby mama said when she walked in the hospital room.

I stood up. I swear I was ready to go another round with this ho. But I quickly saw her daughter staring at me. I just smiled at that bitch.

"Aye, I'm about to go, boo. Call me when this ho leave." I shot that bitch a devilish smile and gathered my stuff.

"Ky, I can't believe you have this bitch up here knowing your daughter was coming up here. Keep playing and lose your daughter behind this bitch."

"Get used to my face, ho, 'cause I ain't going nowhere," I said while I made my way out the door.

I swear that bitch was working my motherfucking nerves. If it wasn't for him being sick, I would've dragged that ho right in that room.

CHAPTER EIGHTEEN

THREE MONTHS LATER

Kymani

I was happy as fuck to walk up out of that fucking hospital. Staying in bed all day was definitely not my thing. The pain was still there, especially where the bullet was still lodged. I noticed that I had difficulty breathing, which wasn't good, because the doctor suggested that I give up smoking. Telling me to do that was like telling me to stop eating food.

"Babe, you a'ight?" Nyesha asked as she walked up behind me and put her arms around my waist.

"Just sitting here, tryna figure out how to make a couple million."

"Shit, sound like a plan to me. What do you have in mind?"

"If I tell you, I'ma have to kill you," I joked.

"Shit, fuck it then. I'll make my own millions." She laughed as she squeezed me.

I stood there thinking of how blessed I was. If you had told me that I would find a chick like shawty, who would make me want to settle down, I would say you were lying.

"Yo, you ever thought of us just getting up and leaving?" I asked her.

"I do, but I need to make some more money. I mean, we can't just leave like that."

"Man, you got money, and I got a good amount stacked up. We can move somewhere, maybe Atlanta, and start up a few businesses."

"Yeah, true . . ."

I was trying to convince her to leave because the truth was, some shit was about to pop off. I knew the niggas who shot me, but I'd been laying low. I planned on getting my revenge on them and on their fucking families. I didn't want to risk shawty and the kids getting caught up in the crossfire between me and these niggas.

"Yo, just think about it, a'ight?" I said.

"Okay, boo."

I walked back in the house. Lately, I had a lot on my mind. The streets were calling my name, and I was ready to get back out there.

CHAPTER NINETEEN

Nyesha

"I'm just happy the life didn't get me." I sang along with K. Michelle as I drove off the car lot in my brand-new Chevy Impala. Shit, I was feeling myself. It was my first car, and a bitch was happy. I was tired of taking Uber or depending on Ky to take me places. I was a bad bitch, and I deserved a bad ride to compliment my new lifestyle.

I parked my car and ran up the stairs to show Ky my car. When I walked inside, I realized that he wasn't there. That was strange because his car was parked outside. I dialed his number, but it went straight to voicemail.

Oh, well. I shook off the strange feeling that I had and decided to take some steak out of the fridge. I would've loved to have gone out to celebrate, but instead, I decided to cook my man a nice dinner. I wasn't the best damn cook, but I knew how to whip up a meal. I also decided to bake the kids their favorite lemon cake.

After I finished cooking, I decided to cut up two ounces of crack. I smiled at myself in the mirror as I dropped a twenty-dollar rock into the bag. I couldn't believe that a few months ago, I did not know a damn thing about selling crack, but there I was killing the game already.

Ky's boy had put me on to this connect that had some butter crack. It took no time for word to get around that I was selling that shit. My crackhead, Kim, was a cool-ass chick, and a lot of niggas fucked with her. I would hit Kim off with some free shit, and in return, she would call me whenever her friends wanted to get high.

I bagged up three thousand dollars' worth of crack, and then I washed my hands. It was almost time to get the kids off the school bus. I made it my business to never hustle while the kids were home. I mean, if they were in bed sleeping, then I would still get calls and go outside to serve the customers.

I ran down the stairs when I saw the bus pulling up. "Good evening, Mr. Jones." I greeted their bus driver. He was a cool old dude who kept trying to holla at me. I just laughed at him because there was no way I would let that old man put those fucking old paws on me.

"Mommy!" Emanyi ran up and hugged me.

"Hey, baby girl." I hugged her.

I noticed my son's face was screwed up. "What's wrong with you?"

"Oh, he mad 'cause Mr. Jones yelled at him for getting up out of his seat while the bus was moving."

"Little boy, what I tell you 'bout that? Keep on playing and I'ma beat yo' ass!" I said.

I was about to walk up the steps when I noticed a nigga named Johnte walking toward me. I didn't care for him too much because the few times that I'd seen him, his face was balled the fuck up like he smelled shit.

"Yo, I need to holla at you," he said.

"Who you talking to?" I looked at that nigga strangely.

"You, shawty," he said, taking a few steps too close for my comfort.

"Y'all go ahead and go inside," I told the kids.

I waited until they walked in and closed the door, then I took a few steps back.

"What the hell do you want?" I asked him.

"Shawty, I'ma need you to stop hustling over here. This Churchill, and you not one of us, so I don't think you should be over here making no money."

"What? So what this is Churchill? I pay rent over here, so I can do whatever the fuck I want to do."

"Yo, shawty, this ain't no joke. I know you fucking with that fuck nigga, Ky, so I suggest you relay this message to him. His bitch can't make no money 'round here."

"Ha-ha, I get it. You not man enough to approach him. You know he would smash that ass, so you feel like you can come at me recklessly," I said.

I took a couple of steps closer to him and stared him down. "Listen to me, you little fuck nigga. I hustle wherever the fuck I want to. There is nothing you or the rest of these fuck niggas can do about it. Get the fuck out my way. Let me go hit Ky up, so he can know what yo' clown ass is saying."

"Bitch, you playing with fire. I see I'ma have to make an example out of you."

I was going to respond, but I was no fool. I walked off on that nigga and his idle threats. Slamming the front door behind me, I walked up the stairs and locked my apartment door. The nerve of that motherfucker. Who the fuck did he really think he was?

I walked in my room and grabbed my phone. I dialed Ky's phone again, but it just rang and went to the voicemail. I was really pissed off at that point. I needed to talk to that nigga, and he was MIA. What the fuck was really going on?

CHAPTER TWENTY

Kymani

I sat in the car, waiting for a text to come through on my cellphone. I was feeling anxious, but I took a few more pulls from the blunt, trying to relax my mind.

"Yo, these fools ain't gon' even know what hit they ass," my nigga said.

"Nah, nigga. I need that nigga J-Roc to see me when I put one in his motherfucking dome." I took a sip of the Cîroc that I had in my cup.

My phone started vibrating. I quickly grabbed it and opened the message.

It read: All set to go. 4 total.

I knew then that it was a go for me. "Yo, let's roll my nigga." I pulled off, and the car behind me did too.

I'ma pull 'round the back. You and Dino can pull up in the front. Make it quick. I just want to get in and get out, I texted back.

See, ever since I got out of the hospital, I'd been plotting and planning. The nigga J-Roc was the nigga that fired at Mo and me. He was also the same nigga who shot me up later that night. They had no idea that I knew it, but I just had to wait until the right time to act.

I put my mask on and jumped out of the car with my gun in my hand. I ran up the back steps and slowly opened the door. There was no light on in the back room, so I used my senses to guide me. My nigga came right behind me. I was careful not to make a sound as I crept through the house.

I heard voices coming from a room. I stood in the hallway for a second, and then put my ear up to the door.

"Fuck me, daddy!" I heard a female voice say.

I busted into the room. "Don't move, nigga."

He threw shawty off of him and jumped up from the bed, but that nigga was two seconds too late. I already had his gun.

"Nigga, didn't I say don't move?" I took a few steps closer to him and pressed the gun against his head.

"Yo, get outta here." I pointed at shawty.

"Man, what the fuck you want? Money? I got plenty of that," he said.

"Nah, nigga, I want your life," I said as I pulled the mask off of my face.

His eyes widened as he realized that it was me. "Yo, dawg, what's good?"

I didn't respond. I just pressed the trigger, not easing up until that nigga's body slumped over on the bed. I quickly turned around and returned to the front room.

"Yo, boss, what you want to do with these niggas?" my man asked.

"Kill them," I said.

Shots rang out back-to-back. Within seconds, we were out of there. I eased out of the back alley without bringing any attention to myself. As soon as I was back on the street, I burned tires, getting the fuck away from there. I knew that the police would be swarming the area real soon.

"Man, fuck them niggas for real. Mo, this one for you, my nigga." I raised my cup in the air. I knew, I couldn't bring my nigga back, but fuck that. Those niggas wouldn't be walking the streets anymore.

We drove over to the James River and got rid of the guns and burned the masks. I always thought niggas were stupid for keeping a gun that had a body on it. There was no way that I was going to get caught slipping like that.

I dropped my nigga off. It was still early, and I decided to go check on my daughter. Her mama had been blowing up my phone for the last couple days. I took off my gloves, pulled into the driveway, and walked up to the door. I rang the doorbell and waited.

"Who is it?" she hollered.

"It's me."

She opened the door, looking at me like I was trespassing.

"Yo, you gon' let me in?" I asked.

"Sure," she said and walked away. I couldn't help but notice how fat her ass had gotten.

"Your daughter is sleeping. So, why are you here?" She bent over to grab a piece of paper off the floor.

"What? Maybe I came to see you," I joked.

"Why is that, baby daddy? Your bitch ain't fucking you right?"

"Yo, chill out, shawty. This about me and you."

"You really think I'm one of those dumb-ass bitches for real," she said.

"Come on, Simone. I just want to chill wit' you for a little bit. I mean, that's still my pussy right there." I snatched her up and pushed her against the wall. I swear my dick was throbbing, and I wanted to fuck.

"Yo, you drunk or something?"

"Nah, boo, I just want you. I miss fucking you for real."

I fondled her breast. She surprised me when she grabbed my dick and started massaging it. My body was in heat, and I needed release right then.

I pulled her little shorts down along with her panties. I wasted no time pushing my fingers inside of her wet pussy. Shawty always had that wet-wet, and tonight it seemed like she was overflowing with pussy juice.

"Awe, fuck me, baby. I knew you missed this pussy," she whispered in my ear as she nibbled on it.

I took my dick out, lifted her up in the air, and pushed my dick inside of her slippery pussy.

"Aarggh," she moaned as I eased my hard dick in and out. She wrapped her legs around me, and I straight stroked that pussy while she was balanced on the wall.

"I love you, baby. Give me that dick. You know this is your pussy, baby!" she screamed out.

Fuck. It wasn't even a good ten minutes and I felt like I was about to bust. I thought about going slower, but Simone was grinding on my dick so hard, I had no choice but to throw her the dick.

My veins got larger, and the throbbing got more intense. I rammed harder inside of her, not caring if I was tearing up her insides.

"Damn, I'm about to bust, yo!" I dug deeper into her soul.

"Yes, baby, fuck meeeee!" she screamed as my juices spilled into her.

I almost lost my balance as I eased her down to the floor. I stumbled to the couch nearby. Damn, that shit was good as fuck. I wiped the sweat off my face.

It took me a few minutes to get myself together. I walked into the bathroom to clean myself off. I felt a little lightheaded, so I walked out of the bathroom and decided to lay down on the couch for a few minutes. I think I was tired as fuck. I had been drinking earlier, and that pussy drained my energy.

I checked my phone and realized that I had a lot of missed called from Nyesha. Fuck, I just needed a few minutes, and then I planned on going home. I placed the phone on my pant leg and laid my head down.

CHAPTER TWENTY-ONE

Nyesha

It was 2 a.m. and I still had not heard from Ky. I was starting to get worried. This had never happened before, so my nerves were torn up. I tried calling his phone a few more times, but he still wasn't answering it.

I called the county jail to see if he was locked up. They told me he wasn't there, which was a good thing. However, that didn't ease my worries.

"Ky, where the hell are you?" I asked out loud as I buried my face in my pillow.

I heard a text come in on my phone, so I jumped up and grabbed it.

In case you wondering where ya man's at. He's here with me and his daughter.

I noticed that the text was coming from Ky's phone. Minutes later, a picture popped up on the screen. It was a picture of him in his boxers, with no shirt on, laid up on somebody's couch.

"Nooooo!" I screamed out as I threw my phone down. Tears started flowing as anger took over my soul. That nigga was laid up over that bitch's house, and that was the reason why he couldn't answer the damn phone? Really, that was how he was doing it?

I jumped up and grabbed my phone. I realized that I had another text.

I hope I didn't hurt your feelings too bad. No worries. I'm pretty sure he will be back over there in the morning. But please know he is my baby daddy, and I can fuck him whenever the fuck I want.

I sent a text back to her.

Fuck you, you low grade bitch. You can keep that nigga over there, and please know every time you kiss that nigga, that's my pussy scent you're smelling. Now go play in traffic and leave me the fuck alone.

She sent me a reply.

Ha-ha. I think you're big mad. No worries. I took care of the dick for you.

I wasn't going to keep going back and forth with that little bitch. Truth was, I whooped that ass once, and I wouldn't think twice about doing it again.

I turned my phone off and sat there with tears rolling down my face. I felt betrayed, and my feelings took me all the way back to when Yohan was cheating on me. Why me? Why couldn't I find a nigga who wanted just me, and not every other bitch?

The kids were not feeling too well. I checked their temperatures, and they had slight fevers, so I decide to keep them home. I made them breakfast, and they went back to their room.

It was still a day that I had to make money, even if I was going through bullshit. I still had to stay on my grind.

I heard the door open, so I jumped up off the bed and ran toward the front.

"Hey, babe," that two-timing ass nigga said when he walked in.

"Hey, babe? Nigga, you need to get yo' shit and get out of my fucking house."

"Yo, what the fuck? I know you trippin' 'cause I ain't call you all day yesterday, but I had some personal shit to handle. I didn't want to get you involved. I'm sorry, boo." He tried hugging on me.

"Get the fuck off me!" I slapped his ass.

He grabbed my arm. "Yo, what the fuck? I said I'm sorry, shawty. I know I should've call you to let you know what was going on."

"Yes, I agree that you're fucking sorry. You couldn't come home 'cause yo' dirty-dick ass was out fucking yo' baby mama."

"What? You really trippin' now. I ain't fucking shawty, and I ain't cheating on you," he lied.

"Nigga, fuck you. I got the fucking pictures that bitch sent me from yo' fucking phone."

"What pictures? Shit can't nobody send you no picture of me." He tried walking off.

I ran in the room, grabbed my phone, pulled that message up, and shoved it in his face. "See this, nigga? Yo' bitch texted me."

He grabbed my phone and scrolled through it. "Man, what the fuck?" His eyes popped open.

"Now, get yo' shit and get out of my house, nigga!"

"Shawty, I ain't goin' nowhere. Yo, you need to tone yo' fucking attitude down." He turned around and walked right back out the door.

I fell to my knees, crying. "No, God! How could he do this to me?" I cried out.

My heart was hurting. How could the nigga that made me so happy turn around and do that to me?

I heard someone knocking on the door. First I ignored it because I wasn't in the mood to deal with anyone. The banging got louder. I knew it wasn't Ky because he had his key.

I stood on my feet, quickly wiped my tears, and opened the door. Whoever it was, they were about to get cussed the fuck out.

"What the fuck you w—" My mouth stayed wide open, but no words came out.

"Yo, what's good? Where are my kids?"

It was like a lump was blocking my throat and I couldn't speak. Did that bitch-ass Yohan just show up on my steps talking about where his kids at? I didn't feel too good, so I leaned against the door, trying my best to deal with the bullshit that was about to take place.

CHAPTER TWENTY -TWO

Nyesha

God, what the fuck did I do to deserve this bullshit that just dropped on my doorstep? I thought as I stared this nigga dead in his eyes. It seemed like the walls around me were closing in. I braced myself against the door, praying I didn't fall out. Was this a dream that my crazy mind done cooked up, or was it real?

I was still trying to digest the present situation when I heard the downstairs door open. I heard someone running up the stairs. It was Ky. He locked eyes with me, then quickly turned his gaze to Yohan. He took two more steps, then stopped on the last stair, where Yohan was standing.

"Yo, who this nigga, and what he doing here?" Ky turned to me and asked with a confused look written all over his face.

I was gathering my thoughts, but I didn't move fast enough, because Yohan couldn't keep his big-ass mouth shut.

"Yo, nigga, I'm over here to see my motherfucking kids. Is there a problem? Oh, you must be the clown that she's been fucking," Yohan said.

Before he could finish his statement, Ky two-pieced him, knocking Yohan into the wall. He almost lost his balance, but he stood his ground and threw back a couple punches. They started fighting.

"Y'all need to fucking stop. Ky, don't do this," I yelled, trying to get in between them. These two niggas were like raging bulls, and they almost knocked my ass down the stairs.

After a few minutes, Ky pulled his gun out and pointed it at Yohan. "Yo, nigga, I should just blow yo' fucking head off right now."

"You better do it, or you won't get another chance, pussy," Yohan said.

Ky cocked the gun back and started to grin. I could sense shit was about to get bloody.

"Ky, stop. What the fuck you doing? This my kid's father," I yelled.

"So fucking what? This nigga left y'all for dead, and you out here defending his bitch ass?"

"Nah, that nigga fronting. He's a bitch. He ain't gon' shoot nobody," Yohan teased.

"Man, shut the fuck up," I yelled to Yohan, then I turned to Ky. "Ky, go ahead with all this shit. You trying to get me put out with all this."

"You know what? You right, shawty. This pussy nigga back, so you happy. Go play house again with his bitch ass," Ky said to me angrily.

He then turned to Yohan. "Pussy, this ain't over." He winked at him before he ran down the stairs and left out the door.

I was so fucking pissed off because these niggas were acting like little bitches. I looked at this nigga, shook my head, and walked off into the house.

The kids must've heard the commotion. They ran to the front.

"Daddy, daddy, daddy!" They ran straight into his arms. He hugged them for a long period as I stood there watching this fake-ass bullshit that was taking place. Now, don't get me wrong. I know in my heart the kids genuinely loved and missed him, but on his part, this shit was bullshit. How can you get up and leave your damn kids for months on end, act like they didn't exist, and one day, they just happen to pop back into your head and here you are?

"Kids, y'all need to go in the back so I can talk to y'all father," I said. To say I was annoyed would be an understatement. I was fucking aggravated. I was breathing hard, and I felt knots all up in my stomach.

"But Mommy, I want to be with Daddy," Emanyi whined.

"Little girl, what the hell did I just say? Get yo' ass back into your room and watch television like you been doing," I said.

"Go do what yo' mama say, baby. I'll be back there in a little while," Yohan told her.

I watched as the kids walked off before I spoke to him. "Yo, what the fuck you think you're doing, walking up in my shit like this? And how the fuck you know where the hell I stay at?"

"Yo, it's not over between that nigga and me. His pussy ass must not know who the fuck I am."

"Listen, I don't care about none of that. I just want to know why you are here."

"Can I come in? I ain't tryna have e'erybody all up in my business like that." Before I could respond, he stepped in and locked the door behind him.

"Yo, Nyesha, I know you pissed off at a nigga, and you have e'ery right to be, but I'm here now, and I want to be in y'all lives."

"What the fuck? You brought us down here from New York, dogged me out, and disappeared. What kind of fool do you think I am?"

"Man, I swear I'm sorry as fuck. I ain't goin' lie. We were just arguing too much, and I was under too much damn pressure. I didn't know what to do."

"So you just up and left us for dead. You went to go play house with the next bitch and left me and your fucking kids to find our own way. Well, guess what, my nigga? I had to pull on my big girl panties and find a way for us, 'cause you left us with nothing. You hear me? Absolutely nothing. No Pampers, no milk. Not even a damn dollar. I really don't see how you can even show yo' face 'round here."

"Man, Nyesha. I swear on my mama, I'm sorry that I did that to you. I will spend the rest of my life making this shit up to you. I brought you some money to help take care of you and the kids." He went into his pants pocket and pulled out a wad of cash and handed it to me.

I pulled my hand back, letting the money drop to the ground. "Boy, you silly as fuck if you think you can just walk up in here and throw a few dollars at my ass and I come running back to you. We ain't hungry no more. Matter of fact, we living good over here, so pick up yo' money and take it to that little young-ass bitch that you been living with."

"Nyesha, c'mon, boo. I know you angry and shit, but I'm begging you, please give a nigga chance. Let me be the man that I know I can be for y'all."

"You had that motherfucking chance and you fucked it up. I got a nigga now, and I've moved on." I walked off on his ass to go check on the kids, who were arguing back and forth. Yohan just followed me into the house.

A while later, I stood at the counter, fixing the kids some spaghetti and meatballs that they had requested earlier. All kinds of different emotions were running through my veins. The kids were overly excited that he was there, but I wasn't feeling that way. Every bit of anger that I had for this nigga just reappeared. And how the fuck he just pop up and expect me to accept him with open arms? It wasn't like I was single. I had a whole nigga that I was in love with even though he did some fucked up shit also. I shook my head from side to side. This whole shit was a big-ass mess, and guess who was in the middle of it? My dumb ass.

After I fed the kids and bathed them, it was time for bed. This nigga walked off into their room. It was getting late, and I was ready for him to go, so I could get ready for bed. After I cleaned up the kitchen, I took me a long shower, trying my hardest to get my thoughts under control. I was shivering inside, nervous and angry at the same damn time.

I sat on my bed, thinking I needed to go in there and let this nigga know it was time for him to go. Before I had a chance to make that move, I heard my room door pushed open.

"What are you doing in here?" I jumped up off the bed.

"Man, come here. I swear to you, I'm sorry for the way I carried you." He pulled me close to him, hugging me tight.

"Get off me. How could you do me like this? How?" I started hitting his chest with my fist.

"I'm sorry, babe. I don't know what I was thinking. But I'm here now, and I ain't going nowhere." He started massaging my back.

I tried to ignore his hands, but I realized that I was still weak for this nigga. My pussy started throbbing as he used one hand to pull my breast out.

"Hmmm, stop, boy. We can't—"

"Shhhh, yes we can. I love you and miss you so much." He started kissing me.

I couldn't resist any longer. My mind was telling me to push him away, but my body was screaming for him.

"Man, quit fighting the feeling. You know you want me as bad as I want you." He didn't give me a chance to respond, he slid his pants down halfway, enough to get his hard dick out. He picked me up and put me on the bed, placing my feet on his shoulders, knees pressed against my chest. I don't know what kind of position the nigga had me in. If it had a name, I'd call it "the pretzel."

Good thing my pussy was wet because as soon as his dick entered my pussy, it took away my breath. It felt like his dick was punching my kidneys.

"Oh Lord, Yohan," I screamed between strokes. I swear I was about to suffocate. Each thrust Yohan gave me took my breath away.

"Oh, shit!" This nigga was trying to rip my insides out. His dick was punching my clit like a drumstick. My juices were flowing through my body. I couldn't resist myself from creaming on his dick.

"Awe, damn, I'm about to bust, boo." He gripped me tight and dug deeper inside of me. I pushed him off me.

"Damn, what you did that for? Shit. It's about time we have another little me running around here again. Little man ain't no baby no more," he said.

"Boy, shut the fuck up. I ain't having no more kids." I got up off the bed, grabbed my robe, and walked out of the room.

I locked the bathroom door and sat on the edge of the tub. Guilt started taking over. "What have I done, God?" I asked out loud. "Oh my God." I was in disbelief that I had allowed myself to fuck him after all the shit he did to me.

I got up and jumped in the shower. I grabbed my sponge and soaped it with Dove body wash. I tried to wash this nigga off me. I started crying because I felt guilty. I shouldn't have done this, not with him anyway.

I got out of the shower and walked into my room to grab some night clothes. This nigga was butt-ass naked, knocked out in my bed.

What the fuck he think he's doing? I thought as I grabbed a pair of pajamas.

"Yohan, wake up. You can't spend the night, nigga." I shook his shoulder.

"Man, I'm tired, yo. I'ma get up in a few."

He was not budging, so I got on the other side of the bed, and before I knew it, I was knocked out.

A few hours later, I jumped up and looked on the other side of the bed. That nigga was still asleep, snoring loud as hell. Fuck! What if Ky walked in? What the fuck was I going to do?

"Yohan, you need to wake up. You got to go." I shook him a few times.

"What time is it? Man, it's early as fuck," he said when he woke up.

"It don't matter what time it is. You shouldn't be here anyway."

"Why not? You worried that pussy nigga you fucking with might show up?" he asked.

"Boy, shut the fuck up already. Matter of fact, Ky do live here, so you need to go."

"Yo, you need to tell that nigga that it's over. This is my pussy, and I'm back to claim it."

"Whatever you say. Just get yo' ass up and go." I regretted fucking him last night, because it only gave him room to talk shit.

He must've sensed that I was serious, 'cause he got up and grabbed his boxers, walking out of the room with his dick hard as hell.

While he was in the bathroom, I quickly made the bed. I knew I was playing a dangerous game because Ky had his keys and could've popped up at any minute. I grabbed my phone to see if I had any missed calls from him, but there were none. However, there was a text.

So this how you playing it shawty. I see ole boy car still parked outside. Man, fuck you. You a grimey-ass female.

I was caught up in feeling guilty, but at the same time, I didn't, 'cause he carried it first.

"You a'ight? You look like you just saw a ghost," Yohan asked as he walked back into the room.

"Yeah, I'm good. You just need to go."

"I know you still ain't worried 'bout that nigga. I done told you, I'm here to stay. Tell that pussy nigga you been my pussy for years. I'ma make a few runs, but I'll be back later."

Before I could respond, he walked out of the room. I followed him to the front door, angry as fuck.

CHAPTER TWENTY-THREE

Kymani

I was pissed the fuck off when Nyesha showed me the pictures that Simone sent her. That bitch was grimey as fuck. I swear I wanted to kill that bitch, but I just knew that I would be the first person that they would look at if anything popped off with that bitch.

I knew Nyesha was mad as fuck with me, so after I stormed out the crib, I took a few minutes to calm down, then I decided to go back and try my hardest to convince her that she was the only one I loved. I ran up the stairs, and that was when I came face to face with a nigga that she was standing there talking to. Instantly, I became suspicious.

Come to find out, it was the fuck nigga that left her and the kids for dead. So, all of a sudden, when she and I are having problems, this nigga just happened to pop up. I was already heated, so once the nigga opened his mouth, I was ready to punish his ass. This nigga had no idea how much anger I had built up in me, but I made sure I showed his ass.

After I was tired of beating his ass, I was ready to drop that nigga right there in front of Nyesha, but surprisingly, she started yelling at me like I did something wrong. Shit, this nigga was up in my motherfucking space! Or did her ass forget that I was the one that helped her pay those damn bills?

After I saw who she was riding with, I figured her ass wasn't worth it in the first place. I looked at Nyesha, shook my head, and ran off, but not before letting that nigga know this was far from over. See, this nigga really didn't know who he was fucking with. Soon enough, he'd find out, though.

I jumped in my car and pulled off. I quickly lit up the half blunt that I had in the ashtray. I cut the music up as Moneybagg Yo Gangsta's *Pain* CD blasted through my speakers. I swear my anger level was elevated, and none of my thoughts were good.

I parked and jumped out of the ride and ran to this bitch's door and started banging on it. "Open this fucking door, bitch!" I yelled.

"Boy, what the fuck you want?"

"Simone, open this fucking door or I'ma kick this shit off," I yelled back.

"You better get the fuck on. I take it yo' bitch done seen the pics of you. Ha-ha!" she laughed.

"You a stupid-ass ho, you know that? Bitch, I hope you die."

"Like yo' dead-ass mama. Boy, grow the fuck up. You got caught cheating. Now the bitch see the kind of dog you are, and now you mad at me. Huh? Go play in traffic, nigga. Me and baby girl don't need you."

I realized the bitch wasn't going to open the door, so I kicked it a few times. "Bitch, lose my fucking number." I kicked it real hard again before I walked off.

"Boy, whatever," I heard her holler.

I just laughed to myself and got back into my car. I swear, I regretted ever fucking with that little-ass girl. I hated the fact my baby girl was part of her.

"Yo, nigga, you look like you goin' through some shit. Ever since you pull up, you ain't say a damn word," my nigga Mikey Q said.

"Huh, what you just said?"

"See, that's what I'm talkin' 'bout. What's good, my G?"

"Man, I hate my stupid-ass baby mother. I just want to put one in that bitch head real quick."

"Damn, it's that bad, my nigga? I mean, I know she likes to play her little games and shit, but this seem a bit more serious."

"Yo, I went over the bitch house, fucked her. I fell asleep, and this dumb-ass ho done took pictures and sent it to Nyesha."

"Damn, dawg. How the fuck you manage that? I told yo' ass stop fucking wit' her ass completely. You gon' fuck around and lose Nyesha," he said.

"Shit, fuck her too. All of a sudden, her baby daddy done popped back up. I almost killed that nigga earlier."

"Man, you got too much shit goin' on. You need to chill before we have bodies from left to right. You know we running out of burial sites." He busted out laughing.

"Nah, I'm cooling now. I just need to get back to the money and stop worrying 'bout these hoes."

"That's what I'm talkin' 'bout. Let's roll up in Daddy Rabbit tonight. You need some new hoes in yo' life."

"Sounds good. I got a run to make, then we can meet up," I told him.

"A'ight, my nigga. Just hit my line when you ready."

I took the last sip of my Grey Goose and threw the cup in the trash before I exited my homeboy's crib.

The weather was getting chilly, and I was out and about in a wife beater. I thought about stopping by the crib to grab a shirt. As soon as I pulled up, I noticed a car parked by the gate. I knew then that nigga was still up in there. I stopped for a second. The mixture of my anger, the alcohol, and the weed had me thinking about going up in there and murdering that nigga and her ass.

I was about to cut the car off when I spotted a police car in my mirror, approaching me. I shook my head and waited until he drove by. I then pulled off.

That bitch grimey as fuck, I thought as I busted a U-turn and headed out to the club.

Daddy Rabbit was jumping as usual. The club wasn't no high-end strip club, but it kept some of the baddest bitches in Richmond up in there. Soon as we walked in, they knew what time it was. The dancers surrounded our table, trying to outdo one another.

"Hey, baby, can I give you a lap dance?" one sexy-ass bitch asked.

"Yeah, gimme a minute." I waved for the waitress to come to our table.

"Hey, fellas, what y'all drinking tonight?" the cute little Spanish chick asked.

"Bring over a bottle of Grey Goose."

"Okay, baby. I'll be right back."

Man, her ass stayed flirting with me e'ery time I came through these doors. *If she don't stop playing, her ass about to get some of this dick*, I thought.

After she brought our drinks, we started drinking and chilling. The chicks on the stage were working for their money, and we sat back, enjoying the show. At first it was cool, but the more I drank, the more Nyesha invaded my mind. I tried to say "fuck her" in my mind, but I couldn't. This was the first female that had a hold on my heart the way she did. Man, I hated to admit it, especially when I was angry with her ass, but I loved that girl.

"Yo, what you doing, my nigga? Man, forget them hoes and have a little fun. If that pussy got you like that, you need to leave that shit alone. My nigga ain't never been bent out of shape like that over no bitch," Mikey Q joked.

"Chill, my nigga. I got it under control." I took a big gulp of the Goose. There was was no way I could let my nigga know that shawty had me weak, so I waved for one of the dancers to come over.

"Hey, boo, do you want a dance?" the sexy little dark-skinned chick asked.

"Yeah, lemme see what you working with."

I ain't gon' lie, my dick got hard instantly as she twerked on me. I pulled her closer and inserted my finger in her tight pussy, which was wet by the time I fingered her.

"You know we can always finish this later, right?" she whispered in my ear.

"Really?"

"Yeah. I'll give you my number, and you can hit me up later. I get off 'round two."

"A'ight sounds good."

I continued fingering her until she gripped me tight and exploded on my fingers. By then, the music had stopped. She adjusted her underwear, smiling at me in a sexy but wicked way.

"A'ight, shawty, I'ma hit you up." I dug into my pocket and pulled out a couple hundred and handed it to her. I definitely planned on hitting her ass up later. I had to get some of that wet-wet.

The rest of the night was spent drinking and entertaining these hoes. I was drunk as fuck and high off the weed. I was ready to get the fuck up outta there.

"Yo, my nigga, I'ma bounce," I said.

"This early? I thought you was enjoying yourself."

"Yeah, but I got some shit to do. It's almost the end of the month, and I need to get my shit together," I lied.

"A'ight. Be easy, my nigga. Hit me when you get settled."

"Bet." I exchanged dap and left.

I had just left the club and pulled onto Broadrock Boulevard when I noticed a cop car behind me. I tried my best to stay within the speed limit, hoping this nigga would get the fuck on. I realized he was on my tail. I figured he was running my license plate, but I wasn't trippin'. I was good. My car was registered in my sister's name, and everything was legit.

I pulled out a Black and Mild and lit it because this nigga was making me nervous. I tried my best to remain cool as possible. All that calmness went out the window the second I heard the siren. I knew then that he was pulling me because I was the only car within his reach right about now.

"Fuck, what this pussy pulling me for?" I asked out loud as I hit the steering wheel. I already knew I was going to jail. I was drunk as fuck, plus I had the fucking burner and some work up in there. I thought about running, but it would only lead them to my sister's doorstep.

I pulled over and braced for whatever the fuck was going to happen. I watched as the black officer got out of the car and walked up on my car.

"Driver's license and registration, please?"

I reached over to get the registration out of the glove compartment and handed it to him.

"I'll be right back," he said.

I knew I was good on that end. I was just praying to God that he didn't smell the alcohol reeking through my pores. I sat there thinking about how the shit was gon' play out if he decided to search the whip. Maybe I should just jump out blasting at that nigga, I thought, but then my daughter's face flashed across my face.

Fuck. I can't do this shit to my baby girl.

I looked up, and there he was, walking back to the car. I swear I was seconds away from pissing on myself.

"Please step out the car," he said as he shined the light inside of the car.

"Get out the car for what? Am I under arrest? And what for?" I was talking fast.

"Sir, I said get out the car," he yelled.

Before I could respond, I saw three other police cars pulling up. The cops jumped out of their cars.

Fuck. This can't be happening right now.

I wanted to cuss at his bitch ass, but instead, I held my tongue. I hit the steering wheel to show my frustration, then I stepped out of the car.

"Put your hands where I can see them," he commanded.

I raised my hands, and the bitch-ass nigga proceeded to search me. He then placed the cuffs on me.

"Kymani Lee, you're under arrest for assault and battery on Simone Facey."

What the fuck is this nigga talking about? I know he tripping. I didn't even see the bitch, much less assault her ass. This dirty-ass bitch did this to me.

My thoughts were interrupted when I saw two officers searching my car. I knew then I was really going down. I had my burner in the arm rest, and I had a couple ounces of coke also stashed up in there.

"Look what we got here." He held up my Glock.

I just shook my head in disbelief. All the years that I had been grinding, I'd been able to stay out of the motherfucking way. Fucking with this bird-ass bitch, I done got caught up in some shit.

"Let's go." The cop grabbed my arm and led me to the police car. I was still under my liquor, so I couldn't walk straight.

"Here. Blow in this," he said.

"Man, I ain't drunk. I only had a few drinks."

"Are you refusing to take the Breathalyzer test? Because if you do, I will presume you're drunk."

"Man, do whatever the fuck you want to do. I ain't blowing in shit."

He shot me a dirty look, opened the car door, and put my ass in. I sat there watching as the officers continued searching my car.

I wished I had a few more drinks, 'cause I needed something to keep my mind off this shit that was going down.

I watched as the officer pulled off. "What the fuck y'all gon' do with my ride?"

"A tow truck is on the way. They will give you the info when you get to the jail."

Just the mention of the jail made my blood boil. I swear, I was gonna kill that ho once I got the fuck up outta there.

He pulled up at the jail and led me into where they process inmates. I was told to sit down. I was about to be in front of a judge. I was sure that I would get a bond, 'cause I didn't have a record.

Shit, I was shocked when the white cracker said, "No bond."

I just shook my head and held my comments to myself. After I was searched and changed into a jail outfit, I made a call to my sister.

"Hello," she answered sleepily.

"Aye, sis, it's Ky."

"What's wrong? Where you at?"

"Down by the lockup."

"For what?"

"Can't get into all that right now, but that little bitch Simone put some bogus-ass charges on me and shit."

"Say what? I'ma beat that ho ass. I told you a long time ago stop fucking with that bird."

"Listen, sis, I tried calling Nia's phone, but it keep going to voicemail. Here goes her number. Hit her up and let her know I got court in the morning. She needs to get up wit' the lawyer right now so he can be there also, and she should bring bond money."

"A'ight, bro. I'm on it now. Please don't worry. I'm calling in from work. I'll be there too. What time is court?"

"I think it's at nine a.m. A'ight, sis, I got to go."

"Love you, bro."

After I hung up, I went to the cell where I would spend the night until they moved me to the jail. As I lay on the hard-ass bench, freezing my ass off, I couldn't help but wonder what Nyesha was doing. She should've been the one that I called, but I guessed she was too busy worried about that bitch-ass baby daddy. I should've killed that pussy when I had the chance.

CHAPTER TWENTY-FOUR

Nyesha

I knew damn well I was tripping. Yohan's ass was dead-ass serious when he said he was not going anywhere, and to make matters worse, he had the kids wrapped around his little fingers. I loved the fact that the kids were happy, but this was way bigger than they understood.

I hadn't seen Ky or heard from him in two days. I tried calling his phone, and it kept going to voicemail. I knew damn well that his phone wasn't dead, so either he blocked me, or he lost his phone. If I didn't hear from him that day, I planned on going over to his old apartment. Even though we lived together, he still maintained that apartment.

After the kids left for daycare, I bagged up some work. Even though shit was going on in my life, I still had to make my money. Yohan came around, throwing money at me because he thought that was the way to make me fall back for him. But truth was, his little chump change didn't move me. I was no longer that broke-ass chick he left. I made my own money.

"You a'ight?" He walked up on me in the kitchen.

"Yeah, I'm just thinking. I still can't understand how you just up and left us. Did you miss the kids?"

"What kind of question is that? Yeah, I missed my damn kids. Man, don't start wit' all this negative shit this morning. I'm here with you and them now. You should be happy."

I stopped what I was doing, turned around, and looked at him. "Are you serious right now? I didn't ask you to be here. My life been going great before you decide to come over and interrupt me."

"Yo, I ain't mean it like that. I got to go. I'ma be late tonight."

Before I could respond, he was out the door. I hurriedly locked the door behind him. Lord, what the fuck was I doing? Was I so stupid that I would allow him to just come back into my life? This shit had definitely gotten out of hand.

It had been days since I'd seen or heard from Ky. I logged on to Facebook to see if he'd been posting on his page. Nothing jumped out at me, until I scrolled down and saw a post that his homeboy posted: **Free a real nigga**.

What? Who is locked up? I scrolled further down, but there was nothing else on his page that might suggest that he was locked up.

I quickly logged out of Facebook and dialed his boy's number. He didn't pick up. I hung up and dialed the number again.

"Yooo," he answered.

"Hey, this Nyesha. Is Ky around?"

"Nah, he ain't 'round. Did you hit his line?"

"Yeah, I been calling him, but he ain't answering. Then I saw your post that talking 'bout free a real nigga."

"Oh, you ain't know?"

"Know what?" I anxiously waited for a response.

"I figured that you knew he got locked up the other night."

"Hell nah, I ain't know. What the fuck happened, and do he have a bond?" My mind was racing.

"Calm down, shawty. The nigga home."

"This is fucking crazy, yo. A'ight, I got to go." I didn't wait for a response. Instead, I hung the phone up in his face.

I dialed Ky's phone again. Still no response. I grabbed my car keys and rushed through the door. I pulled off in a hurry and drove a block over to Ky's crib. I saw his truck parked on the street. I parked behind it and jumped out.

I ran up the stairs started pounding on the door. I waited a few minutes, but no one came to the door.

"Ky, I know yo' ass in there. Open the fucking door, yo," I yelled. Still no response. I started kicking the door. I was angry as fuck. How the hell did he get locked up and I wasn't even notified? This shit seemed real suspect. I knew he was in there. All kind of crazy thoughts started invading my mind.

"Ky, open this fucking door before I kick the door in!" I yelled at the top of my lungs.

"Yo, what the fuck you want?" Ky opened the door, looking rough as fuck. His hair wasn't done, and his beard needed to be cut.

"Really, this what kind of time we on? I just came to check on you because I heard you was locked up."

"Really?" He laughed.

"What that supposed to mean?"

"Yo, you don't need to worry 'bout what's going on wit' me no mo'. You got yo' baby daddy, the love of yo' life, to worry about."

"Boy, you tripping. You act like I wanted this. You know damn well I love you."

"Man, go ahead wit' yo' dramatic ass. I only got one question for you. Knowing you, you might lie. Did you fuck this nigga?"

My heart sank. Why would he ask me this? "Listen, I didn't want the nigga 'round, but the kids want their daddy. What the fuck I'm supposed to do?" Tears started rolling down my face.

"You silly as fuck, shawty. You sat up there telling me how much you hated this nigga, how this nigga carried you for another bitch. Shit, he left you and your fucking kids for dead. But all it took was this nigga showing up for you to open yo' fucking legs and fuck him in our bed. Bitch, get the fuck away from me." He shook his head and turned to walk away.

"Ky, please. It ain't like that." I grabbed his arm.

"Bitch, you heard me. Get the fuck up off me. You know, motherfuckers told me I was stupid to fuck with you. I didn't care that you had two kids. I loved you. I stepped up like a man's supposed to, and this is what I get. You a dirty bitch. But guess what? Lose my fucking number."

"You think you know everything, nigga. Go ahead, disrespect me some more. Yeah, I fucked it. Shit, a few motherfucking times. But didn't you just fuck yo' baby mama? What make what I do so fucking wrong? We both did the same shit. Stop sitting up screaming you a real nigga, but yet you can't accept real shit. I ain't never been a fake bitch, and I ain't gon' start now. What about you, my nigga?"

"Bitch, fuck you." He stepped inside and slammed the door before I could even get another word in. I stood on the steps, crying my eyes out, not giving a fuck who was passing by.

I realized he was not coming back out, so I slowly walked down the stairs and got into my car. I sat there for a few seconds, trying to digest all this shit. I was shocked that he was carrying me like this. Yeah, I was wrong as fuck, but I thought the nigga would at least try to see that I really did love him, and the only reason why I let this nigga Yohan back in was because of my kids. Yes, my kids. I tried to convince myself, because what other reason would there be? Ky had more money than Yohan, his dick game was A plus, and he treated me like a queen.

I glanced at the time and realized it was time to get the kids off the daycare van. I gently pulled off, hoping I would see Ky running out the door after me. I kept looking in the rearview mirror until his street was in the distance.

I pulled up just in time to get the kids. I parked and waited for them to get off. They wasted no time with telling me all about their day. I tried my best to pay attention to what they were saying, but the truth was, my heart was broken, and there was not a damn thing I could do about it.

After I got the kids in the house, I gave them a snack and got them settled in. My phone was ringing nonstop with plays. In about an hour, I made almost two grand. I was happy because I'd been slacking and needed to get back on my grind.

"Baby girl, what's going on wit' you and Ky?" Kim, my crackhead runner, asked when she came by.

"Why you ask me that?" I quizzed as we sat on the steps outside of my building.

"I notice he ain't been coming around, and I also notice you ain't as bubbly as you used to be."

"Well, Ky and I are no longer together. I'm quite sure you'll see him with a new bitch soon."

"Boss lady, I'on't know 'bout all that cause I know him since he was a little boy. I watched him grow into a man, and I could tell he was all into you. I done heard him bragging 'bout you. I don't mean to be in y'all business, and honestly I'on't care, but y'all need to get it together. Y'all make the perfect couple."

"Kim, I'on't know 'bout all that, and honestly, I'm good. I just need to make my money and take care of these damn kids. If the right nigga comes along, then I'm all for it. But right now, I'm back on my grind."

"I hear you. Well, here come my white boy. He the one that want the eight ball. I be back," she said.

"A'ight, cool. Be safe." I sat there and watched while Kim jumped into the truck, and they pulled off.

I swear Kim was a cool-ass chick, even though she was a crackhead. I had to say she was the reason why my shit jumped like it did. She was not only a crackhead, but also a trick. You should've seen how many niggas came through to fuck with her. I ain't talking 'bout no crackhead niggas either. These were niggas that had businesses and, I'm pretty sure, wives also.

These niggas ain't shit, I tell you. I laughed to myself.

A while later, I was in bed when I heard someone knocking. I was so hoping Yohan would stay gone that night. I was in my feelings and really didn't feel like dealing with his shit either.

My phone started ringing.

"Hello." I pretended like I had been sleeping.

"Man, come open the door. You know how long I'm out here knocking," he said with an attitude.

I didn't even respond. I hung the phone up and dragged myself off the bed. I unlocked the door and walked off. I made my way back to the room. I heard him in the kitchen, then I heard him walk toward the room.

"Yo, you ain't cook?"

"Nah, I ain't cook. You do know I be busy making my money, right?"

"Man, I'm hungry as fuck."

"Okay, why is you telling me? You a grown-ass man. Go make some noodles or eat some damn cereal," I said.

"Did you at least feed the kids? I know you ain't send them to bed hungry like that," he stated.

"Yo, yo' ass ain't been worried about what they're eating when you left us. Matter of fact, you left us with nothing. I made sure they didn't miss a meal. So don't come here trying to act like I'm the type of mother that would let them go to bed without food." I was very annoyed with his ass.

"Man, chill the fuck out. When you gonna stop bringing that shit up? I ain't gon' keep listening to this shit e'ery time you get mad. You act like yo' ass ain't do shit. I ain't been gone that damn long, and you already had a lame-ass nigga around my kids, playing daddy and shit."

"You know what, Yohan? Fuck you. A nigga can't play daddy if the real daddy was in the picture taking care of his kids. Now, get the fuck up out of my shit if you feel like that."

"Ha-ha, you finally grew some balls, huh? Must be the little paper that you making. The old you would never come out of your mouth like that to me. You know damn well I'd beat that ass."

"Yeah, well, how 'bout you try doing it now?"

"Man, Nyesha, chill the fuck out. You already know I ain't no chump."

He gritted on me before he grabbed a pillow and stormed out of the room, mumbling something under his breath.

I waited a few minutes, then I got up and locked my bedroom door. I buried my head into my pillow, allowing the tears to fall. I was missing Ky something serious. Just a week ago, everything was going good as hell. Now suddenly, here I was, back with this old disrespectful fool.

CHAPTER TWENTY-FIVE

KYMANI

I couldn't believe a nigga like me allowed a bitch to get into my head like this. It had been days since I last saw her, and we exchanged words. I tried not to show it, but when that bitch stood in front of me admitting that she fucked her baby daddy, only one thought was in my head, and it was just to body her ass. I believe in death before dishonor. That was my pussy. How the fuck she just gon' throw that shit around on a nigga that left her for dead?

The only thing that had been able to help me was smoking and staying drunk. It was like e'erything around me was fucking up. I lost my bitch to a south side nigga, and not just that, the nigga was living in my shit. Nah, fuck that. I was gon' show that bitch and that nigga that this was all a big mistake. Nobody, and I meant nobody, disrespected Ky like that and got away with it.

I took a few more drags off the blunt that I was smoking. My phone started ringing.

"Yo, my nigga, where you been?" Beenie quizzed.

"Yo, I'm at the crib, cooling. What's good, though?"

"Ain't shit. Was hitting you up 'cause we low and need to probably make a run this weekend."

"A'ight, let's do it then. I'll hit my peoples up."

"You tryna go out later? Shoot some pool or something?" he asked.

"Nah, I'ma stay in and politick for a few."

"A'ight, my G. Be easy."

I hung the phone up and threw it on the bed. Before I could get up to go get me another drink, it started ringing again. I grabbed it up without looking at the caller ID.

"Yo."

"So, this how your dumb ass gon' play it, huh?"

I know this stupid-ass bitch did not call my mother-fucking phone after she lied on me.

"Yo, bitch, if this ain't about my motherfucking daughter, I ain't got shit to say to you."

"You a dumb-ass nigga. Your only child ain't seen yo' ass in over a week, but you laid up with that ho, playing daddy to another nigga kids."

"Maybe if yo' dumb ass ain't lied that I hit yo' ass, my daughter would be able to see her daddy. Quit pretending, bitch. This ain't 'bout my daughter. You only give a fuck about yo'self. Matter of fact, don't call my mother-fucking phone no more."

"What the fuck you mean, don't call your fucking phone? You know what? I ain't gon' beg yo' ass to be in my child's life, but I promise, my black ass will be down by the child support office first thing in the morning. Let's see what the fucking white man think," she threatened.

"Bitch, fuck you." I hung the phone up in her face before she could get another word in. That bitch made me sick to my motherfucking stomach. I swear I wished she would just die so I could get my daughter.

I cut the phone off and walked to the kitchen. I grabbed the bottle of Goose out of the cabinet, opened it up, and took it straight to the head. Images of my mama falling to the floor flashed across my face. I took two more big gulps as tears rolled down my face.

"Damn, Ma, I miss you. I wish you was here right now. I need you, Ma. I need you," I cried out.

I held my chest as I felt a sharp pain. I swear I was ready to go be with my mama. I staggered back into my room and grabbed my .380 that was under my mattress. I took it out and placed it on my lap. I ain't never been no weak-ass nigga, but I didn't deserve to live. I had killed the only person that loved me, even though I was born a piece of shit. My mama never judged me and was always there to hold me down.

I got up and walked to the dresser where I had her picture hanging on the mirror. I took and brought it to my face and started kissing it.

"Ma, I miss you. Why did you leave me, Ma?" I took the gun and aimed it to my dome.

I'm ready to go. I'm ready to be with you, Ma.

My mind was racing. Tears were rolling down my face. I was seconds away from pulling the trigger when my daughter's face flashed across my face.

Man, I can't do this to you, baby girl, I thought before I lowered the gun. I fell to my feet, crying like a baby. I was broken as fuck and had no idea how the fuck I was going to get through it.

Fuck it, I thought as I stumbled to my feet. I grabbed the bottle and put it to my head. This wasn't working. I need something stronger. Something that would numb all this pain I was going through.

I grabbed my bag of coke and poured a small amount on my nightstand. Then I grabbed a dollar bill. I wasn't thinking. My only goal was to numb this pain. I took one drag, then another. Within seconds, my emotions started to change. The tears quickly dried up, and I was feeling happier. I snorted a few more lines, until all the coke disappeared up my nose. My energy level skyrocketed as I felt energized.

Damn, is this what I've been missing? I thought as I folded up the dollar bill and put it in my drawer. The feeling of desperation quickly disappeared. I stood up and started laughing. I couldn't believe that a nigga like me, a boss nigga, was contemplating suicide.

Man, fuck that. I'm this nigga out in these streets. Fuck my baby mama. Matter of fact, fuck Nyesha ass too. Them bitches can die for real.

I was ready to go back to the old me, to get my money and get pussy. Fuck trying to wife a bitch. Shit, none of these bitches were loyal anyways.

I reached for my phone and searched for the stripper bitch's number. Kaley. Yup, that was her name. Shit, let me see if she was about that life.

"I thought you wasn't gonna call me. Shit, it's been almost a week since I gave you my number," she said as she walked into my crib an hour later.

"Yeah, you know a nigga stay busy. Plus, I know you was on yo' grind too."

"Yeah, I understand. So, what's going on with you?"

"I'm good. I'm tryna see what's really good with you, you know?" I shot her a sexy look.

"Hmmm, I'm trying to see if this is business or personal."

"It can be whichever one you choose. If it's money you want, I got that. If you looking for a special friend, I can be that too," I told her.

"Sounds interesting. Well, I could be at the club working right now, but I'm here with you. So I'm missing out on money."

"No worries. I got you. Put your price on the table. How much would you make on a regular Sunday night?"

"Well, on an average night, I bring home 'bout twenty-five hundred."

This bitch was tripping. I was seconds away from telling this bitch she was a liar, but I was tipsy and horny as fuck. She had a fat ass, so I was trying to fuck. I mean, it ain't tricking if I got it, right?

This chick wasted no time in pleasing me. I lay on my back as she made love to my dick. I ain't talking about no amateur dick sucking. Shawty knew what the fuck she was doing. She held my dick and licked all over, at times deep-throating it until it touched the back of her throat. I swear my toes were curled up as I tried my best not to explode in her mouth.

"Aargh, aargh, arrgh." I grabbed her head and pulled it down on my dick. She didn't resist. She opened her mouth wider as my juice shot out of my dick into her throat. She wasted no time in cleaning me up with her tongue.

"Yo, come here." I picked her up and turned her on all fours. I reached over and pulled a rubber out of my drawer. I then eased into her wet pussy. I tried to calm my anxiety level down because shawty was so wet. I felt like I was about to cum that fast. After I got myself under control, I used my hand to hold her stomach and pulled her up to me. I wasted no time in beating the pussy up. She wasn't the tightest pussy that I had, but her shit was so wet and slippery, it made the pussy good as fuck.

"Daddy, give me the dick. Yes, fuck me nigga. Fuck me. Show me you ain't scared of the pussy," she teased.

That only made me beat that pussy up more. I showed no mercy as I thrust my nine-and-a-half-inch dick in and out of her pussy.

"Yessss. Oohwee, yes, daddy, oh," she whined as she threw the ass back at me.

I grabbed both hips with my hands and thrust deep as my dick allowed me to go. She gripped the sheets and moaned in pleasure.

"Oh my God. You tearing my pussy out," she screamed.

"Oh, yeah, this what you want, right? This what you want, right, baby?" I didn't ease up none. My dick was throbbing hard, and my veins stood up.

"Damn, arrgh, aarghhh!" I gripped her tighter as I exploded in the condom.

Sweat dripped from my face onto her back. After I caught my breath, I eased out of her. I was careful to grab hold of the condom before I slid out. There was no way I was going to make a mistake to get another trick pregnant. Not after all this shit I was going through wit' Simone's stupid ass.

"Man, you sure know how to tear some pussy up. My shit is hurting."

"My bad. I thought that's what you wanted, right?"

"I ain't complaining. I can appreciate a man with a nice-size dick and one that also knows how to use it the right way."

"Uh-huh, I hear you, baby girl." I walked off to get some water out of the fridge. Once I stepped in the kitchen, I realized I was tripping. My money, my work, and my gun were left in my room. I didn't know this chick like that to leave her alone around my shit. I used the bathroom and hurried my black ass back into my room, hoping shawty wasn't up to anything suspect. She was fully dressed when I got into the room.

"You a'ight?" I quizzed.

"Yeah, I got to get my daughter from my friend's house. She just texted me, saying she's been crying that her stomach hurting. My daughter has lupus and needs around-the-clock care."

"Damn, sorry to hear that."

"Nah, you good. That's why I bust my ass e'ery day to make sure all her doctor bills and medicine are taken care of. Trust me, I ain't up in that club shaking my ass for nothing. I got a plan."

"Even though I don't know you, that make me respect yo' grind even more." I walked over to my drawer and pulled out a wad of cash. I peeled off three grand

and handed it to her. Nah, the fuck wasn't worth three grand, but I could see that shawty was struggling to make it.

"Oh my God. Are you serious? I ain't even spend an hour. No, I can't take this." She tried to hand the money back to me.

"Man, chill out and take the money. Matter of fact, you need to boss up and know yo' worth," I told her.

"I swear I appreciate you. You can call me anytime you feel like having a great time."

"Okay, for sure. Now, go ahead. Go handle yo' business."

"I am, and I swear I'll never forget this."

She grabbed her purse, and I let her out the door. I was tired from beating that pussy up and all that drinking and smoking. I was ready to call it a night.

I checked my phone and saw that I had two missed calls from Nyesha.

Man, fuck her, I thought before I threw the phone on the other side of the bed.

CHAPTER TWENTY-SIX

Nyesha

I'd been calling Ky's ass nonstop for weeks, but this nigga kept on ignoring my ass. I swear I was not the one to be chasing after no nigga, for real. I knew the situation was kind of fucked up, but how could he just say fuck me like that? I sat on the edge of my bed, pondering.

The water was running from Yohan taking a shower. I swear this was his normal routine. Get up, eat my damn food, take a shit, shower, and then bounce. Besides the money that he threw at me when he first came back, he hadn't given me a dollar or asked about one damn bill.

My phone started ringing. That might be some money, so I reached over and grabbed it up.

"Aye, bitch." It was my sister.

"Hey, boo. What's up wit' you?"

"Nothing. Sitting here trying to decide if I want to go get my hair done or wait 'til tomorrow."

"Knowing yo' saddity ass, you gonna go get it done today." I busted out laughing.

"Don't be analyzing me, little bitch. Where my damn brother-in-law at?"

"Which one?" I blurted out without thinking. I wished I could take it the fuck back.

"Hold up. What? You cheating on Ky?"

I was frantically searching for the right words to explain this situation to my sister.

"Sis, listen. Yohan is back."

"What the fuck you mean, he's back? Back in the kid's lives? 'Cause I know damn well yo' ass did not start fucking with that old bitch-ass nigga again."

"Sis, shut up and listen to me. I know you don't like Yohan because of what I've told you about him, but he is the kids' daddy, and they love him. You know I'll do anything for my kids."

"Yo, I really can't believe you right now. Kids? He left them for dead. His wicked ass came up here, packed you and the kids up, and brought y'all down there and left y'all. Did you lose your fucking mind? All of a sudden that you're doing good and have a nigga that loves you, he just happen to pop back up?"

"You know what, Meisha? I can't talk to you right now. You're being judgmental and don't know what's really going on. It's my life and my decisions, so let me deal with them."

"Do you forget who the fuck you call crying to when that bum left yo' ass? Do you remember who was by your side? Me, bitch. But you right. It's your life. Just don't expect me to be there for you the next time that cheating-ass nigga walk out on you and the kids." Before I could respond, she hung up in my face.

I knew she was angry as hell with me. Shit, I was angry with my damn self. How the fuck did I allow this to happen? I knew I fucked up. I just didn't want to hear it from anyone else. Not right now anyway.

"Who was that on the phone?" Yohan quizzed when he walked into the room.

"That was my sister. Why?"

"I know I heard my name, so I was wondering what y'all was talkin' 'bout."

"It's nothing."

"Oh, okay."

"Yo, I'm curious. Where do you go every day? I mean, you claim that you back over here for yo' kids, but they leave in the morning, and by the time you come home late night, they're sleeping. So, how are you there for them?"

"Man, you know I got shit to do. I can't sit around here e'ery day not making money."

"Hmmm. I hope you getting ready to pay some bills up in here 'cause the first of the month coming up," I said.

"Yo, I see you tryna argue and shit. You'll have money, so don't start tripping on me. I got to go. See you later. Love you."

I didn't respond to him. Instead, I sat there shaking my head. I was still in my feelings about my sister's behavior. I loved her to death, and she was the closest person to me, so I was disappointed that she couldn't at least try to understand where I was coming from. Shit, she was sitting up there defending Ky and shit like he was some saint or something. That was because I didn't tell her ass what the fuck he did. Shit, if you ask me, none of them niggas weren't no damn good.

My phone rang three times, and I picked it up. No one answered, but I could hear someone breathing hard into the phone.

"I know it's a stupid-ass bitch playing on my phone. You better go find you another bitch to play with, 'cause I drag bitches," I said before I hung up.

"Bitch, you ain't gon' drag nobody. I'm just trying to see if my baby father is over there. He supposed to be taking K'asia to the doctor, and now he ain't picking up the phone."

"Why would yo' baby father be over here? Bitch, I got my own baby daddy."

"I see you don't know who you talking to. This Zaria. We spoke a while back. And Yohan is my daughter's father, and I'm looking for him."

"Oh, I remember you. You the silly bitch that he was fucking."

"Was fucking? Bitch we live together, and we have a three-month-old daughter. You better get yo' life."

"If y'all so much together, why the fuck you calling my phone, little girl? Keep yo' little ass off my fucking phone before this shit gets crazy." I hung up in that ho's face and immediately called Yohan's phone.

His phone went to voicemail. This bitch-ass nigga had a daughter and didn't tell me. Yo, I couldn't wait to get my hands on him.

My day went from great to shitty real fast. I lit a Black and Mild and smoked it while pacing from the front of the apartment to the back.

Fuck my life, I thought as tears streamed down my face. After all these years and dealing with this nigga and his lies, I thought he was trying to change, only to find out his ass done made a motherfucking baby that he failed to mention, even in those late-night talks where he claimed he was keeping it one hundred.

Fucking liar, man, I said in my mind.

After the kids ate dinner, I bathed them and got them ready for bed.

"Good night, baby girl." I kissed my daughter on the cheek.

"Mommy, why do you look sad? Is Daddy hurting you again?"

I shot her a surprised look. I quickly changed my frown to a smile.

"No, baby. Mommy just a little bit tired. But I love you. Get some sleep."

"I love you too, Mommy."

I tucked her in, turned the light off, and walked out of her room. I was shocked by what she had said. I knew she was getting older, and sooner or later, she was going to have a lot of questions. Her ass was already nosey as hell. I had to be careful what I said around her.

I was so pissed off that I couldn't eat. I had a banging-ass headache that I needed to get rid of so, I made some ramen noodles. After I ate that, I popped a Percocet and smoked a blunt. My heart wanted to cry, but my mind was stronger.

After I counted how much money I had made for the day, I cut the television on. I needed something to get my mind off all this negative shit. I thought about calling Ky, but what was the use? He never picked up his phone for me.

I lay in the bed, twisting and turning, thoughts all over the place. I was also listening for the door 'cause I was going to dig into Yohan's ass when he popped up here that night. I knew his old lying ass was gon' deny e'erything.

I heard a loud banging on the door. I knew it was Yohan's ass. I grabbed my robe and put it on. I unlocked the door and waited for him. As soon as he stepped in, I smacked him in his face.

"Yo, what the fuck you did that for? You fucking crazy bitch!" He lunged toward me, but I was quick on my feet this time.

I ran into the kitchen and grabbed my big knife. I ran at him, trying to stab his ass.

"Yo, you got a fucking baby?" I yelled.

He looked at me like he saw a wild animal. "Yo, shawty, chill out. You tripping with that knife."

"Am I, nigga? Answer my fucking question. Do you have a fucking daughter wit' that bitch Zaria?" I lunged toward him. I planned on getting a few cuts in.

"You stupid bitch. You cut me. Yo, I'ma beat yo' moth-erfucking ass, yo."

"Answer my fucking question, nigga."

"Man, I was gon' tell you."

"What you was gon' tell me? You don't think that was the first fucking thing you should've said out of yo' mouth when you walked yo' ass up in here? You went and made another baby with the bitch that you cheated on me with?" The tears started to flow.

"It wasn't like that. Shawty told me she was on the pill, but she wasn't. I asked her to have an abortion, but she was totally against that 'cause her mama and them are Christians."

"Are you fucking serious right now? How could you do this? I mean, I could forgive you for anything else, but to get another bitch pregnant. Nah, I can't fuck wit' you anymore."

"Yo, listen, Nyesha. I know I lied to you, but I was scared. I didn't know how to come to you and tell you this. Look at how you behaving right now. See, look, you fucking cut me." He tried showing his hand that was dripping blood.

"I really hate you, dude. I swear everything that comes out of yo' mouth is a lie. The bitch even said y'all is living together. Now it all make sense to me. I kept asking you where were the rest of your clothes, but you keep saying at yo' homeboy house. Nigga, you a fucking liar."

"That bitch lying. How do I live wit' her if I'm here wit' you e'ery night? You acting real slow right now. Can't you see she just mad 'cause I'm with you? She only tryna break us up. I know you smarter than that."

"Man, fuck you, Yohan. I swear, I can't believe I fell for yo' shit a second time. I fucked up my relation-ship for this?"

"Yo, fuck that. I'm tired of you bringing up that bitch-ass nigga. If you miss fucking him that bad, go be wit' him. I'on't need no bitch that keep bringing up the nigga she was fucking e'ery time we get into it. Matter of fact, I'm good. I'on't need no bitch."

"Yo, I ain't gon' be all these bitches up in my shit. You been slinging dick all over Richmond. You got a nerve to be in yo' feelings 'cause I was fucking wit' one nigga."

All I felt was this nigga's hand across my face. I grabbed my face and ran toward him with the knife still in my hand.

"I told you about talking to me crazy. You my bitch, so you need to show some motherfucking respect!" he yelled.

"Boy, fuck you. I can't believe you just put yo' mother-fucking hands on me."

I grabbed my phone to call the police on his ass, but before I could dial the number, I remembered that I had all those drugs up in there.

"I want you out of my shit. You hear me? I want you out."

"You know what? I'm sorry that I hit you. This ain't even me, hitting on no broad. But you begging to get yo' ass beat. How the fuck you gon' go off on me 'cause what a bitch told you? I love you, not her. I'm here with you, not her. That bitch only tryna start beef with me and you, and your dumb ass feeding right into it."

"I swear to God I'm done with you." I walked off.

He followed me into my room. I tried to shut my door into his face, but he blocked it.

"Nyesha, baby. I swear, I'm sorry I put my hand on you. I swear, baby. I'm just pissed off. I fucking love you. You my soulmate. You know e'erything 'bout me. You the mother of my kids. I want to marry you, baby."

"I ain't the only one wit' your kids. That bitch can have you. I don't want you no more. I gave you too many damn years of my life. I stuck with you when no one else did. All you ever did was lie to me, play me like a fucking fool. Do you know how stupid I felt when you left me and my kids without shit? Do you know what the fuck I had to go through to buy milk and Pampers for your fucking son? No, nigga, you have no idea how much you hurt me."

"And I'm sorry, bae. I promise I will spend the rest of my life making it up to you and the kids. I will never hurt you like that, ever again. Can't you see I'm trying? I just want a life with you and my kids."

"Don't you forget that other little bastard you got out there," I snapped.

"Man, I ain't worried 'bout all that right now. My main concern is you and my kids that I have with you." He reached over and grabbed me. He started hugging me.

"Let me go. I can't do this anymore. This ain't the first time you put yo' hand on me, but I promise it will be the last time, though." I wiggled my way out of his grip.

Part of me was falling for the bullshit he was feeding me, but the other half knew he was a pro at this lying shit. As crazy as it sounds, I still loved this nigga, and it was hard for me to walk away again.

Days turned into weeks, and finally months, and I hadn't seen or heard from Ky. I knew he was still around because I would drive by his house occasionally and his truck was parked outside.

One day, I was on my way from the bank when I decided to drive by his house to see if he was outside. As I approached his house, I saw two people standing by his car. I realized it was Ky and a female. I watched as he leaned over and hugged her, gripping her ass. I stopped the car dead in the street and jumped out.

"Yo, who the fuck is this bitch?"

"What the fuck you doing?" this nigga turned around and asked me.

"Ky, who is this chick?"

"Bitch, don't worry 'bout who the fuck I am. Who the fuck are you?" she said.

"Nyesha, you need to go. Don't be bringing no drama where I'm at," he said in a serious tone.

"Yo, fuck you. I can't believe you're doing this."

"Doing what, Nyesha? Don't you have a nigga that live with you? Yeah, this my hood. I know e'erything that goes on 'round here. Now, get in yo' car and go home," he said.

"Boy, fuck you and this bitch."

I was waiting for the bitch to respond, so I could take out some of this anger on her ass, but that ho stood there looking unbothered, which made me even angrier. I stared that bitch down, trying to find whatever fault I could.

"Listen, bitch. I don't know what he told you, but if I was you, I would go get tested, 'cause this nigga got the bug," I told her.

"The bug? Ky, what the fuck she talking about?" that bitch said in a high-pitched voice.

"Bitch, HIV/AIDS. Yes, ho, I hope you been using condoms."

"Yo, Nyesha, what the fuck? You trippin'. Yo, get the fuck on before I blow yo' fucking brains out," he said.

"You right. I have no right telling yo' business like that. I just want to make sure you're not infecting another young lady like you did me. I'm sorry, y'all. I'm gone."

"Ky, what is she talking about? Do you have HIV?" she asked as I was walking away.

I got into my car and sped off. I wished I could've stayed to hear his response to that ho. I knew I was playing a dangerous game with him, but I had to get his attention somehow.

Even though I did that to Ky, I wasn't satisfied. I wondered who the fuck that bitch was and how long he'd been fucking her. It hadn't taken him too long to replace me.

Tears filled my eyes as I thought back on how much I loved that boy. The thoughts of him being with someone else made me hate him. I now knew that it couldn't be us anymore.

CHAPTER TWENTY-SEVEN

KYMANI

"Yo, what the lawyer talkin' 'bout? I need to holla at the motherfucker to see what he think my chances of beating this case is," I asked Nia.

"I spoke to him yesterday, and he was saying if you can get that bitch to retract her statement, then you would only be looking at the gun and coke charge against you."

"Shit, that's the most serious charge. Matter of fact, the feds can pick that shit up if they get wind of the charge. You know them motherfuckers been trying to bring the crew down."

"Yeah, that's what I was thinking about too. I just can't believe that bitch would do that knowing what could possibly happen. I swear if that wasn't yo' baby mama, I would beat that ass so bad."

"Man, fuck that dizzy bitch. She made it bad on herself because I was taking care of my daughter. The other day, she call my phone talking crazy and shit 'bout she about to put me on child support. Man, I'm at the point where that ho could die and I wouldn't give a fuck."

"Yeah, I feel you," she said.

"Anyway, I need you to make a bank run in the morning. Make sure you keeping e'erything clean. We don't know how this case goin' turn out, so we got to be prepared for whatever. I got enough money to come home and bounce back. You feel me?"

"I don't even want to talk like that. You gon' beat this shit, my nigga."

"Yeah, I'm hoping I do, but I'm mentally ready for whatever. You feel me? I'm a real nigga," I said.

"I know."

"Listen, set up an appointment for Thursday with the lawyer. And don't forget the bank run. I'm about to go handle some business real quick. Hit my line if you need me."

"Okay, boss."

We hugged, then I jumped in my truck, busted a U-turn, and headed down 32nd Street. I lit the blunt up and blasted Yo Gotti's song "Law."

I was definitely in the zone, just smoking and riding. It had been months since I visited my mama, and this was definitely one of those days that I just needed to holla at her. I was still having these dreams and feeling guilty. I wished I could bring my mama back just for one day so I could let her know how sorry I was that I shot her. I swear I was trying to kill that nigga.

I pulled into the cemetery and took the last few drags off the blunt. I put that shit out then got out of the truck. I felt like my chest started tightening up on me as soon as I started approaching the site where Mama was buried. I thought about turning around, but I needed to talk to her. I needed to let her know that my life wasn't the same without her.

I stood there, just staring at her name engraved into the stone. I felt a tear drop onto my face. I used everything in me to stop myself from crying. E'erybody that knows me knows I don't shed tears over nothing, but this shit was ripping through my soul. I probably could bear it if she was sick and died, but to know I pull the motherfucking trigger was really tearing me up.

I don't deserve to live. I deserve to be in the ground alongside my Mama.

I knelt down beside her grave. "Hey, Ma, it's yo' baby boy." I wiped the tears from my eyes. "I know it's been a while, but it's just so hard to come see you, knowing I did this to you. Ma, I ain't blaming you, but why would you jump in front of the gun? Why would you try to save this nigga? Ma, he didn't love you," I cried out, clinging to the side of her grave.

"Listen, Ma, it's so much that I have to tell you. I just wish I could come over to your house and hear you tell me to pull up my pants. I can still hear you telling me that you don't want no drug money, but I still sneak and put a stack in your drawer when you turn your back." I busted out laughing at the thought of her cussing me out when she would find the money days later. "Man, woman, I miss you. I swear I do."

I just sat there waiting to get some sort of response from her, but none came. I saw a bird fly right in front of me and I just stood there. My mind was telling me that was Mama. I just smiled at it, hoping I was right.

After I left Mama's grave, I was feeling weak as fuck. I swear I didn't want to leave her, but I had to go.

I stopped by my sister's crib. I rang her doorbell and waited.

"Who is it?" she hollered.

"It's me, sis."

"Boy, you know I was just thinking 'bout you a few seconds ago."

"Really? See, I told you we connected spiritually. You'on't believe me," I said as I gave her a long, tight hug.

"Damn, bro. You okay?"

"Nah, sis, kind of fucked up. Just came from Mama grave."

"Oh Lord, I was up there a few days ago. I had to go see her after you got locked up. I need her to watch over you 'cause God knows you all I got."

"Sis, I'm good. You gon' always have me."

"Bro, I can't lose you too. That's why I wish you just leave them damn streets alone. You too smart to be out here just wasting your talent. You can rap. You need to get into somebody studio or get into college so you can produce music."

"Sis, I hear you. I just got some shit to do out here. Then I'm done."

"I hear you, but do you know every time a dude say they got shit to handle, that's when they either get locked up or killed? You the only person I got in this world, and I don't want either one to happen to you."

"Aye, sis, do you think Mama will ever be able to forgive me?"

"Forgive you for being out in the streets? Trust me, baby boy, we all know you was her favorite. Yeah, she didn't approve of what you was out there doing, but she love the hell out of you, and there's nothing in this world could let her see her baby boy in a negative light," she said.

"Nah, sis. You just don't know. This shit is deeper than you know. I swear." I started crying again. I knew I shouldn't be saying this, but I had to let it out.

"Boy, come over here and sit down. What in the world are you talking about?" She used her hand to wipe my face. I swear my sister was only three years older than me, but she always acted like she was a second mama to me.

"Sis, I got something to tell you, but you got to promise me that you won't look at me any different."

"Boy, what the fuck you talking about?"

"You know the day Mama got killed?"

"Yeah, some motherfucker went up in there and killed her and Deano."

"Well, I was there . . ." My words trailed off.

"You was there? What you mean, you was there when they got killed?" she asked.

I was having second thoughts about cleansing my soul to my sis. I was reading her body language, and I could tell she was feeling uneasy.

"I went over there earlier that day. Mama had a black eye. That nigga hit Mama. I tried to confront him, and he laughed, sis. He said some old crazy shit, that he gon' beat my ass like he beat that bitch ass. I snapped." I paused.

"And what happened, Kymani?"

"I pulled the gun, sis. I was about to body that nigga when Mama jumped in the middle. The shot was already fired. . . ." My voice trailed off.

"What! Oh my God. Y—you killed Mama?" Her face turned to hot pink.

"Sis, I swear I didn't mean to. I was only trying to protect her. She die protecting that bitch-ass nigga." I tried to touch her.

"No! Don't touch me. How could you kill yo' own Mama? That lady gave you life." She started crying.

"It was an accident. You should've seen her face. That nigga beat her like she was a trick out in the streets."

"How are you different? You took her life away from her. Oh my God. I can't. You need to go. Get out."

"Sis, come on. I swear it was—"

"I said get out!" she yelled.

I looked at her, shook my head, and walked out the door. As I walked down the stairs, I heard when she slammed her door shut. I wiped my eyes as I made my way to my truck. Shit, if it was someone else, I might have to worry, but my sister wasn't gon' call the people. I just needed to give her some time to digest what I just told her.

I lit a Black and Mild up before pulling off. My life was spiraling downhill, and I needed to get it together fast.

CHAPTER TWENTY-EIGHT

Nyesha

Old habits die hard, I saw. First Yohan start staying out one night, then two nights, and now it had been days since I last saw him. I called him numerous times, and the phone just rang.

"Mommy, where is my daddy? I hope he didn't leave again," Emanyi said as we sat at the table eating dinner.

"No, baby. Your daddy is just out working," I lied.

I can't say I was shocked this nigga was pulling his disappearing act again. I was just mad at my fucking self that I was stupid as fuck. I knew what he was about, but I fell for his tricks a second fucking time.

"All right, y'all. Put the plates in the sink." I got up, trying to hide the tears that were about to roll down my face.

After the kids went to their rooms, I hurried up and washed the dishes. I decided to take a shower. The minute I got in, that's when I broke down. I bawled my eyes out as the cold truth hit me. This nigga didn't love me. He was still with this bitch and playing games. His words echoed in my head—all the lies he told me, and all the fake promises he made to me. Now it was hitting me in the face, and I swear it was a very hard pill to swallow. I mean, I knew my pussy was good, my head game was great, and I made my own money. What could be the reason why this nigga kept carrying me like I wasn't shit? I was confused, hurt, and in my feelings.

***

A few days later, it was the first of the month and a Friday, so it was jumping. I was out making my rounds to my regulars. You'd be shocked to see some of the people that smoke crack—people who lived in big-ass houses, have good-ass government jobs and shit. I mean, I wasn't complaining because they spent big money with me. I kept their little secret, and they continued spending with me.

I dialed Sean's phone and sat there waiting for him to respond.

"Yo."

"Hey, babe. What's up? You straight?" I said.

"Yeah, what you tryna get?" he asked.

"I need five of them thangs."

"A'ight, bet. But listen, you gon' have to meet me at the McDonald's at the bottom of the hill. I told you them niggas too hot over there, and I ain't tryna get caught up in their shit."

"Okay, that's cool. Just let me know when you're on the way," I said.

After I hung up the phone, I got out of the car. I noticed this bitch-ass nigga Johnte and his crew standing by the building. I swear I couldn't stand his ass, and I knew his ass was mad 'cause I was making money.

I locked my car and sashayed past their asses. I looked him dead in the eyes as I walked into my building. I knew my little gun wasn't nothing compared to the guns niggas were carrying, but on my mama soul, if that bitch-ass nigga tried me, I would pull it out quick without even thinking. I locked my door as I walked into my apartment.

I opened my safe and counted the money. After I got the money straight for the weed, I counted how much money I made today, and it was still early. I did pretty good. I smiled at myself. I remembered when I was broke as fuck. Nowadays, I could spend without having to worry about anything. I swear I was proud of my motherfucking self.

The phone started ringing. It was Sean.

"Hello."

"I'm on the way. I be there in about twenty-five minutes."

"Got you."

I looked in the mirror, made sure my hair was straight, then I left. I clung to my purse tightly as I stepped out of the building. I didn't trust that fuck nigga and didn't put anything past him. No one was outside, so I carefully made my way to my car.

I got to the McDonald's and looked around for Sean's car, but it wasn't in the parking lot. I parked and got out. I was starving, so I decided to grab me a Southern style chicken sandwich and two kid meals for the kiddos.

As soon as I stepped outside, I saw him pulling in. He parked beside my car. I put the food inside and got into his car.

"Yo, what's good with you, beautiful?"

"Nothing. Same shit, different day." I smiled at him.

"The bag right there by your foot."

I pulled out the money and handed it to him. "It's all there. Count it."

"Nah, ma, we good. Yo, you look sexy as fuck in them tights. When you gon' let me slide in them drawers?"

"Boy, stop. You know we ain't on them type of times no more."

"You act like I'm asking for a relationship or some serious shit. I'm just tryna fuck. Don't act like you don't miss this dick, B."

"I don't be on no dick. I'm just focused on making this money and taking care of them kids," I said.

"I hear you, but if you ever need that pussy touched, hit me up. I'll come burn you up real quick."

"Bye. I'll hit you up when I need this work."

I got into my car, and he pulled off. I swear, that boy was a trip. But that was my nigga, though. There was nothing I wouldn't do for him, except keep fucking him. I was way past that. I did some shit I had no business doing. I wasn't proud of it, but not embarrassed either. I had to do what I had to do to feed my kids, including giving the pussy up. Those days were long gone, and I don't plan on revisiting them.

I pulled up a few minutes before it was time for the kids to get off the bus. I hurried and took the weed in the house. That shit was so strong, it had my car smelling like a weed field in Jamaica.

I then hurried back out to get them off the daycare van. After we got into the house, I fed them, helped them with their homework, and they were off to their rooms to play their games.

I had been ripping and running all day, so I had to sit down for a quick second. My phone started to ring as soon as I flopped down on the couch.

"Hello."

"What's good, shawty?"

"Who is this?"

"This Trell. You straight?"

"What you tryna get?" I asked.

"Two pounds."

"Okay, I got you."

"Cool. I'll be there in a few."

Trell was a dude that been copping weed from me since I moved over here. At first, he was liking on me, but I had to shut that down real fast. It was crazy because up until now all he'd been getting was a quarter pound. Let me find out he done upgraded to pounds and shit. I got up and went to grab two pounds.

Something didn't seem right to me. My mind was telling me that something about his call was off. But I'd been dealing with him for some time now, and from what I heard from Ky, he was a real thorough nigga, so I pushed those thoughts out of my mind.

I sat in the living room, waiting on him to pull up. I heard a knock on the door, so I knew that was him. I looked through the hole and saw him standing there. I opened the door.

"Hey, you."

"What up, shawty? You got that for me?"

"Yes, it's right here in the kitchen."

I walked off into the kitchen to put the weed on the scale to show him. I sat on the counter, waiting for him to walk in. My head was down.

"Give me this shit and e'erything else you got in here," he said as he walked in the kitchen with a gun pointed at me.

"Boy, what the fuck you doing with that?' I laughed, not knowing this nigga was really serious.

"You heard what the fuck I said. Bitch, give me this shit and go get the rest of it before I kill you and them fucking kids." He pointed the gun to my head.

If I thought it was a joke at first, but my ass saw the seriousness as soon as he mentioned killing me and my kids. "Okay, man, chill out. But this all the weed I got. I just got it today, but you can have it." I took it up and shoved it to him with my trembling hands.

His eyes were glossy, and his hands were shaking. I could tell that nigga was on something, which was making him act irrational. I just needed to get him the fuck out of my shit before me and my kids became victims.

He grabbed the weed from me and started walking through my shit, making his way to my room. He opened the closet and looked around, looked under the bed.

He said something under his breath before leaving out the back door. I ran and locked the door as soon as he left. I then ran to my kids' room to make sure they were all right. I saw they were both occupied doing their thing, so I didn't disturb them.

I walked into the kitchen, taking a few seconds to digest what the fuck just happened. *This bitch-ass nigga just robbed me? A nigga that I've been dealing with just came up in my shit and threatened me and my kids' lives.*

I grabbed my phone and dialed Ky's number. It went straight to voicemail.

Ain't this some shit? I need this nigga and he got his damn phone off. Fuck it.

I dialed Yohan's phone.

"Yeah."

"Where the fuck you at? Some nigga just came up in here and robbed me."

"What you mean, he robbed you? How much money he got, and who the fuck is he?" he asked.

"He ain't get no money. He took pounds of weed from me and put a gun to my head," I said, still shaking from the ordeal.

"A'ight, I'm on my way."

I rolled me a big blunt. I swear I hated this nigga who did this. I felt like it was only because I was a female. I also knew that if I was still with Ky, that nigga would've never tried me like this. I was angry as fuck, so I tried smoking to calm my nerves.

I heard a banging on the door, so I got up to go look. It was Yohan, his cousin, and two other niggas.

"Aye, you know this nigga and where he stay at?" Yohan asked.

"I only know that he be out here. I been serving him since I moved over here, so I didn't think anything when he called and say he want some work."

"Man, this why I tell you, you need to stop grinding outta yo' crib. This nigga could've killed you and my damn kids."

"I only let a few people come up here. Everybody else, I go meet."

"Man, fuck all that. I need to find this motherfucking nigga. I'ma let these Churchill niggas know that they need to stay the fuck away from my kids," he said. "We'll be back." All of them left out.

I knew it was about to be some shit, but truthfully, I didn't give a fuck. That nigga didn't think twice to come up in here and take my shit and threaten to kill my damn kids. I hoped they found that bum and killed his ass for real. I was done sparing niggas' feelings.

About an hour later, I heard gunshots. I knew it was Yohan and them. I was too scared to go to the window and look. Instead, I went into my kids' room, making sure they were fine. I just prayed their father made it out alive, for their sake.

I heard a loud banging on the door. My heart dropped, but then I heard Yohan's voice, so I got up and opened it.

"Yeah, I ain't seen the pussy nigga, but I sprayed the whole motherfucking block, sending these niggas a message. If they want it, they definitely can get it, 'cause we definitely 'bout that life. You need to think 'bout moving from over here. You already know how grimey these niggas are. That nigga you used to fuck wit' might've set yo' ass up. You don't know, 'cause it's kind of suspicious that soon as you stop fucking wit' his ass, one of them come up in here and rob you."

"I know Ky ain't like that, but I hear you." I wasn't gon' sit up there arguing with him. I already knew he didn't care for Ky.

"A'ight, we gon' spend the night to see if anything pop off tonight," he said.

"Okay." I got up off the sofa and walked back to my room.

As I lay down, I couldn't help but wonder about what Yohan said earlier. Could Ky have something to do with this? I mean, I did carry him in front of his bitch the other day. Was this payback? Hell no, I decided. I knew Ky, and I knew he wouldn't do no shit like that to me. My mind was racing, I felt uneasy. I swear this trap life was turning out to be too much for me.

The next morning after the kids left for daycare, I took a shower and got dressed. I had court that morning, and my nerves were torn up. I spoke with my attorney the day before, and he told me that he was going to ask that the case be thrown out because they didn't find the drugs in my house. I agreed with him. Shit, all they found in my house was money.

I got dressed in a pair of slacks and a nice blouse. I put on a pair of my Michael Kors pumps, along with a matching clutch purse. I was going in there like a boss bitch.

I walked in and immediately spotted my lawyer.

"Good morning, Miss Smith. Are you ready?" my lawyer asked.

"Good morning. I'm not, but hey, I'm here."

"Okay, I'm sure the DA is going to come up with all the reasons as to why the case shouldn't be dropped, but I will be all on it. I'll show the judge that they have no case and it's waste of time to even continue."

I loved this lawyer. She was on point with her shit. Ky was the one who recommended her to me. At least he was good for something.

"Here go the judge," I said.

"All rise. The Honorable Judge Tashell presiding. Please be seated. Your Honor, this is case 145 on the docket. The defendant, Nyesha Smith, is charged with possession of marijuana, with the intent to distribute."

"How do you plead?"

"Not guilty, Your Honor."

The argument started with the prosecutor. The bitch tried to paint me as this big-ass drug dealer that their confidential informant bought drugs from. She was asking the court to carry the case over to trial.

My Pitbull-in-a-dress-ass lawyer wasted no time and went in for the kill, explaining to the judge that I was a single mother of two children. She explained no drugs were found in my apartment and that the CI lied to save himself from the police that were pressuring him. I tried to read the judge's face, but he sat there without giving off any sort of vibes.

They both stated their cases, and then the judge spoke. "I've listened to both parties carefully, and I've examined the evidence. I want to say the burden is on the state to prove that the defendant had these drugs in her possession, but I don't see that here. With that said, I must drop the charges against the defendant."

"But Your Honor, I have a CI that bought drugs from the defendant on numerous occasions," the prosecutor argued.

"Is your CI prepared to testify that he bought drugs from the defendant?"

"No, Your Honor."

"Well, sorry, you have no case," the judge said.

I could tell the bitch was mad as fuck. I was waiting to see if her boy was going to testify. I knew his bitch ass was going to stay a secret so he could set more people up. Crazy thing was, niggas in the hood still was fucking with this man like he was working with the people. That was their dumb asses. They'd learn once he told on their asses.

"Well, your client is free to go. Case dismissed," the judge said.

Wow! That was simple and fast. I let out a long sigh of relief when I exited the courtroom. I waited for my lawyer to come out, so I could thank her before I got the hell away from that place.

"Miss Smith, you're a free woman. Now you can go home to those babies," she said.

"Yes, thank you so much. You definitely know what you were doing in there." I shook her hand.

"Thank you. Take care."

She walked off, and I went in the opposite direction. I was feeling happy. It was the best damn thing I did when I threw that weed across the fence. I mean, it was found outside, and no one witnessed me throwing it out there.

I walked hurriedly across the street to the parking lot. "Thank you, God," I said out loud as I got into my car.

CHAPTER TWENTY-NINE

KYMANI

I heard someone at my door, banging loud as hell. I jumped off the bed, grabbed my gun, and peeped through the corner of the window. I shook my head and went to the door and opened it.

"Man, why the fuck you banging the door like you the motherfucking police for, nigga? I almost pissed on myself," I said to Beenie.

"Man, I been calling yo' ass. Why you ain't answering the damn phone? Got me worried and shit. I know you heard all them motherfucking shots that were ringing out earlier."

"Shit, I was in here listening to the Gotti and shit. What happen out there?"

"Yo, I heard that Trell ass ran up in ya girl spot."

"What girl?" I looked at him for clarification.

"Nyesha. And her baby daddy and them south side niggas came through and sprayed the block."

"Nigga, what the fuck you talkin' bout?"

"I just told you, nigga. Man, it sound like Fourth of July out that bitch. I was tryna to make sure it wasn't none of my niggas. That's when Stalky ass told me what the fuck was going on," he said. "Yo, that fool trippin'. How the fuck you gon' run up in a female shit? He weak as fuck for that."

"I mean, I can't even ride wit' the nigga on that one. I'm glad he ain't hit me up with that shit. He on his motherfucking own wit' that," I said.

"Yeah, same shit I was thinking. I know he aware that you used to fuck with shawty."

"Yeah, well, that's dead. See, her nigga came to her rescue. Them south side niggas bold as fuck, coming over here like that. They lucky I wasn't out and about. I would definitely send them back to their maker, just 'cause they in my hood trying to start some shit. That's just mad disrespectful. How would they like for me and my crew to come through and shoot they entire spots up?" I shook my head, trying to make some sense of this bullshit.

"That's the same shit that I was thinking, for real. These niggas trippin', dawg."

"Where Trell at right now?" I asked.

"That nigga took off somewhere. I swear his ass was high off them damn Xanax. He couldn't even think straight when I saw him, talking 'bout he about to cool off 'til this shit die down."

"You got that nigga number?"

"Yeah. Hold on, lemme get it."

After he gave me the number, we decided to chill. We smoked a few blunts and drank a couple beers together before he bounced.

After Beenie left, I dialed Trell's number. I needed to holla at the nigga, 'cause that was foul shit he did. Plus, how the fuck was he going to bring drama where we laid our head at? I was irritated to say the least.

"Hello."

"Yo, my nigga, I need to holla at you," I said.

"Who this?"

"Nigga, this Ky."

"Oh, shit, dawg. I didn't recognize the voice." He laughed.

"No worries. Yo, I'm tryna to holla at you."

"Go ahead, boss," he said nervously.

"Nah, meet me on Chimborazo, where we be at in about a hour."

"All right, boss. I got you."

After I hung up the phone, I decided to play the new XBOX game that just came out. I needed to think some shit through. Lately my mind had been all over the place, at times interfering with my grind. I swear, I had too much going on to be slacking.

I played for a while, and then I glanced over at the time. It was nearing an hour, so I took a quick shower and got dressed. I grabbed my Glock and placed it in my waist and left out the crib. I dialed Beenie's number.

"Whaddup, boss?"

"Yo, I'm on the way down the street. Make sure ain't nobody out there hanging around and shit."

"I'm sitting out here on my car, and ain't nobody out here. Wait, this nigga Trell just pulled up. You want me to tell him to leave?"

"Nah, he good. I'm on my way."

"A'ight, boss."

I cut my cell phone completely off and got into my ride, heading toward Chimborazo. I pulled up in front of the trap. I spotted Beenie and Trell sitting outside, rapping.

"What's good wit' y'all niggas?" I said. We exchanged daps, and they followed me inside the house.

We gathered in the living room. Beenie pulled out some weed and started rolling up. We started doing small talk, like it was business as usual.

"Yo, Trell, my nigga, I heard you had a situation the other day with some south side niggas. What's up with that?" I asked.

"Damn, I was gon' hit you up 'bout that, but . . . but." He started stuttering.

"So, what did happen, though?" I looked him dead in the eyes while I took a few drags off the weed.

"Man, you know the bitch from up top. The one you used to fuck with. I ran up in the bitch shit and took a few pounds of weed from her ass. I mean, I heard she did you wrong, my nigga, so I was like fuck her. Let me get back at her ass," he said.

"Damn, my nigga, so you saying you ran up in this bitch house, rob her, all because she dissed me?"

"Yeah, boss, that's exactly how it goes."

Beenie shot me a look as if he was reading my mind. I switched my full attention back to Trell. This nigga sat there feeding me this garbage.

"My nigga, how long have you known me?" I scratched my head before I continued. "What, since we both were in Pampers running around in dirt? With that said, my nigga, you should know that I don't play that shit. Bitches and kids are off limit, period. For you to sit here and say you did this for me, my nigga, that's straight up bullshit. You did it 'cause you wanted to, and then bring us unnecessary drama back this way. The block was already hot, and now you got it blazing. This where I make my living, so you fucking with my money," I said.

"I ain't know that bitch would call them niggas over. I swear, boss, I ain't mean to bring no heat to the spot."

I was tired of hearing his bitch-ass voice. He knew better, but he allowed his ego to lead him. This was some sucka shit he pulled off. I stood up and walked over to the window. I stared into space while I put my gloves on. The time was now. I let out a long sigh before I walked back to where they were sitting.

"Boss, wh—what you doing with that?" Trell asked nervously as I stood in front of him.

I didn't respond. My mind was made up, and nothing he could say or do would change my mind. He must've caught on. He tried reaching for his gun, but Beenie was too fast for him.

"Lemme get this off you, partner." He removed Trell's gun off his hip.

"Y'all can't be serious right now. We family. What happened to never letting no bitch come between us? Ain't that the law that we live by?"

I looked him in the eyes, then raised the gun. I stepped forward and fired two shots into his dome. He fell backward onto the sofa.

A few seconds later, I checked his pulse to be sure that nigga was dead. I shoved his ass off my leather sofa.

"Yo, call the cleaning crew and clean up this shit. Make sure his ass can't be found two lifetimes from now."

"Got you, boss," Beenie said. "Man, I saw that look in yo' motherfucking eyes and I knew what's up then. What's crazy is that nigga thought he could sell you that bullshit story about doing it for you."

"Well, you know these niggas too stupid to understand. Just make sure y'all clean up this mess." I removed my gloves. I was dressed in all black. Even my boots were black. I knew blood might splatter, and I didn't want that nigga's body parts anywhere on me.

"A'ight, hit me up after y'all handle that. We need to make some moves late tonight," I said.

I swear the more niggas I buried, the easier it had become for me. I remembered the first time I killed someone. I was nervous and shaking. Shit, I was only fifteen, and one of the old heads placed the gun into my hands. I remembered pulling the trigger. I jumped when I realized my bullet hit the nigga. I was frightened, but I had to put on a brave show. I had a point to prove to the O.G.s.

That night, when I got in the crib, I threw up all over the place. I kept seeing that nigga's face in my dreams for months to come. After that, I made my mind up that I was a G, and I wasn't going out like that no more.

The second and third kills were easier. Now, I could do that shit and spit on the nigga and walk away like nothing happened.

CHAPTER THIRTY

Nyesha

After that shit happened with Trell, I was more aware of my surroundings. That shit really opened up my eyes that these snake niggas really didn't fuck with me. I wasn't one of them, and they showed it. Every time I went out, I would see if I saw the nigga, but he was nowhere around. His pussy ass was somewhere hiding. If they knew Yohan well enough, they knew his ass wasn't nothing to be played with. I swear, they didn't want those kinds of problems.

As if I didn't have enough on my table to deal with, Yohan was back on his bullshit. Some days he would be there, and other days I couldn't find his ass. I would confront him about the shit, and all he would do was lie, accusing me of being insecure and shit. You damn right a bitch was insecure because everything that came out of his mouth was a damn lie.

It was Friday night, and he was at the house, surprisingly. After the kids went to bed, we sat in the living room, eating some spicy shrimp that I had bought earlier that day. For the first time in weeks, we were able to sit down and talk.

Everything was going good until his phone started to ring. At first he ignored it, but I was fully aware that he heard it.

"Whoever that is, they are really trying to reach you," I said sarcastically.

"Yeah, that's a switch trying to get some work, but I'm chilling with my lady, so that can wait."

"Oh, okay," I said, pretending like I believed his lying ass.

A few minutes later, he got up and walked into the kitchen to grab his bottle of Grey Goose. I knew I only had seconds before he'd return. I grabbed his phone and checked to see who was calling. I quickly realized it was his side bitch. I knew it was going to be a fight between him and me, but I ran out of fucks to give. I called the number back.

"Hello. I know you see me calling you," she said with an attitude.

"Chill, sis, this ain't yo' baby daddy, but I want you to listen to something."

"B-bitch, I—"

"Shut up and just listen." I cut her off.

I heard the fridge closing, so I hurried up and put his phone back in place, turning the face down so he wouldn't notice that it was on a call. I was nervous as hell, but I needed to let this little bitch know that he was playing her, lying to her that he no longer fucks with me. Let the games begin.

"Aye, boo, can I ask you a question and you answer me truthfully?" I said when he came back.

"Yeah, what's up, bae?" he said as he took a few sips of his drink.

"I heard rumors that you still fuck with Zaria."

"That's bullshit. I told you I only fuck the bitch a few times and then she say she pregnant. I already told you, I'm not one hundred percent sure that's my baby."

"Oh, okay. I mean, you left once before, and I just don't want the same thing happening again. I'm tired of sharing you."

"I told you, you ain't sharing me. You the only woman that I love. If I didn't want you, I would not be right here with you. Stop stressing. You ain't got shit to worry about."

"Okay, I hear you, boo. Can you check on the kids, make sure they sleeping?"

"Yeah, sure." Without question, he jumped up and walked toward the back.

I tiptoed toward the kitchen to make sure he was gone. I then quickly picked up his phone. "You got proof that he doesn't want you. You be a stupid-ass ho if you continue fucking with him."

Without responding, that bitch hung up. I guess she was big mad. Shit, I tried to tell that little bitch what's really good, but she didn't listen, so I had to prove it to her.

"Who was you talking to?"

"Huh?"

He caught me off guard.

"I thought I heard you talking to someone."

"Nah, I was on Facebook watching a video, and I was saying how stupid it was," I lied.

"Oh, okay. Well, both of them are knocked out."

"Good. Now I can really relax."

We ended up talking, smoking, and drinking way into the wee hours. It really felt like old times, but I was still aware that this shit was temporary. Even still, in my heart, I was praying this nigga would just change his cheating ways and remain faithful to me.

The next day was like any other day. The kids were home for the weekend, so I really wasn't doing anything. I got up, made them and their daddy breakfast, and they all ate. He hung around with the kids for a little while before he left.

"Boo, I got some run to make. I'll be back later." He kissed me on the cheek. He also kissed the kids and left.

I went about cleaning the house and doing laundry. Boy, I tell you, ain't nothing like a house smelling like

Pine Sol. Kids' rooms were spotless, bathroom was cleaned from top to bottom, and the kitchen was also on point.

My phone started ringing. I grabbed it without looking at the caller ID.

"Aye, cuz."

I removed the phone from my ear to look at the number because I didn't recognize the voice at first.

"Who is this?"

"This Yohan cousin. He locked up."

"What you talkin' 'bout?" I asked.

"Twelve locked him up down there by Willow Lawn at a hotel."

"What the fuck was he doing at a hotel, and who was there with him?" I quizzed.

"He was making a play, and yeah, he was by himself. I got to go. Just hit me up and let me know if you need me to do anything."

"Okay." I took a seat at the kitchen table. I needed a few seconds to digest the info that was dumped on me.

After I gathered my thoughts, I picked up the phone and dialed the Henrico County Jail to inquire about him. The lady informed me that he was arrested for distribution of crack cocaine. He didn't have any bond. As soon as I heard no bond, my heart sank. He wasn't coming home that night.

The next thought that popped in my head was that I needed to get a lawyer to schedule a bond hearing. I called the lawyer that I previously used because her ass was a beast. I was disappointed that she couldn't take the case, but she passed me on to one of her colleagues. I called him right away and set up an appointment for Monday morning.

My mood was fucked up by this news because I knew I was going to have to spend money. I rolled me a blunt to help calm my nerves. I took a few drags.

When my phone rang, it was a prepaid call from Henrico County Jail. I quickly pressed 5 to accept the call.

"Hey, boo."

"Hey, you. How you holding up?" I asked.

"I'm straight. I need you to get a lawyer so I can go up for a bond hearing."

"Yohan, you know a lawyer cost money, right? Do you have a stash somewhere?"

"The money that I had on me, they took it and the other shit. Them motherfuckers set me up," he yelled.

"A'ight, I'll go see a lawyer and see what I can do. I don't have a lot of money," I told him.

"I know, boo, but if you get me out of here, I'll have the money back to you in a few days."

"I hear you. Um, what about your cousin? Don't he got some money?"

"Nah, that nigga be with me and shit. I doubt he got anything."

I was getting really irritated. These niggas stayed in the motherfucking streets all day, or so they said, and not one of them had any bond or lawyer money for days like these.

"Boo, you still there? Why you so quiet? You know I love you, right? I swear, when I get out of here, me and you gonna take a trip, maybe go to the beach or something or maybe go to New York for the weekend. I know how much you miss home," he said.

I wanted to respond, but I didn't. I was hoping that this nigga wasn't trying to feed me his bullshit again. "Listen, after I meet with the lawyer, I will let you know what's going on."

"Aye, boo. Make sure you keep the pussy warm for a nigga. Can't wait to come home so I can eat it up for ya."

I swear I loved when his ass talked dirty, because I knew he was a freak in the bed, and I loved when his tongue made contact with my body.

"I love you, boo. Call me tomorrow evening, and I'll let you know what's going on," I said.

"All right, love. Kiss the kids for me."

Before I could respond, his time was up, and the phone was cut off. That nigga was a certified fool, I thought before I put the rest of the blunt out. I went to bag up some work. I had some shit to pay for, so I needed to make some money.

As I sat there cutting up the crack, Ky's ass jumped in my head. After the way he carried me that day, I'd tried to put him out of my mind forever, but I ain't goin' lie. That shit was hard as hell.

Sometimes I wondered if I ever crossed his mind. Did he ever miss me and all the great times we had together? The memories of him were causing me to tear up. Damn, man, I missed that nigga.

I quickly tried to put him back out of my head. Yohan and I were together. Ky had moved on with his new boo, whoever the fuck that bitch was.

The weekend was spent quietly. I took the kids to the park so they could release some energy. They both kept asking for their daddy, and I kept lying that he was out working. I couldn't tell the kids their daddy was in jail.

After we left the park, we headed to McDonald's, grabbed two kids' meals, then headed home. I was taking the kids out of the car when I saw Ky's car approaching. I was hoping like hell he would stop when we saw us. Instead, that nigga looked me dead in the face and rolled by. I felt like my heart was ripped open. I couldn't believe he just passed us like we didn't matter to him. I tried not to show any emotion, but deep inside, I was hurting.

"Mommy, that's your friend Ky's car," my daughter said as I pulled them inside.

"Really? I didn't see it, baby," I lied.

That nigga was behaving like I was a fucking stranger. Maybe it was time I treated his ass like the piece of shit he really was. I was hurting and I missed him, but I wasn't going to allow him to keep bossing up on me like it wasn't just months ago he had his head buried deep into my pussy or his tongue buried in my butthole.

I got the kids bathed and settled in, then rolled up a blunt. Kim was on her way to make a few plays for me with her white dudes. I didn't care what anyone said. Money always kept the pussy moist . . . better than a nigga and his antics.

The next day, I watched as the kids got on the school bus, and then I got in my car. I was in a much better mood this morning. After seeing Ky yesterday, that kind of let me realize that he had moved on one hundred percent, and I needed to do the same.

I wasn't no righteous bitch, but this morning before I took a shower, I got on my knees, and I prayed to God to remove anyone or anything that wasn't for me, and I meant that. I was tired of crying, tired of niggas' lies and every little game they played. I swear to God, I just wanted to focus on securing the bag and taking care of the kids. Anything or anyone else was just in my motherfucking way.

I was so caught up in my thoughts that my ass forgot to pull off. I had put the address for the lawyer's office in the GPS before I pulled off. I turned around to get back on track.

I sat in the waiting room, waiting for the lawyer. It seemed like forever. Shit, I had a million things that I could be doing instead of sitting up in there, I thought.

"Miss Smith, Attorney Blake is ready to see you now," the receptionist said.

I walked into the office. I was shocked to see this big, tall nigga as a lawyer. It seemed like he could barely stand straight because of his weight. I wondered how the hell his ass was gon' stand up in a court and defend someone.

"Miss Smith, nice to meet you. I'm Attorney Blake. Please take a seat."

"Good morning. Thanks." I took a seat across from him.

I watched as he read something off his computer. "So, I did go down to see Mr. Ellis at the jail."

"Okay, so you are familiar with what's going on then?"

"Yes, he filled me in on what he was charged with. He told me you would be who I need to discuss the fees with," he said.

"So, how much is the fee?" I held my breath, hoping this nigga didn't read off no outrageous-ass figures.

"He's been charged with possession, and he allegedly sold crack cocaine to an undercover officer. With that said, we're going to have to fight to prove his innocence. My fee is sixty-five hundred."

"What?" I shot him a strange look.

"I understand that sounds a little steep, but I am one of the best criminal attorneys out here, and I fight for my clients. You will need to put down two thousand today, and we can set up a payment plan, commencing on the final day of the case."

"Okay," I responded reluctantly.

"You can make the payments to my secretary. Now that that's out of the way, I will request a bond hearing a week from today. I have to tell you these judges are tough, especially with drug cases. It's a fifty-fifty chance that he will get bond. Either way, my team and I gonna fight with everything in us to get your husband home to you and them babies."

"Okay."

We talked for a while before I left his office. I counted off two stacks and gave it to his secretary. She handed me a paper to sign, saying I would be responsible for the remainder of the money that was due.

No the fuck I won't, I thought.

I decided to head home so I could make some more money before it was time for the kids to arrive. On my way home, something popped in my head. I mean, I wasn't the only bitch that this nigga was fucking, so why was I the only one to foot this bill? I grabbed my phone and pulled up his bitch's number that I had saved.

"Hellooo," that ho answered with an attitude.

"Hey, girl, this Nyesha."

"I know who you are. What do you want?" she responded with an attitude.

"I was calling to see if you had your share of money."

"My share of money? What the fuck you talkin' 'bout?"

"I mean, you know Yohan locked up and he needs a lawyer. The lawyer is charging sixty-five hundred."

"Okay, and?" this ignorant bitch asked.

"I mean, let me get to the fucking point. We both fucking him, so how 'bout we split the cost of the lawyer fee?" I was tired of playing with this bitch.

"I ain't got no money. He knows that."

"Damn, bitch, you broke? Now tell me why the fuck he cheating with you? You can't even come up wit' a dollar to get his ass outta jail." I laughed.

"Bitch, you always screaming he your nigga. How about you pay your nigga lawyer money? You a boss bitch, so you shouldn't be concerned if I have a few coins or not," she said.

"Broke bitches always got the most to say. How about you get off yo' ass and go make something shake, hoe?" I lashed out at this bitch.

"Why, when yo' nigga bring me stacks at a time? Shit, I ain't got no worries over here. I can get up, look cute every day, and still pull yo' nigga. Now, bitch, go get that money so you can get my man home. I promise I'll send him back after I finish sitting on his face. Shit, you might be lucky if I send him back that night."

I didn't have a chance to respond. That scary-ass ho hung up the phone in my face. I tried calling her back, but she blocked me. The phone kept going to voicemail. I was mad as fuck. I couldn't wait until me and that ho met up so I could beat that ass once and for all.

It was visitation day for Yohan. I got the kids all dressed up nicely. They talked my head off the entire ride to the jail. They were too excited to see their daddy.

We were early, so we had to wait about twenty minutes before it was time for visiting to start. To be honest, I wasn't feeling too enthusiastic about this visit. I mean, I had to spend all that damn money.

I walked up and gave them my name and identification. I was cleared and instructed to walk back to where the visitation was being held. I swear, the kids were so damn hype they almost tripped over each other trying to get to the booth first.

"Y'all need to calm down," I yelled.

Their father was already seated behind the glass. I picked up the phone so we could talk.

"Hey there, gorgeous." He smiled, revealing his set of pearly white teeth.

"Hey, you. How you feeling?"

"Shit, I'm feeling great now that I get to see you and my nuggets."

"Hey, Daddy," the kids chimed in.

"Mommy, can I talk to Daddy?" Emanyi asked.

"Sure, let Mommy talk to him real quick, and then y'all can talk to him."

"Okay," she said.

"I went and saw the lawyer yesterday," I told Yohan. Without wasting time on small talk, I got straight to the point.

"Oh, yeah? Did you pay him?" That nigga wasted no time in inquiring about money like he had left some with me. That irritated my damn soul.

"Yeah, I paid him the down payment."

"A'ight, thanks, babe. I'll deal with the rest. What that nigga talkin' about? He think he can get me out on bond?"

"He said it's a fifty-fifty chance."

"Fifty-fifty? That nigga don't sound too sure. Shit, maybe we need to find somebody else who is a hundred percent sure that he can get me up outta here. I got shit to do," he said.

"You need to chill out. I don't have all that money to get multiple lawyers. He seems to know what he's doing, so why don't you wait and see before you start going off?"

"Yeah, you right, babe. I just hate it in here, and I'm ready to come home to y'all."

"Here. Talk to the kids," I said.

"A'ight. Listen, girl, just be patient. Your man will be home soon to tear that pussy up for you. Love you, girl."

I didn't respond because the kids were right there. I just handed the phone to them and took a seat. I could hear them telling him everything they ate or did since he left. These kids didn't forget a damn thing.

The guard informed us that visitation was over, and it was time to say goodbye. Now, here goes the boo-hooing.

"Daddy, please don't go," Emanyi and Kyle screamed.

His eyes watered up as the guard informed him he had to go. I saw when he snatched his arm away and muttered "I love you" to the kids as he disappeared behind the double doors.

"Come on, kids. Daddy will be home soon." I tried my best to console them.

They were not trying to hear that shit. Instead, they continued crying all the way into the car. You would've thought they had just gotten a severe-ass whooping.

I pulled off and cut the music up a little to drown out some of the crying. I didn't get a chance to hit the highway before they fell asleep. I guess my babies were worn out from all the crying they did.

I was happy that they were asleep. I put my window down, let the cool breeze in, and cued up Megan Thee Stallion's new album, *Good News*. I needed to get my shit together. I couldn't keep living like this.

Change gotta come, I thought as I sped down the road.

The week flew by, and Yohan's court date was here, which also mean if he got bond, I was gon' have to fork out more money. He had been calling every day, trying his hardest to convince me that I was his one and only. Where had I heard all this shit before? Oh, from his ass. It's safe to say I was hoping it would change, but I wasn't banking on it.

The lawyer was already in the hallway when I walked in. "Good morning, Miss Smith. How are you this morning?"

"I'm good, and you?"

"Can't complain, thank God. The case is gonna be heard in courtroom C in front of Judge Jonas. I was hoping that we had another judge because he is known for denying bonds. Nonetheless, I'm going in here to do my best," he said.

I just nodded my head. I didn't know which way it was going to work out, but I was prepared for whatever.

We walked in the courtroom. I took a seat behind him and waited. I watched as Yohan walked in and nodded his head at me.

Soon after, the judge entered the courtroom. The DA told the judge that Yohan was a flight risk and should be denied bond. When it was Mr. Blake's turn, he wasted no time painting Yohan as a child of God, a hard-working family man who had two small children to support. The judge listened to both sides, then he gave him a $20,000 bond with a curfew.

Yohan smiled at me as he walked out. I walked out of the courtroom and waited for the lawyer. After a few minutes, he exited the courtroom and walked over to me.

"This judge plays no games. Mr. Ellis has a bond, so you can go ahead and get him out, and I will meet with both of you guys on Friday at three."

"Okay, thanks," I replied as I walked off.

I had mixed emotions about this. Yes, I was happy he was getting out, but I wasn't thrilled about spending another dollar on his ass.

I got into the car, and I called the bondsman that I was familiar with. He agreed to bond him out for ten percent, but before I could do anything, I needed to make it home to get the kids off the bus.

I pulled up a few minutes earlier than the bus. I sat in the car, just gathering my thoughts. When my phone started to ring, it was Yohan's worrisome ass.

"Did you post the bond yet?"

"Boy, you really tripping. I just got back to Richmond."

"I'm not trying to wait until it get late. You know how slow these motherfuckers are."

"Yohan, listen. I'm going to bond you out, okay? Chill the fuck out. I got to get my damn kids first. Is that okay with you?"

"All right, boo. I know you got me. But you know your man is a little impatient."

"Okay." I was annoyed as fuck at this nigga. All he did was call from jail, being demanding and shit.

Like, nigga, go call your other ho. Let that bitch boss up and handle some shit.

After the kids got off the bus, we made our way into the house. I straightened up the place and made the kids dinner. They wanted baked chicken and macaroni, so that's what dinner was. Ain't nothing like making those babies happy. After they ate, they took their baths and got dressed.

Before I left out, I sat down to smoke a blunt. I needed something to calm my nerves down a bit. I took a shower and got dressed. I went into my little stack and pulled out two grand. I was feeling some kind of way about this, but I put my feelings aside and placed the money into my purse.

"Come on, kids. We got to go get your daddy."

"Yay, Daddy coming home!" they yelled in unison.

"Mommy, are you happy that Daddy coming home?" Kyle asked.

"Umm, yeah, baby," I lied to him. I just didn't want to hurt his feelings.

The traffic wasn't bad, so I made it to Henrico in no time. The bondsman's car was there when I pulled up. I waved to him as I parked. We talked, and I paid him the money. He then left to go in the building to handle the paperwork. I knew it was going to be a long-ass wait time before they brought him down. I never understood why their processing took so motherfucking long, but when they lock yo' ass up, it happens quickly.

We sat in the lobby, waiting. I was browsing Facebook and just thinking, while the kids sat quietly on their tablets. Nothing interesting was on Facebook. I decided to hop over on Ky's page to see what was going on with him.

Add friend? What the fuck, this nigga unfriended me? Wow, it's that serious huh?

"Mommy, Daddy right there." My daughter shook my hand, interrupting my thoughts.

"Huh, baby?"

"Daddy right there."

I looked where she was pointing, and there he was, standing at the window, signing papers. I got up and waited until he was finished. I thanked the bondsman, and he left.

"Your nigga free, babe." Yohan hugged me tightly.

"Welcome home."

The kids were so damn happy, they just kept hugging him.

"A'ight, y'all, it's getting late. Let's go. Y'all have school in the morning," he said.

"You driving?" I threw the keys at him.

After getting in the house, I gave the kids an hour with their daddy. They were behaving like he was gone for a few years or something.

"A'ight, you two. Tell your daddy good night. Y'all have school in the morning," I said.

"Mommy, can Daddy tuck us in?" Emanyi asked.

I looked at him, and I looked back at their sad puppy faces. "Okay, I guess so."

I went to my room while he tucked them in. I lay on my back across the bed. I should have been happy that my man was home, but instead, I was feeling burdened. But why? This was what I wanted, right?

"Yo, you a'ight?" Yohan asked as he entered my room.

"Yeah, just a little tired," I lied.

"You got some weed?"

"You know I got weed." I got up off the bed, went into my stash, and broke him off a twenty.

"You want to blow?" he asked.

"No, I'm just going to take a quick shower and call it a night."

"A'ight, I'ma smoke then hit the shower after you."

"Cool."

After I took my shower, I peeped in on the kids. They were knocked out. It had been a long-ass day, so I decided to hit the bed. I grabbed the remote and turned the TV on WE. They had a *Law & Order* marathon on. I have no idea why I was engulfed into crime shows when here I was breaking the law daily.

I was sleepy as hell, but this episode was interesting, so I tried my best to stay awake. While I lay there, I couldn't help but notice that Yohan's ass had been out of the shower, but he had disappeared for a good thirty minutes.

I got up and tiptoed toward the front of the apartment. The closer I got to the kitchen, the louder I heard his voice. I stopped in the kitchen and leaned up against the wall where I could hear him clearly.

"Man, you trippin'. You know I only love you and you only. Don't be paying that shit she saying no mind. When all this shit over, you know it's me and you, baby."

I couldn't hear what the bitch was saying on the other end. I could only assume based on what he was saying to her.

"Girl, you know you my bonnie and that ain't gon' ever change. Man, block her number. She just miserable and want you to break up with me. Shit, even if you left me, I still won't be with her ass. That bitch pussy so damn dry, shit has me scraping my dick up."

The tears rolled down my face as I clung to the wall for support. I couldn't believe what I was hearing. I thought about running up on him and hitting him, but I tried my hardest to control my anger.

I heard enough, so I tiptoed back into the room. Why didn't God let me hear this before I spent my money on this fuck nigga? Now I had to be quiet until he paid me my money, every last cent of it. This snake nigga was the worst fucking kind. All that crying and professing his love to me were all fucking lies, and my dumb ass couldn't seem to get enough of it.

I must've dozed off. I felt Yohan's hands trying to massage my breasts.

"What the hell you doing?" I pushed his hands away.

"Man, I'm trying to rub on my lady. I miss you. You know a nigga ain't had no pussy in a minute."

"Well, that's a personal problem. I'm tired and don't feel like getting fucked," I said.

"Man, come on. Let me eat it then." He grabbed my leg.

"No, I'm straight on that too."

"Man, you bugging. What, you been fucking another nigga?" he quizzed.

"Only yo' stupid ass would think that, but you know what? Think whatever you want, my nigga."

"Man, you trippin'. I see a nigga don't get no love no mo'."

I really didn't care to listen to his fake whining. I just heard him professing his love to his ho, and now he was acting like he wanted me. I wiped my tears that were flowing down my face. This shit was ridiculous, and I was the only one to blame. I kept showing up at the fucking circus this nigga created.

I guess he was in his feelings after not getting any pussy. He left out early the next day without saying a word. It was 12 a.m. the following day, and I still hadn't heard from Yohan. He was supposed to report to the probation office. Now it was the wee hours of the morning, and this nigga had not called to let a bitch know he was alive or anything.

I thought about calling him but changed my mind. This nigga know part of his release was 9 p.m. curfew, and he damn sure know where he lived at, so why the fuck should I call him to chase him down?

I tried to go to sleep, but it was hard as hell. I knew my sister probably was just leaving the club. I really missed talking to her. I really didn't see why we were beefing anyway, not over no nigga. She was my blood, and she knew that I might not like what the hell she said, but I respected her because I knew she had my best interests at heart and vice versa. Sometimes, I wished my relationship with my mama wasn't strained because at times like this, I needed my mama's love. But we all knew how her ass behaved in the past. I swear, I didn't have the patience to deal with her dramatic ass right now.

Two days had passed, and still no sign of Yohan. I got the kids dressed and out the door. Now that I was by myself, I dialed his number. The phone rang until the voicemail came on.

"So, this is how we playing, huh? No calls, don't come home or nothing. I see you back to yo' old tricks."

I hung the phone up, feeling betrayed. I had just spent all that damn money on that nigga, and he done disappeared on my ass. I figured his old grimey ass was laid up with that old broke-ass bitch that couldn't put a dollar toward his lawyer or bond payment. But that was the bitch he was loving on. I got angrier as I remembered what the fuck he was saying on the phone the other night to that bitch. I grabbed a Black and Mild and lit it up, trying my best not to break down and cry as the sad truth crept up on me.

I rushed to my surround sound system and cut on the music. I needed to hear K. Michelle's "Can't Raise a Man." I swear, the words were piercing through my soul. I don't know what this bitch was going through when she made this song, but she was speaking the truth.

CHAPTER THIRTY-ONE

KYMANI

"Man, so what you saying, I need to plead out? I mean, you my motherfucking lawyer, and it seems like you just want to give up. Shit, I pay you big money to do yo' damn job, which is fight these motherfuckers, not tell me to cop a plea. Shit, if that's what I wanted, I could do that on my own," I stood up and yelled at my attorney.

"Mr. Lee, please calm down and listen to what I'm saying. I have been doing this for years. I am remarkably familiar with these kinds of cases, and I spoke to a few of my colleagues. If you can get your child's mother to drop the charges, then that would be great. The gun was found in your car, along with more than an ounce of cocaine. The feds could easily pick this case up. That's why I'm suggesting to you, plead out. The gun is a mandatory five years, so I would ask for that for both charges."

I stood there listening to this nigga talk like it was his motherfucking life on the line. I looked him in the face and said angrily, "I hear what the fuck you saying, but I ain't pleading to shit. I ain't touch that ho. She straight up lying, and I ain't pleading guilty to the rest of the shit 'cause they pulled me behind a lie anyways. I mean, I can find me another lawyer if you feel like you can't go in there and fight for me."

"You're the client," he said, "so if you want to go to trial, then that's what we're going to do. Just tell me how you want me to move forward. Give me everything you can on your baby mother, so I can rip her apart if she decides to testify against you."

"I ain't no rat, so you gon' have to get that shit on yo' own. That bitch lying, but she is my daughter's mother."

"Okay, I gotcha. I just want you to know, you must start thinking about yourself, 'cause these prisons are waiting for young men like you. Our next court date is in two weeks. I am putting the request in for a speedy trial. In the meantime, you need to get a job to show the judge you're not out here breaking the law and you are a valuable member of society."

"A'ight, cool. Just let me know."

I didn't wait for a response. I just got up and walked out of the office. He had been handling cases for my team for a minute, and he was one of the best niggas out there for the job, but I was just irritated as fuck when he mentioned a plea. I wasn't telling on my motherfucking self. Them niggas wanted me, then let them do their motherfucking jobs.

I pulled up at the trap where the niggas were waiting. I had got some new work that I needed on these streets. I let one of my dopeheads check it out, and that nigga said that shit was straight fire. That's what the fuck I wanted to hear, since I bought a couple keys. I planned to get rid of all of it before my court date. I needed to make sure all my shit was secured.

I walked in where the fellas were sitting and rapping. "Y'all really slipping. Didn't even hear when I walked in the door. All y'all niggas would be dead." I pulled them up on game.

"Bullshit, nigga. I saw when you pulled up. Plus, I keep my hand on my trigger at all times," Beenie said, showing the burner that was on his lap, hiding under his fleece.

"I see you, nigga." I exchanged daps with them before joining them. "Pass the blunt, nigga," I said.

"Nigga, you look like you been up for days," the youngest nigga of the crew, Javon, said.

"Nigga, I been grinding nonstop. This that money look, you feel me?"

"I hear you, boss man, but you making me look bad. You know I stay fly." He laughed.

"Nigga, I will pull yo' bitch and fuck her looking like this. These hoes don't care 'bout how a nigga look. They just want to know yo' paper long."

"Nigga, if my bitch fuck you, I'ma body that ho after I bust in her mouth."

We all bust out laughing. That little nigga was too young to be that cold and ruthless. We joked around, smoking and drinking for about an hour. After that, we got in the kitchen. My nigga J Money was in the kitchen, whipping up that work. I swear, the snowman Jeezy ain't got shit on my cook. That nigga could bring any crack back to perfection. That nigga be having that shit so buttery and soft, having these crackheads running around Richmond, geeking and shit.

After I concluded business, I left. I was supposed to meet up with shawty for dinner. We had been chilling hard lately. I wasn't taking it too serious 'cause I knew she was a stripper, and I couldn't wife no ho, but I needed to get over Nyesha, so shawty was definitely the help I needed to accomplish that. She was a certified freak and knew how to keep a nigga satisfied. I had told her we could go out to the restaurant, but she insisted she'd cook dinner. I love a woman that knows how to fuck and cook also. Shit, I might keep her ass around since I didn't plan on getting in no relationship no more.

I put her address in the GPS. She stayed over the north side on Barton Avenue. I rarely fucked with the north side 'cause them niggas were bums and loved robbing niggas. E'erybody knew north side niggas wasn't making no paper, so if you was a nigga making major moves, your best bet was to stay clear of them niggas.

Young Boy NBA's song was blasting through the speaker as I drove.

This shit got crazy when Lil Dave died. When my grandma left, couldn't do nothing but cry.

This little nigga wasn't nothing but seventeen, but his ass was spitting some real-life shit. The GPS notified me that the address was coming up on the corner. I pulled over, then sat in the car and finished smoking a Black. I then called shawty's phone.

"Hello," she answered in a sexy, seductive voice.

"Yo, quit playing answering the phone like that, trying to let a nigga come up in there and tear that pussy up. I'm outside."

"A'ight, come on, boy."

I took my gun out and tucked it in my waist, looked around, then hopped out of the ride. I peeped shawty standing in the doorway with her sexy self.

"What's up, love?" I kissed her cheek while cuffing her ass cheeks.

"Boy, you better stop playing before you let me have to jump on yo' ass."

"Shit, I'm pretty sure I would love that shit."

"I'm sure you would, but you need to eat first," she said.

"Yes, ma'am, feed me," I joked. I followed her into the tiny but neat apartment.

"Come in here," she said. "Space is a little tight, but it works."

I sat down at the table while she put the food on the plates. Then she joined me. She made baked chicken, cabbage, and rice. This reminded of my mama's home-cooked meals. I took the first bite, not knowing what to expect, but surprisingly, it was delicious. I was shocked a little bit. Maybe I was judging her because she worked at the shaky booty club.

She got up and walked to her cupboard. "Look. I got your favorite."

I turned to see what she was talking about. She held up a bottle of Grey Goose.

"That's my girl. You know how to make a nigga feel special."

"But of course. Your meal wouldn't be complete without your favorite drink," she said as she poured me a shot. "I ain't got no glass but this. It's kind of big, but it'll work."

"You good. You know I don't get drunk that easy no way."

"Don't worry if you get drunk. I have a big queen size bed for you to crash on."

"It takes a lot to get me drunk. But thanks for the offer."

"I mean, give me some credit for trying."

We busted out laughing. We ate, laughed, and talked. I was feeling a little tipsy, which was strange because I was a drinker, which I know sounds bad, but I could outdrink more than the average person without getting drunk. So, I was kind of puzzled about why I drank a glass of liquor and I was already feeling drunk.

"You a'ight, babes?" she quizzed as she got up from the table.

"Yeah, I'm straight. Just feel a little fatigue."

"Well, it's call *niggeritis*. You know the shit that black folks get after they finish eating. Plus, you drank that liquor. You might want to relax for a little while. Come on. Let's go upstairs," she said.

"A'ight." I got up, and she held my hand, leading me up the stairs.

Something felt off. I didn't like the way I was feeling. However, I convinced myself that I just needed to lay down for a few, then I'd be straight. We didn't set foot in the room before she started kissing on me aggressively.

"Damn, shawty, you in heat, huh?" I joked as I kissed her back.

She wasted no time in unbuttoning my pants, dropping them to my ankles. She released my dick out of my boxers and started massaging it gently. All along, I was feeling like my muscles were giving out on me. I tried to brush off that feeling and keep up with her. She was hungry for this dick, so I had to show up and show out.

"Lay down," she instructed.

I obliged and lay on my back while she licked the tip of my dick slowly and massaged it with her other hand. "Damn, aargh," I groaned as she performed magic with her warm mouth.

"Relax, babe, I got you."

Those were the last words I remembered.

I tried opening my eyes, but I was having a hard time doing so. I tried to figure out what the fuck was going on, but I was drawing a blank. The last thing that I remembered was when shawty was giving me some head.

Wait, where the fuck she at?

I placed my hand on the left side of the bed, but no one was there. I finally managed to open my eyes and look around. I was still in the room, but the room was dark, and I was the only one there. I was feeling disoriented.

It took me a few minutes to ease myself up off the bed. I assumed she was in the bathroom or something. I fumbled around for the light switch, but when I found one and flipped it on, there was no light.

What the fuck is going on here?

"Kaley! Kaley!" I hollered her name a few times, but there was no response. I fumbled my way through the dark to what I believed was the bathroom. It was empty.

All kinds of crazy shit started running through my mind. I rushed back to the bed, holding on the walls for support. I looked around for my pants. I was about to put them on when I noticed they were a little bit lightweight. I reached into my pockets. The stack of cash that I had was gone.

"Fuck! I been robbed," I blurted out. I quickly turned around to look for my gun.

You won't be needing this right now.

I remembered that bitch saying that to me before she placed it on a stand. I quickly looked over to the stand, but my gun was gone.

I hurriedly put on my clothes and dashed down the stairs. There was no light in the entire house. I tried to look around, but it was obvious that bitch was long gone. The bitch did leave my car key, so I stumbled outside into the cold weather. I felt like I was going to throw up, so I hurried to my car.

I sat in my car, pissed the fuck off. My iPhone was also missing. This bitch had robbed me, and I was pretty sure she didn't do that shit by herself. But how? I started my car and pulled off, thinking of how many ways I was going to kill that ho.

I lit me a Black. My head was spinning, and I felt like I needed to vomit. I really wasn't in shape to drive, but I needed to get back to my side of town ASAP. I let out a slight laugh 'cause I knew how grimey these north side niggas were. I had just been fucking around with this bitch so long that I didn't see this shit coming. They got me for about four stacks, my phone, and my gun.

This bitch had to be the dumbest. She betrayed a nigga that had been showing her mad love. I knew the bitch was a ho, but I didn't look at her ass no fucked up way. I had to give it shawty, though. She played a good game.

CHAPTER THIRTY-TWO

Nyesha

It had been over a month that I had not heard from Yohan. I thought about revoking his bond numerous times, but it wasn't in me to be no grimey-ass bitch. I was back to being by myself again, but that didn't stop my flow. I ain't goin' lie. For days, I cried and cried, praying to God to bring him back to me, but days passed, and my prayers were falling on deaf ears. I couldn't eat, and I barely slept. I had to put my best out for my kids. I didn't have anyone to talk to about what I was going through.

The weekend was here, and the kids were fast asleep early. I was up grinding, so I was in the living room, waiting on Kim to come back through. I smoked a blunt and drank a glass of Bailey's.

I was on Facebook, chilling, when I heard a loud banging. It scared the fuck out of me. The first thought that came to my mind was that it was the police. I quickly put out the blunt and jumped off the couch. I tiptoed to the door and looked through the peephole. I saw two big, burly-ass dudes posted outside my door.

"Who is it?" I yelled nervously.

"Bail bondsman. I'm looking for Yohan Ellis."

"Well, he's not here," I yelled back.

"We need to talk to you, Miss Smith."

I opened the door, looking at them with an attitude. "He's not here, so what y'all want with me?" I asked.

"Do you know where he's at? This is his address, right?"

"Yes, it is, but like I said before, he ain't here."

"You signed this bond, so we can arrest you if we don't find him or if we find out you're hiding him."

"Arrest me for what?" I took a few steps back.

"You signed his bond, which means you're assuring us this bond would be paid, and if not, we can revoke it."

"That man is grown, and he's not here. I'll sure let him know y'all looking for him."

"Miss Smith, this is serious, and we're not playing around. Turn him in, or risk going to jail with him."

I was going to respond but didn't feel the need to keep going back and forth with these niggas. I already peeped that because I was a female, they felt like they could apply pressure on my ass. They had the wrong bitch.

After I locked the door, I dialed that nigga's number. Still, there was no response. I texted him.

While you want to play possum, just know the bail bondsman an' them is looking for yo' ass.

I put the phone down. This nigga was stupid as hell. He didn't pay them niggas their money, and now they were after him. I shook my head in disgust. His ass was not gon' learn until them motherfuckers locked him up and threw away the damn key.

It was a chilly November day, but I was sitting outside, catching some sales and kicking it with Kim. This other crackhead, Jean, walked up. Jean was from the south side and was friends with Yohan. Nowadays, she was in Churchill, hanging with the crackheads over here.

"Hey, y'all," she said as she took a seat on the wall beside us.

"Hey, you."

"Here comes my big dude. I got to go New York." This was the code Kim used when she was selling for me.

We watched as Kim hopped into a Black Denali and they pulled off.

"So, what you been up to lately, girl?" Jean asked.

"Nothing. Grinding and taking care of these kids."

"Where that baby daddy of yours? I ain't seen him in a few weeks," she said.

"Me and you both." I knew her ass was just fishing for information, so I kept quiet about Yohan.

"Hmm. I ain't messy or nothing, but did he tell you him and Zaria got a new baby on the way?"

I started coughing. The piece of ice that I was sucking on slipped down my throat.

"Girl, you a'ight? I ain't made you choke, did I?"

I managed to get my coughing under control. "Did you just say he got that bitch pregnant?"

"Girl, yes. She 'bout four months pregnant. Wait, Yohan ain't tell you?"

My body froze as I trembled inside. "Are you high, Jean?"

"Girl, nah. I ain't had nothing to smoke since last night. I was just gon' ask you to front me a fifteen. You think I'm high, that's why I'm saying that? I'm for real. Everybody know they having another baby."

I didn't respond to her. Instead, I handed her a dub bag of crack.

"A'ight, girl. I'll be back later if my sugar daddy come through. And don't tell Yohan I tell you anything. You know that nigga be tripping," she said.

"Nah, you straight."

I watched as she walked off down the streets. When she was out of sight, my mind went to work. This dirty-ass nigga done went and got this bitch pregnant again.

I let out a nervous laugh, trying to prevent myself from crying.

My thoughts were quickly interrupted when I saw two police Dodge Chargers speed past me, going up 32nd Street. That was my cue to bring my ass in the house. Whatever was going on up the street wasn't my business.

I locked my door and dialed Yohan's number, but still no response. The phone rang until the voicemail came on. I thought about leaving a message but changed my mind.

Months later, I still hadn't heard from Yohan. This nigga didn't even bother to check on his kids. I tried to bury myself into my grind, but deep down, I was broken. I gave this nigga a chance when I shouldn't have. I fucked Ky over for him, and now look how he did me again.

My phone started to ring. I didn't answer it, but it started ringing again. It might have been some money, so I reached on the carpet to pick it up. It was a number that I didn't recognize, but I answered anyway.

"You have a prepaid call from Henrico County Jail. Press five to accept and zero to ignore."

I thought of hanging up my damn phone, but something stopped me.

"Hey, Nyesha," Yohan ass said.

"Hey," I said dryly.

"Man, they fucking got me."

"Okay," I responded nonchalantly.

"I just told yo' ass I'm in jail, and all you can say is okay? What's wrong with you, yo?"

"Nah, the question is what the fuck is wrong with you? You con my ass into bonding you out and paying for a damn lawyer so you can get out and be wit' yo' ho. Nigga, why the fuck you calling me?" I yelled.

"Man, you need to chill the fuck out. I ain't been with nobody."

"Nigga, fuck you and that ho. Please lose my mother-fucking number, bitch-ass nigga." Without waiting for a response, I hung up. It had been months of me trying to track his ass down. There could've been something wrong with his kids. He never answered; instead, he ducked me. Now that they done caught up with him, he was calling me. This nigga really thought I was a mother-fucking clown.

I needed a blunt to calm my nerves, so I wasted no time in rolling up a fat one. With all this stress that I had going on, I was turning into a weed head little by little.

I wondered what Mama would say if she saw me with this blunt in my mouth. Her bougie ass would proba-bly collapse. The thought of her ass collapsing made me laugh out loud. It didn't make no damn sense that woman was so selfish. I couldn't help but wonder who the fuck was going to take care of her ass when she got old. I guess Meisha was the oldest, so she would do it.

The phone started ringing. I looked at the caller ID. It was the same number that Yohan had called from earlier. Hell no, I was not talking to his ass. I was going to ignore him, just like he did me when I was calling him.

That nigga had too much time on his hands, I saw, because he was calling back-to-back without ceasing. I held out, though, and put the phone on silent. I was not folding this time.

I hadn't been shopping in a while, not for myself or the kids. I decided to hit the mall up. I waited for the kids to get home, then we drove to Chesterfield Town Center. Their stores were much better than what was in the city. I ain't gon' lie. I splurged on the kids and got me a couple of designer purses. I copped two pairs of the lat-est Jordans for me and two apiece for the kids also. I got them some winter clothes and jackets. By the time we were finished, I spent well over three stacks on us.

"Mommy, I'm hungry," Kyle whined.

"You know what? I am too. Let's go. The food court is upstairs," I said.

We decided we wanted Chinese food, so that's what we had. The kids sat there, eating and messing with one another, and I was browsing Facebook—more like stalking Ky's page. That nigga hadn't posted nothing for a while, which was kind of strange 'cause when we were together, that nigga stayed posting shit on social media. His ass was probably hiding on Snapchat or something.

I swear, each day that went by, I missed that boy more and more. I still couldn't believe I fucked him over for Yohan.

By the time we got home, I was past exhaustion, but I couldn't rest. I had some sales that I was expecting. No matter what I was going through, I still had to grind for me and the kids. So, after they got settled, I hit Kim up so she could come through.

This nigga had been calling every day for a week straight. I still didn't pick up the phone. Then the lawyer called.

"Hello."

"Hello, Miss Smith. This is Attorney Blake."

"I know who you are. Just for the record, Mr. Ellis will be paying the balance on his bill," I said.

"Okay, he informed me his bond was revoked, so now he has to sit until his trial date."

"Yes, it is, but like I was saying, you can talk to him about the remainder of your fee. We're no longer together, so I want to relieve myself of all his obligations."

"I understand what you're saying, but Mr. Ellis didn't sign the agreement. You did. Therefore, you're responsible for the remaining balance," he said.

"Well, stop representing him then, or get his other bitch to pay his bill. But like I said, I ain't paying another dollar to benefit his ass." I removed the phone from my ear and ended the call. This nigga was a fool if he thought he could bully me into paying him. Without delay, I went as far as blocking the lawyer's number.

An hour later, Yohan's ass was calling me. I guess he had got the news that I wasn't helping him anymore. I decided to answer the phone. Wasn't no need to keep ducking him. I was ready to let his ass have it.

"Helloooo," I answered with an attitude.

"Yo, where you been? I been calling you for days now."

"I been doing me. Ain't that what you been doing when you was out here?"

"Man, chill out wit' all that unnecessary drama. I know you mad wit' a nigga, but that don't give you the right to keep my kids away from me."

"Your kids? Nigga, how many times since they were born that you been around them? How many times have you left them? You need to find something else to use as an excuse," I spat.

"Nyesha, I ain't perfect, but I love my kids. I swear, if you don't do anything else for me, can you bring them to see me? I might be in here for a minute, and I just want to see them. Please, shawty."

Was this nigga crying? Not this macho-ass nigga.

"A'ight, man. I will bring them down there. You know my fucking kids deserve better than this."

"Babe, I swear I love you. I don't know why I keep messing up."

I was sick and tired of him and his fucking sorry-ass apologies.

"Listen, Yohan, cut the bullshit. You ain't got to do all this. I said I will bring them to see you on Thursday."

"A'ight, that's cool. If it's possible, can I talk to them before they go to bed tonight?"

"Sure. You can call them."

As angry as I was at this nigga, I wasn't going to keep spiting my kids. They had been asking for him almost every day, and I had to keep telling them he was working. To be honest, I was tired of lying to my kids. Sometimes I wished they were older so I could just tell them the truth about his no-good ass.

It had been a long, stressful-ass day, so after Kim brought me back my money, I decided to call it a night. These nights were getting lonelier. I didn't know how some bitches had all the luck in this world, but not me. Shit, I had to change some things real fast. I didn't even want no relationship, just possibly a friend who could come over to eat this pussy up real fast and then lay the dick on me. What them hoes call it? No strings attached.

Thursday got there fast, and I wasn't looking forward to visiting this nigga. After all this nigga had put me through, I really couldn't care less. I got the kids dressed. We stopped by Waffle House for breakfast, and then we headed to Henrico County. As usual, they were overly excited to see their daddy. Kids are so innocent. No matter how this nigga dragged them, they still loved him unconditionally. I shook my head in disgust 'cause this nigga didn't deserve their love.

"Mommy, I thought you said Daddy was at work. How come he at jail now?" Emanyi's smart ass asked.

"Baby, it's a long story, okay?" I hated lying to her.

I pulled into the jail and parked. *Kids these days are too damn smart,* I thought as we exited the vehicle.

After I signed in, we walked into the visitation area. The kids ran up to the glass as usual. My daughter grabbed the phone and wasted no time letting her daddy know how much she loved and missed him. Her brother was standing by, nervous as hell to talk to his daddy too.

While the kids talked to him, I stood there watching. My eyes caught someone walking up. I looked behind me.

This bitch can't be serious.

I recognized the hoe's face from me going through his pictures. The bitch resembled a mongrel dog, so I couldn't forget. I stepped toward the bitch, not caring about where I was.

"What the fuck you doing up here?" I asked.

"Bitch, don't question me. I'm here to see my baby father."

I quickly realized her big-ass stomach busting out the small-ass shirt she was wearing. "So, I see you pregnant. Who is the daddy?"

"Why don't you ask him?" She pointed to Yohan.

I snatched the phone away from my son's ear. "Yo, this is how you do? And who the fuck she pregnant for?" I yelled, not giving a fuck who was listening.

This nigga's eyes popped open. He sat there looking like he saw a ghost.

"Answer me, dammit. This your baby?"

No sound came out that nigga's mouth.

I smiled at him. "You know what, Yohan? You can have that bitch. Enjoy your fucking life." I looked over at her and said, "Here, bitch. He's all yours." I shook my head in disgust.

"Come on, kids."

My daughter was saying something, but I wasn't trying to hear shit.

"I said let's go!" I yelled while walking fast as hell. I needed to get the fuck out of there. I needed some cold air to calm me down.

I busted out the door and started gasping for air. It took me a few minutes to get my breathing under control. I guess the crackhead bitch wasn't lying when she had said that bitch was pregnant. What fucked me up was this nigga didn't even deny it. He just sat there like he didn't give a fuck. His silence spoke louder than his words. Tears welled up in my eyes as I pulled off. I had gotten all the confirmation that I needed.

CHAPTER THIRTY-THREE

KYMANI

It was my court date, and to be honest, even though I didn't want to be locked up, There was no other way out. My lawyer worked out a sweet-ass deal for me. Instead of getting the five years, I got eighteen months up in Goochland. The judge ordered my bond revoked immediately, which was surprising because I been doing good while I was out.

I heard my sister crying out. I was shocked that she showed up that day because she had not spoken to me since the day I confessed that I accidently killed Mama. The deputies walked over and placed the cuffs on me. As they walked me out, I turned to my sister and whispered, "I love you." I hated to see her hurting like that.

By the time I got to the jail, reality had set in. I had some homies that greeted me soon as I stepped in the door. I wasn't gon' sit there and cry. Shit, I was a real street nigga, so I was gon' deal with whatever the fuck was thrown my motherfucking way.

I had to adjust to a certain routine quick. I would wake up early in the morning and do pushups, then I would bathe. I was binging on ramen noodles. My homeboy, Jigga, that was also my bunkie, would whip up tuna, and we would eat that with crackers. I would then spend time on the phone. Shit I was a boss and had a business to run, no matter where the fuck I was.

I tried not to let this jail shit get to me, especially being around some of these niggas up in there. The other day, I was taking a shower when this bitch-ass nigga walked in. I continued washing myself off, trying not to let this fuck shit bother me. I stood there soaping up when I spotted the nigga from the corner of my eye. I noticed that he wasn't getting in the shower, but instead, stood there staring.

"Yo, nigga, what the fuck you looking at?" I yelled at him. I must've caught him off guard.

"What are you talking about?"

"Nigga, this a shower room, and you ain't showering, so again I ask, what the fuck you doing?"

"Boy, chill out. Ain't nobody checking for yo' ass with that little-ass dick. Trust me, I've seen bigger," he said to me in a girly-ass tone.

I grabbed my towel that was nearby, wrapped it around me, and stepped in that nigga's face. "What the fuck you said to me, faggot?"

"I'll show you a faggot, bitch-ass nigga," he said in a manly voice. It was crazy how a second ago, he had no bass in his voice.

I balled my fist up and just kept pounding this nigga's face in. Don't get me wrong, he was holding his own, but I wasn't easing up.

"Fight, fight!" I heard someone yell.

I then heard the door opening and feet running. I knew it was the correctional officers coming. A crowd had gathered.

"Move out the way!" one CO hollered while he made his way toward us.

"Stop it now! Let him go." Another one grabbed me and threw me on the wall.

"Nigga, get the fuck off me," I yelled and tried to hit his ass.

"Go ahead so I can beat yo' ass down," the white CO said to me.

"Nigga, I ain't scared. You got all the motherfucking power right now, but I bet yo' pussy ass a bitch out in them streets."

He didn't respond. Instead, he yanked my arms and placed the cuffs on me. "Get him out of here," he ordered the female CO.

"Come on. Let's go," she said.

"We need medical down here now. Greene is bleeding," one of them said into a radio.

I tried to get a glimpse of the nigga I'd beat, but the crowd was too thick.

"Go back to y'all cubes. Unit on lockdown," the CO ordered.

Niggas were yelling some shit, but I couldn't make out what they were saying. I was pretty sure they were mad that they were on lockdown. Me, on the other hand, I didn't give a fuck. This nigga violated me and deserved every lick he got. He was lucky we were not in the streets. I would've bodied his ass.

"What happened up in there?" the bitch CO asked.

"Ain't shit. I was bathing, and that faggot ass nigga stood there staring and shit. Y'all lucky I ain't killed his ass before y'all got to him."

"You too handsome to be talking like this. Ain't you trying to go home?" she said.

"The nigga disrespected me. I don't tolerate no type of disrespect."

"I hear you, but if you trying to leave up out of here, you might need to check that attitude. Gay people are everywhere, especially up in these jails and prisons. You can't go around beating every last one of them up."

"Listen, shawty, no disrespect, but you the law, and I ain't tryna hear all this shit you talking."

"Okay, have it your way." She led me to the hole and opened the door. "The lieutenant will be down to write you a shot, and your things will be down in a few. Take care."

I shook my head and took a seat on the mat. I was still heated. I noticed my right knuckles were bruised. That nigga was lucky as fuck 'cause I was trying to rearrange his face.

It took me a minute to calm myself down. I was ready to get shipped. I had never been to prison, but I preferred to go instead of being cooped up with these bitch-ass niggas.

I was in the hole for 45 days. Each day that went by, I wondered when the fuck I was getting shipped. I ain't goin' lie. Being in the hole was way better than being on the pod with all them niggas. The one thing about being in the hole was that I couldn't get visitation or talk on the phone. I had a business to motherfucking run, even though I knew my nigga and Nia were holding me down. I still loved to stay on top of my shit, especially when a lot of money was involved.

When I was finally out the hole, my nigga showed me mad love.

"Yo, they finally let a real one out, huh?" he said.

"Yeah, you know they can't hold a real nigga down forever. What's good though, my nigga?" We exchanged daps.

"Ain't shit. Man, you put a beating down on that faggot. I ain't seen his ass, but I heard he might need a few surgeries to get his shit back right. Man, what the fuck happened?"

"That bitch-ass nigga stood there watching me while I was tryna shower. You know I'on't play that faggot shit. I step to the nigga, and he started running off at the mouth, so I went in. On the real, I was tryna murder that nigga."

"Nigga, I already know how you get down. You shouldn't be here longer, though. After what happened, I think they gon' make sure you get shipped asap," he said.

"That be good. Shit, I'm ready to get this time out the way so I can get back to these streets."

"Yeah, I feel you, bro," he said in a somber tone.

"Yo, my nigga, what's going on wit' yo' case?"

"Man, I'on't even know."

"What yo' lawyer saying?" I asked.

"Man, that dumb-ass nigga talking about shit don't look good. You know how them court appointed lawyers be."

"I thought you hired a lawyer."

"Man, I had some money when I got caught up. 'Bout fifteen stacks. Fucked around and gave the code to the bitch I was fucking with. I'm embarrassed to even say it. That's the last time I heard from the bitch. No visit and phone cut off. My mama went 'round by the crib, but she said ain't nobody come to the door. The bitch took my money and bounced," he said.

"Really? That ho grimey as fuck. Is that the bitch from Creighton?"

"Yup, that's her. Been fucking with her for 'bout two years, so I never thought that bitch would fuck me over like that. I'ma kill that ho when I get out. I swear that's all I dream about e'ery day. A slow death. Might torture that ho for days."

I heard the coldness in his voice, but I couldn't blame him. That bitch was dirty and deserved everything coming to her.

"Aye, yo, I'ma let my peoples get you a lawyer and put some money on yo' books. You already know how we roll. I don't know why you ain't hit my line. I coulda been got you a lawyer."

"Bro, I know you got a lot going on, so I ain't want to put that burden on you. You feel me? I treated that bitch good, dawg. I can't believe she did me dirty like that." His voice cracked.

"My nigga, you can't trust these bitches nowadays. Bitches only fuck with you when you there in they face. Soon as some shit pop off, they ain't nowhere to be found. Man, fuck a bitch. I just want to knock this little time off so I can get back to the money. You feel me, nigga?"

"Hell yeah, I feel you. I'm trying to get on yo' team when I touch down."

"That's what I'm talkin' 'bout. Get wit' the money team, my nigga."

"What you about to get into?" he asked.

"Gonna do a few pushups and get on the phone. I'ma come fuck wit' you later on."

"A'ight peace."

We exchanged daps, and I walked off. I was acting like e'erything was cool, but truth was, I was ready to get the fuck on up out of there.

After I took a shower, I got on the phone. Trying to get shit going from the inside was hard, but I was still the boss and couldn't let up or let these walls hinder what I had going on. I was a boss no matter where the fuck I was at, and e'erybody would know that soon enough.